Now You See It...

Teresa Roblin

Cerridwen Press

What the critics are saying...

ɞ

"Teresa Roblin is a fairly new author, but you cannot tell by her great writing style!...a refreshing new author on the block..." ~ *Novelspot*

"Following in the same style as the first, with the same warm and witty characters, this book takes you away for an entertaining afternoon read. A combination of humor and secondary characters made Now You See It come alive and kept me reading." ~ *Romance Divas*

"NOW YOU SEE IT was a sweet romance." ~ *Love Romances*

"A hilarious comedy of errors and enchanting titillation, Now You See It compelled me into reading it from the first page to the last. I think I spent a majority of the book laughing my head off; every few paragraphs had me in fits." ~ *Ecataromance Reviews*

"This was a great read that had me laughing, crying, and sighing over the many hijinks that Sarah and Anthony found themselves in. Teresa Roblins did an amazing job of pulling together two people that should never have been apart in the first place. Not only were her characters engaging and real, but the descriptions of the various places they visited were awesome." ~ *Fallen Angels Review*

A Cerridwen Press Publication

www.cerridwenpress.com

Now You See It…

ISBN 1419905422, 9781419956119
ALL RIGHTS RESERVED.
Now You See It… Copyright © 2006 Teresa Roblin
Edited by Kelli Kwiatkowski
Cover art by Willo

Electronic book Publication February 2006
Trade paperback publication May 2007

With the exception of quotes used in reviews, this book may not be reproduced or used in whole or in part by any means existing without written permission from the publisher, Ellora's Cave Publishing Inc., 1056 Home Avenue, Akron, OH 44310-3502.

This book is a work of fiction and any resemblance to persons, living or dead, or places, events or locales is purely coincidental. The characters are productions of the authors' imagination and used fictitiously.

Cerridwen Press is an imprint of Ellora's Cave Publishing, Inc.®

Also by Teresa Roblin

∞

Hocus Pocus

About the Author

∞

Teresa welcomes comments from readers. You can find her website and email address on her author bio page at www.cerridwenpress.com.

NOW YOU SEE IT...

Dedication

To my husband and two sons, for their wonderful support and patience.

And to my critique partners — Mary, Maureen, Michele, Molly, Sinead and Susan. You are the wind beneath my wings.

To the lovely people at Sunquest Cruises, who answered all my questions.

To Kelly Hanley at Travel Pro Network who helped with the train schedules.

Trademarks Acknowledgement

The author acknowledges the trademarked status and trademark owners of the following wordmarks mentioned in this work of fiction:

Carlton: Ritz-Carlton Hotel Company, L.L.C.
Lear: Learjet Inc.
Lycra: Invista North America S.A.R. L. Corporation
Jack Daniel's: Jack Daniel's Properties Inc.
Ouija board: Hasbro Inc.
Ping-Pong: Parker-Brothers, Inc.
Romance Perfume: PRL USA Holdings, Inc.
Sea-Doo: Bombardier Recreational Products Inc.
Sopranos: Time Warner Entertainment Company

Now You See It…

Chapter One
ஐ

Sarah had it all figured out.

Climbing out of her little red sports car, she smoothed her black miniskirt over her long legs and re-tucked the gauzy white shirt that hinted at the lace bra beneath. Throwing her purse over her shoulder, she grabbed a grocery bag in each arm.

"Damn long lines." She'd left the house bright and early to avoid the Saturday morning crowds, only to find the gourmet shop she loved for its delicacies packed because of a sale. Hot and sticky, and running two hours behind schedule, she'd finally made it back home just before lunch.

Lack of time wouldn't dent her plans. With a swing of her hips, Sarah shut the car door. Her long black hair swung from side to side, brushing the base of her back with each confident step she took to the front door.

She went over the facts. Fact one—her seventy-five-year-old Aunt Lilly and her new seventy-year-old friend, Emily, wanted to go on a cruise. Fact two—Emily's grandson was being difficult about his grandmother's impending trip.

Solution—she'd pile on the charm. Sweeten him with wine and goodies, then steamroll the pain in the ass into letting the dear old ladies go by themselves. What harm could they come to on a cruise ship?

Sarah would convince him that they could look after themselves with one hand tied behind her back. She'd have him eating out of the palm of her hand in no time. Then it would be goodbye Aunt Lilly and Emily, sayonara to the jackass of a grandson, and hello to a week of peace.

Juggling the groceries, Sarah opened the front door. "Aunt Lilly, I'm home."

"Crap." Her aunt sounded pissed off.

She could hear Aunt Lilly continuing to swear and mumble from the kitchen. Her accident-prone aunt swore often, usually when she had just made a mess of something. Sarah hurried to the kitchen to make sure everything was still intact, the heavy grocery bags nearly slipping out of her grasp.

"Made it!" Dropping the bags onto the glass tabletop, Sarah glanced over the tidy, cream-colored kitchen with its large arrangement of colorful, dried corncobs above the kitchen window. No problem here.

Sarah turned around. "Guess what I bought—" She started, her grin disappearing when she caught sight of her aunt.

Aunt Lilly's short gray curls were hidden under a large turban. The red gentleman's smoking jacket she'd slipped over her flowered dress barely fit her short, ample body. Flowers, candles and an open magic book lay on the granite countertop as she waved a lit barbecue lighter.

Sarah didn't like the look of this.

"Who are you putting a curse on this time?"

"You."

"Oh, no, you're not." Sarah rushed over to her aunt. "Give me that," she said, grabbing the lighter out of her aunt's hands and dropping it onto the counter. "Haven't you learned your lesson yet about meddling in other people's lives?"

"Doesn't everything I do turn out right? Besides, how is a skinny thing like you going to stop me?"

"Watch me," Sarah stated. Besides, she wasn't skinny — just slim.

With a gentle shove, Sarah propelled her aunt past the sink toward the table. Aunt Lilly tried to dig her heels into the polished granite floors, but they only slid.

"Instead of blowing up the house, help me unpack these bags," Sarah said, pushing one toward her aunt and started to unpack the other. She needed to get her aunt's mind off this ridiculous nonsense of playing with magic.

Ever since Aunt Lilly had found her dearly departed sister's spell book in the attic, she'd decided she would solve Sarah's and her sister's man problems with magic. But mixing magic with her meddling aunt's good intentions was, is and always would be a huge mistake.

The last time her aunt had experimented with magic, Sarah's normally quiet sister had lost control of the words that came out of her mouth. Amanda had confronted anyone who challenged her and ended up telling her boss that she loved him. There was no way in hell Sarah was willing to let her aunt do something similar to her.

"What's all this for?" Aunt Lilly asked, pulling a bottle of champagne and a box of chocolates from the bag.

Sarah set a tray of hors d'oeuvres on the table, pulling off the plastic lid that covered them. "These are to celebrate your upcoming trip."

Aunt Lilly shook her head regretfully. "If Tony keeps complaining, I don't think we'll be going."

"You leave Tony to me," Sarah replied, empting a bag of wrapped toffees into the glass bowl in the middle of the table. "There, all done. Emily and her grandson will be here any minute now so why don't we watch some TV?"

Aunt Lilly crossed her arms over her generous bosom and lifted her chin. "Not interested."

Sarah felt her eyebrows brush against the tips of her bangs. "Since when? I can't tear you away from that thing most of the time."

"I've got more important things to do, like straightening out your life," Lilly said, easing closer to the candles.

Sarah blocked her way. "If you're thinking of casting a spell so that I can get a man, think again. I've got more than my fair share of them."

Aunt Lilly pushed her out of the way and waddled back to the counter. "And you scare them away within a month." She planted her hands on her hips and faced Sarah. "Now, we can do this the easy way or the hard way."

"What's the difference?"

"The hard way is I cast the spell when you're not around," Aunt Lilly said, picking up the lighter, flicking on the flame and waving it in front of her face. "And the easy way is you stick around so I don't blow anything up."

"Oh God." The last time she was left alone, her aunt nearly set the house on fire trying to rewire the toaster. She must have crossed the wires—the electric shock had knocked her off her feet, making her hit her head and pass out.

Sarah was damned if she did and damned if she didn't. Taking a deep breath, she sealed her fate. "Fine. Get this circus act over with." By the time their guests arrived she'd have hidden all evidence of her aunt's idiosyncrasies. Besides, like the chances of lightning striking the same place twice, what were the odds that Lilly would make magic work a second time?

Aunt Lilly clicked on the lighter again. A bright flame jumped into the air. "You won't regret it."

"I already do." Drawing closer to her aunt, Sarah continued, "Just remember, if anything crazy starts to happen while you're away on that cruise, I'm going to track you down."

"No problem."

Sarah felt like she had just made a pact with the devil. Gripping the cold edge of the granite counter for support, she watched her aunt light a row of red, yellow and white candles. "Did you follow the instruction of the spell book or have you improvised?"

"I'm ad-libbing."

That's what she was afraid of. Her aunt never did anything by the book. With dramatic flair, Aunt Lilly held her hands over a small dish that held one of Sarah's scarves.

"Where the hell did you find that?"

"In one of your drawers, now shush so I can get this ball rolling."

Rolling? That's what Sarah's stomach was doing at the moment. This was bad — really bad. Aunt Lilly's off-the-cuff approach to magic worried her. How could she explain to her aunt that her good intentions always landed short of the mark? Sarah drew closer and prayed this would be over quickly.

Aunt Lilly cleared her throat and Sarah knew there was no turning back. The candles flickered in readiness and the air grew thick with tension as Aunt Lilly read the first verse of her spell.

"Under layers you will find,
a special person with a mind."

A rustling sound drew Sarah's attention from the swaying flames of the candles to the candies she had placed in the bowl on the table. Her mouth dropped open as the hairs on her arms stood on end.

The candies were bouncing about like jumping beans as one by one they stripped themselves of their wrappers.

"Holy crap." The blood drained from her head only to come rushing back, leaving a ringing in her ears. The room tilted away from her. She kept her eyes glued to the chaotic movement of the candies as they clattered onto the table's glass top. "Oh God." She desperately wanted to stop her aunt but knew that if she did, Lilly would only try again when she wasn't around and hurt herself.

"Keep on peeling, one by one,
for your journey has just begun."

From the corner of one astonished eye, Sarah caught site of the champagne bottle unraveling its top, and she dodged the cork as it rocketed past her head. She was under attack.

"Help!"

Without skipping a beat, her aunt continued.

"'Til you reach the inner core,
then you'll see there's so much more."

Sarah's ears were popping. Looking around the room, she watched the hors d'oeuvres explode, spraying mushrooms and cheesy spinach everywhere. The almond-lacquer cabinets and the gleaming, blue-pearl granite countertops looked like a child had run free with a paintbrush. The little wieners stood naked as the puff pastry surrounding each one unwrapped itself. The smell of melted cheese and overcooked mushrooms made her stomach roil.

"Stop, stop, stop!" Sarah shouted. She couldn't move for fear that something would hit her. Before she could complete the thought, tiny pellets hit the back of her head.

"Now what?" Taking a deep breath, Sarah turned around and gasped. The colored corn decoration over the kitchen window was popping flurries of white missiles. They rained over her and covered the room in a fragrant layer of white disaster.

"What you see is what you get,
then the spell has been met."

With a final clap of her hands, Aunt Lilly leaned forward and blew out the candles as her last words hung in the air.

Silence.

Stillness.

Nothing and no one moved.

The heavy pounding of her heart vibrated throughout Sarah's body, shaking her very bones. With quivering fingers, she pulled the popcorn out of her hair and stared at it in disbelief.

Befuddled thoughts and feelings assailed her as she tried to get over her aunt's latest disaster. Gathering her courage, Sarah took a deep breath, looked up—and screamed. The shock of what she saw hit her full force.

Aunt Lilly covered her heart with her hand. "What's gotten into you?"

With a shaking finger, Sarah pointed to the kitchen doorway. "What have you done?" The erratic beat of her heart pounded in her ears.

Had her aunt somehow conjured up her ex-boyfriend?

Aunt Lilly's frown dissolved and her eyes lit up. "Tony, Emily—you're here."

"We did knock," said a deep, familiar voice, "but no one answered. The door was unlocked so we walked in."

"Anthony?" Sarah exclaimed. Her mind couldn't grasp the evidence in front of her eyes. What the hell was her ex-boyfriend doing walking nonchalantly into her kitchen?

In disbelief, Sarah watched the top of his head almost brush the apex of the doorframe as he crowded into the kitchen. He was still the same attractive devil she had known two years ago.

Dressed in a black designer suit, the pants tailored to the muscular lines of his legs and tight hips, he carelessly carried his jacket over his shoulder, holding it there with the tip of a finger. His white shirt stretched over a wide, firm chest—a chest she remembered caressing, kissing and falling asleep on.

But there were breathtaking differences between then and now. He used to wear his dark brown hair cut short to his head. Now it reached his shoulders and was tied back. A diamond earring sparkled in his right ear. An *earring*, for Pete's sake. Her pulse spun out of control. When had the conservative workaholic been replaced by a pirate?

A little white-haired woman peeked around his body. Emily, she presumed.

Anthony's eyes were openly amused as he surveyed the aftermath of her aunt's attempt with magic.

"How do you know Aunt Lilly?" Sarah asked. Popcorn crunched under her sandals as she made her way to the table and dropped into a chair before her knees could collapse.

The moment she sat down, her sandals seemed to drop off her feet, her soles landing on something squishy on the cold floor.

Frowning, Sarah tentatively moved her foot around, trying to find her sandals. Nothing. She widened the circling motion of her foot and cringed when she brushed up against an exploded hors d'oeuvre. She tried a side-to-side motion, hoping for success, but grasped a wiener with her toes instead. Gross.

Anthony took a handkerchief out of his breast pocket and wiped the cheesy spatters off a seat so his grandmother could sit down, then did the same for himself. "We met your aunt and Amanda at Mark's barbecue, just before your sister and Mark got engaged."

The pieces were falling into place. Her aunt was always talking about Tony and his Italian family. It could have been anyone, for all she knew. Every Italian family has a dozen Tonys. She just never dreamed Aunt Lilly was talking about *her* Tony. No wonder he hadn't looked surprised when he'd walked into the kitchen. He had been prepared while she had been ambushed.

"What happened here?" Anthony glanced around the kitchen.

His deep resonating voice shocked her back to reality. Resentment slowly bubbled into anger. She had worked him out of her system two years ago and now he had the nerve to show up again.

It wasn't enough that he had placed his work above her when they were dating. She had always come last. He'd held an iron grip on the day-to-day management of his business in fear of other companies attempting a takeover. Now he'd walked into her home as if nothing had happened, looking absolutely fabulous and sexy as hell.

"We had a food fight," Sarah replied. Let him think what he wanted, she wasn't going to tell him the truth.

Anthony chuckled. "Still the same impulsive Sarah."

His condescending tone grated on her nerves. "You haven't changed, either. Still a suit and stuffed shirt."

Not waiting for his reply, Sarah ducked her head under the table and searched for her damn sandals. She couldn't find them anywhere. *Where the hell are they? They couldn't have just disappeared—*

As soon as the thought formed, a lightning bolt of shock traveled up her spine and exploded through her body.

No way.

Sitting up, Sarah stared at her aunt and toward the mess of candles and flowers on the counter. Her mind refused to acknowledge what her eyes were telling her. Forget it. She wouldn't let herself believe it. There was no such thing as magic and her ex-boyfriend was not sitting casually in front of her.

Perplexed, Aunt Lilly looked between the two of them. "You know each other?"

Sarah glared at Anthony. "*Knew.* Briefly."

"And you never brought him home so I could meet him?" Aunt Lilly complained.

"He never had the time," Sarah replied. It had been work, work, work—and snatches of hot sex in between.

"Oh well," Aunt Lilly said, "now that he knows it's you, if you come with us, I'm sure there won't be any problems."

"I'm sorry, but I don't think Sarah is competent enough to look after the needs of two elderly women," Anthony said, his scathing glance zapping Sarah's nerves before returning his distasteful stare to the catastrophic conditions of the room. "I couldn't faithfully put my grandmother's safety in the hands of someone so unreliable."

Sarah sat forward in her seat. "Faithful? Unreliable? Those are two words *you* shouldn't be using in the same sentence."

Anthony shrugged. "Just an intuitive opinion."

"If you make such poor judgments, I'm surprised you're such a successful businessman."

"Oh dear." Aunt Lilly picked up one of the exploded hors d'oeuvres and popped it into her mouth.

"Why are you so against your grandmother going on this cruise?" Sarah demanded, drumming her fingers on the table. "She's old enough not to need your permission."

"The last time my dear grandmother went on a seniors' bus tour to a museum, she wandered off. If it happened again overseas, I wouldn't be able to find her."

Emily gave an unapologetic shrug.

"I can't waste any more time on this foolish idea of theirs, and I'm sure that, with your busy schedule, neither can you," Anthony said.

Really? "Who said anything about a busy schedule?" No one—especially not her ex—was going to tell her what she could or couldn't do. Sarah crossed her arms over her chest and smiled. "On the contrary, I've already reorganized my clients because I was thinking of joining them." So she was lying. It was a woman's prerogative to change her mind and that's exactly what she'd do. "So, you see, there's nothing to stop us from going."

"Well, reschedule your clients back. This trip is too ludicrous to even contemplate." Anthony challenged her with a smile of his own. "I mean think about it—two seniors and an impulsive woman?" He shook his head. "Not good."

"Our minds are set," Sarah stated, nodding to her aunt and Emily and receiving an answering nod from each.

Anthony continued to push. "There's nothing I can say to change your minds?"

"Nothing. We three ladies are off on a cruise."

Aunt Lilly and Emily grinned at her.

Anthony picked a chocolate out of the box, flicked a piece of spinach off and dropped it in his mouth. "You're making a big mistake."

The biggest mistake she'd ever made was sitting in front of her. Sarah smiled. "A cruise will be a pleasure," she said, hoping he choked on the chocolate.

Anthony crossed his arms over his white silk-covered chest. "Fine then, book your cruise. But don't say I didn't warn you." He tipped the chair back, balancing it on its back legs and grinning across the table.

The bastard! Sarah didn't trust his look of satisfaction. How the hell had he turned the tables on her? Sarah fisted her hands under the table and smiled back at him.

This was terrible. The kitchen and her life had been turned upside down. She'd lost control over her reasoning the minute Anthony had walked through the kitchen door.

Not to mention the fact that she couldn't find her sandals. Sarah glanced at the candles and shivered. She wanted to get up and leave, but crunching and sliding out the door on bare feet was not her idea of a grand exit.

So much for having it all figured out.

Sarah launched a sweater across her bedroom. How the hell did she get herself into these predicaments? "I should have kept my big mouth shut," she mumbled, slamming a drawer closed.

It never failed. Every time she was backed into a corner, she came out fighting. Was it any wonder she was kicking herself? If she'd kept quiet, she wouldn't be packing for a European cruise. "Stupid cruise."

Oh, the cruise wasn't why she was upset. It was the feeling that she had been railroaded that really bothered her. "Stupid, stupid cruise!"

Seeing Anthony again put her through hell. The fact that he was headstrong, Sarah could handle. That he was bossy, domineering and a complete workaholic, she could also handle. That he was her ex—that she could *not* handle.

"I shanghaied myself into this," Sarah sighed, tossing clothes in the direction of her bed, where they landed next to her suitcase. The more Anthony had insisted that it was unreasonable for his grandmother and her Aunt Lilly to travel, the more determined she'd become that nothing would stand in their way.

"Incompetent!" Sarah yelled, remembering the words he'd used. She balled her bathing suit and jammed it into a corner of her suitcase. "Unbelievable!" She'd let him get under her skin and had sealed her own fate. "He has some nerve saying those things to me."

Sarah frowned at the sweater she was holding and couldn't remember picking it up. "What the hell am I doing?" She sent the sweater flying across the room to join the growing pile of clothes stacked on a wicker chair in the corner.

"Did you know that talking to yourself is the first sign of madness? Either that or you're getting old," Amanda said from the doorway.

Startled, Sarah found her sister leaning against the doorframe, her arms crossed over her chest, smirking at her. "I was thinking out loud," she retorted.

"Yeah, right. Either way, you'll fit in like an old shoe with Aunt Lilly and Emily on this trip," Amanda said.

Sarah couldn't get over the changes in Amanda. After Aunt Lilly had cast a spell on her, she had blossomed from a frumpy, quiet mouse into an outspoken, confident woman. Amanda's transformation may have been the result of the spell, but Sarah knew that all her sister had needed was a push in the right direction. It was utter nonsense to believe in magic.

Dressed in cream-colored suede pants, a mauve top and cream pumps, Amanda exuded chic sophistication. These days, she wore her curly auburn hair loose about her shoulders instead of tying it back in the no-nonsense bun she had once preferred. Her gold-framed glasses had been traded in for a pair of contact lenses to show off her beautiful green eyes.

While Amanda had taken after their Irish mother, with her petite stature and voluptuous curves, Sarah had inherited their Sicilian father's brown, almond-shaped eyes and volatile temperament. Tall with slender curves, Sarah tended to be bluntly outspoken. It was that delightful trait that had landed her in this mess.

"Is Mark staying here while we're away?" Sarah asked.

"You betcha," Amanda replied, wiggling her ring finger and showing off the emerald engagement ring. "Said he didn't like the idea of me being alone in this big house."

Sarah winked at Amanda. "Don't do anything I wouldn't do."

"While I concentrate on Mark here, see if you can get laid on this cruise," Amanda chuckled. "You might come home more relaxed."

"You may think this is funny, but I don't."

Amanda walked into Sarah's room. "You know, for someone who's about to go on vacation, you don't sound too thrilled."

"I am…and I'm not." Sarah took clothes from her overflowing suitcase and set them on her bed.

"Care to elaborate?"

Sarah didn't meet her sister's penetrating stare. Instead, she hid her mixed emotions behind an indifferent shrug. "Both

Aunt Lilly and Emily wanted me to go. I couldn't disappoint them."

"Really? That's the only reason?"

Sarah clipped a skirt onto a hanger and hung it back in her closet. "Oh, all right! I'll admit I was adamant about going on this trip because Anthony insisted that it wasn't a good idea."

"Jeez, that sounds just like you."

"Besides, I've always wanted to see Europe," Sarah continued, carrying a pile of clothes to her drawer and stuffing them back inside. Who was she trying to convince with that load of bull?

Pulling her hair away from her face, Sarah surveyed the room. It was a mess. Just like her life. Anthony was the only man who could affect her this way. If she didn't know better, she'd swear she had met her match. "When hell freezes over," Sarah mumbled and heard Amanda laugh.

Sarah refolded a skirt from the pile of clothes beside her suitcase. "Why are you smirking? I'm a basket case here," she fumed, throwing the garment back down. "Oh, that's it!" This was ridiculous. She'd packed enough clothes to last a month.

"You really have it tough. A week-long cruise." Amanda shook her head. "Poor Sarah," she said sarcastically, pointedly staring at the overflowing suitcase.

"Amanda?" Sarah growled.

Her sister innocently smiled back. "What?"

"Shut up," Sarah snapped, pushing long strands of her jet-black hair off her face.

"Tell you what, if you really don't want to go, I'll explain it to the others," Amanda said, turning to leave.

Sarah grabbed her by the arm. Amanda was turning her words around. "I never said that. It's just that I'm a little nervous."

Now You See It…

Amanda hid her smirk behind her hand as she tried to keep a straight face.

Sarah threw her hands in the air. "Oh hell, who am I kidding? Try a lot nervous."

"About the flying?" Amanda asked.

"It's just the takeoffs and landings that bother me."

"What about Anthony?"

Sarah snorted. "Ancient history. The only reason he's here is to give us a ride to the airport, then it's a done deal." *And good riddance.*

She knelt in her closet to see which shoes she'd like to bring and in the middle of all her pumps and stilettos were her missing sandals. She'd worn flip-flops during the week to do her running around, and hadn't even bothered to look in the closet. No wonder she hadn't been able to find them since the day her aunt had cast the spell. "How the hell did they get back here?" she wondered aloud, lifting them and staring in disbelief.

"You're talking to yourself again."

"Stress." Sarah threw the sandals to the back of her closet. She knew she hadn't put them there, so who — or what — had? The spell? Ridiculous.

"You know, one of these days you're going to come across a man who isn't scared so easily by your quirkiness or your blunt backtalk," Amanda said, shaking her head. "He'll see past your tough exterior to the diamond beneath."

Sarah gave a nervous chuckle. "If he's stubborn enough to get past my defenses, I'll put him out of his misery and keep him," she said, standing up and brushing her knees. "Any more sisterly advice you care to dish out before I finish packing?"

Amanda laughed. "Okay, I get the message. I'll get out of your way, but before I go I brought you a present," she said, handing Sarah a small bag.

"Why did you do that?" Sarah asked, accepting the carrier and noting the prestigious store's logo on the front.

"I'm returning the compliment. Think of it as a small thank you for the time you hid my old clothes and replaced them with new ones. You forced me to change my image and how I saw myself."

Sarah pulled out a bottle of Romance perfume with a scroll attached. She took off its cap and sprayed her wrist. A rich, exotic fragrance filled the air. "Oh, how lovely," Sarah sighed, hugging Amanda. "Thank you."

"Read the scroll."

Sarah unraveled the small piece of parchment paper and groaned. "Not that stupid spell Aunt Lilly cast on me? Where did you find the spell book? And why did you copy the spell?" Sarah rolled the paper back up and held it out to her sister. It brought back the horrible memory of how this had all began.

Blushing, Amanda waved her sister's outstretched hand away. "I popped a button on Mark's shirt the other day and went looking for Aunt Lilly's sewing basket. That's where she hid the book. When I flipped through it I found the spell she made up for you written on the back page, next to the one she wrote for me. Keep it. I copied it because you never know if it'll come in handy."

With a shrug, Sarah jammed the spell into the side pocket of her suitcase. She was positive the spell hadn't worked on her, even if Amanda's had taken on a life of its own.

Sarah flipped the lid of her suitcase shut and sat on top. "Aunt Lilly cast a whopper on you. I thought it was hilarious."

Amanda tugged the bag's zipper closed while Sarah bounced on the top. "There was nothing funny about it. I stepped on a few people's feet," Amanda replied. Once the suitcase was shut, she stepped back. "What about you? Anything happen yet?"

"Besides misplacing a pair of shoes? Nah," Sarah said, hopping off the bag. "I figure if nothing has happened by now, nothing ever will." From her mouth to God's ears.

Amanda picked up a shirt from the floor and hung it back in the closet. "I think it's just a matter of time before Aunt Lilly's spell kicks in."

"What, are you nuts? I've got enough to deal with. Just forget about the spell, I already have," Sarah replied, not sounding too convincing, even to herself. "Give me a hand here." The two of them grabbed the handle and heaved the suitcase off the bed, letting it land with a loud thud.

From down the hallway, Aunt Lilly called out, "Lord have mercy, what fell?"

Sarah listened to the sound of her aunt's feet running on carpet. Aunt Lilly charged into the room with her hands clasped against her heaving, ample chest. When she saw that no one was hurt, her anxious expression dissolved.

Her sweet aunt was dressed in a slip that was partly tucked into the girdle valiantly attempting to squeeze her rotund body. A baby blue box hat tilted precariously on her head of gray curls. "Why aren't you dressed yet?" she asked Sarah.

Sarah looked down at her faded blue jeans and her white T-shirt. "There's nothing wrong with what I'm wearing."

"I thought people were supposed to dress up when they traveled," said Aunt Lilly.

"You've been watching too many old black-and-white movies. If you intend to wear that girdle for the whole eight-hour flight, you won't be able to eat any of the food and champagne they'll be serving us in first-class." Sarah knew that would get her aunt's attention.

"To hell with that!" Lilly exclaimed, wiggling out of the girdle and smoothing her slip over her round figure. "Ah, now *that's* more like it." She waved the girdle like a flag on her way out. "By the way, I just happened to be looking out the window when a big-ass limousine drove up with Anthony and Emily," she called over her shoulder as she left the room.

Sarah sighed. "Here goes nothing." She strapped her watch onto her wrist before putting on a pair of gold hoop earrings and an ankle bracelet.

"Quit griping," Amanda said. "Nothing is going to happen."

Sarah had a queasy sensation in the pit of her stomach that wouldn't go away. "My gut is telling me this trip is going to be a disaster."

"At least you weren't stripped of power over your tongue. Your situation couldn't get any worse than mine did. Now come on," Amanda said, pushing Sarah toward the stairs.

Sarah reluctantly entered the parlor and glanced at the assembled people. The lamps had been lit, casting a soft glow over the occupants and accenting the rich red walls. Amanda joined Mark on one of the sofas flanking an ornate, marble-top table sitting in front of the cast-iron fireplace.

Emily sat in one of the two Queen Anne armchairs in front of the lace-covered windows, tapping absently on the table beside her as she waited. With her short, curly white hair, laughing blue eyes and short stature, she was the picture of absolute delight.

And then there was Anthony. The minute Sarah's gaze landed on him, she felt claustrophobic. Just watching him sit there casually on the piano bench, his legs stretched out and crossed at the ankles, made the air shrink around her.

His presence charged the air with electricity as sparks flew whenever he was near. It was the constant control Anthony held over everything that frightened Sarah. She shrank away from the temptation he exuded.

His black silk shirtsleeves were rolled to his elbows, showing his sculpted arms to perfection. Black tailored pants fitted him snugly, emphasizing his narrow waist and muscular legs. His hair was tied back and his diamond stud glittered. Sarah could swear it winked at her.

"Hello Anthony, where'd you leave your suit?"

Anthony turned his attention to her and smiled. "Same place I left my cell phone."

Sarah crossed her arms over her chest. "Since when are you without your cell? It's normally attached to your hip."

"At the moment, it's not on me." He raised his hands. "You want to check?"

The suggestion tightened her every nerve ending. Sarah threw her hair over her shoulder with a slow practiced move, building her barriers. "I'll pass." She peeked at her watch. One hour—just one more hour and she'd see the last of him.

She sighed. What a hell of a package. No wonder women always chased him, but Sarah wasn't going to add herself to the growing list. He wasn't what she wanted.

She wanted a man she could rely on. Someone who would enrich her life with a loving, passionate relationship and children. She wanted a man who wanted to spend more time with his family than his work.

Sarah felt his dark, piercing eyes watching her, probing past her invisible walls. Yet, when she tried to decipher his emotions, he masked his face of all expression, as though burying his feelings deep within himself. Sarah recognized that mechanism—she also used it often.

Anthony took a moment to glance around the room, appraising his surroundings. "They don't build houses like this anymore. If one were to come on the market, I'd buy it." His eyes returned to Sarah, torching a trail down her body. "I see you've dressing up for the occasion."

"I don't need to impress anyone," Sarah retorted, walking over to Anthony's grandmother and planting a kiss on her soft, wrinkled cheek before sitting down in the chair beside hers. Emily was a woman of few words. No wonder she and

Aunt Lilly got along so well. One never stopped talking while the other one just listened.

"Are you ready for the cruise?" Mark asked Sarah as he wrapped his arm around Amanda's shoulders.

"As I'll ever be."

Sarah watched her sister stroke a finger over Mark's chin and felt a deep yearning inside of her. She wondered how much courage it would take to expose herself to another human being like that. Security was one of the rewards, but at what cost?

"Is this house haunted?" Emily asked. "Where I come from in Italy, the houses are so old that we automatically expect them to be haunted."

Lost in thought, Sarah almost missed the question. "Excuse me? What's haunted?"

"The house," Emily repeated.

"What's haunted?" Aunt Lilly asked, walking in at the end of their discussion. Sarah noticed her aunt had changed into a flowing, flower-print dress and grinned.

Sarah stood up to give her aunt her seat. "I was just about to explain to Emily that our home isn't haunted."

Aunt Lilly sighed. "Too bad. Think of all the fun I could have communicating with the dead."

Sarah perched herself on the armrest of her aunt's chair. "You cause enough trouble for the living. Leave the departed alone. They wouldn't be able to handle you."

"I never cause trouble," Aunt Lilly said. "Just look at how good Mark and Amanda look together."

Mark grinned. "That's right, Amanda revealed a side of herself she wouldn't have dared show me if it wasn't for your spell." He lifted her hand and kissed near the emerald ring he had given her. "Thanks, Aunt Lilly."

Aunt Lilly laughed. "You see, I always know what I'm doing."

Now You See It…

Shocked by Mark's openness about the spell, Sarah glanced at Anthony and found an amused gleam in his eyes. "Anthony knows about this?"

"Who else could I have told but my best friend?" asked Mark. "I didn't understand what was going on."

Sarah was astonished that someone outside her family knew about her aunt's spell. "And his response?"

Mark chuckled. "He said to go with the flow. That there were some things in life you couldn't explain but they sure made it more interesting. Just like women."

"So when's the wedding?" asked Anthony, turning his attention to Mark and Amanda. Sarah inhaled deeply and slowly let out her breath.

"We've decided on the end of October," Mark smiled down at Amanda. "That way the summer heat is over and the leaves have started to change colors."

Sarah gasped. "That's just over a month away."

Amanda laughed. "We know. We figured you'd come back from your holiday all rested and ready to be put to work," she said then nudged Mark.

"We were also wondering," Mark cleared his throat, "if you and Anthony would be our best man and maid of honor?"

Aunt Lilly clapped her hands joyfully. "Yes, yes, yes! It'll make us one big happy family."

Sarah quietly snickered. "Imagine that."

"I can't wait," mumbled Anthony.

"That makes Sarah and Anthony a *comare* and a *compare*," Emily said.

"What does that mean?" asked Sarah.

"Directly translated, it means godmother and godfather," Anthony said. "However, according to Italian tradition, once a family classifies you as such you have been welcomed into the fold and all that it entails."

Sarah narrowed her eyes. "What exactly does it entail?"

"Since I'm the only other male member of this family, it's my duty to join forces with Mark and make sure you women stay out of trouble, and that trouble doesn't find you," Anthony finished, with a satisfied look on his face.

"Hot damn, two men for the price of one," Aunt Lilly said.

"Bravo, Antonio!" Emily beamed.

What nerve. Who the hell did he think he was? Sarah walked purposely toward Anthony and glared down at him. "We've been looking after ourselves just fine. We don't need any man tucking us into bed at night."

Anthony leaned forward and whispered, "When was the last time someone tucked you in?"

"Last night."

The insufferable man chuckled. Sarah peeked at her watch—fifty-five minutes and counting.

Aunt Lilly leaned sideways in her seat. "I can't hear a damn thing you two are saying."

"I just told Sarah that in time everything will work out right," Anthony said, without looking away from Sarah's outraged stare.

"And what did you say, dear?" Aunt Lilly asked.

Sarah refused to look away. "I said we have to catch our flight."

Aunt Lilly looked at Mark and Amanda then back at Sarah. "Speaking of flight, you booked it, so when do we leave?"

"Right now," Sarah said. The sooner the better, in her humble opinion. After this she wouldn't have to set eyes on Anthony again.

Anthony stood up, his body too close for Sarah's comfort. "Where's your luggage?"

Now You See It…

She took one quick step back, making him smile. She'd forgotten how tall he was. She looked up to make eye contact. "Upstairs in our rooms. Are you sure you'll be able to carry them?"

"Mark, lead the way," Anthony said.

Both men left the room as the women moved toward the front hall. She grinned at Anthony's retreating back. Just thinking how annoyed he'd get when he lifted her suitcase gave her pleasure.

"Why do you smile like that?" Emily asked.

"Oh, no reason. It's just that I might have overpacked just a tad." Sarah chuckled as they walked out onto the front porch. He'd always complained about lugging her heavy suitcase whenever they'd snuck away for a weekend. For once, she wasn't sorry she was a habitual overpacker.

Outside, twilight covered the city as lights slowly came to life in neighboring homes. Spotlights illuminated the surrounding trees and shone down on the flagstone walkway leading to the waiting limousine. A cool, gentle breeze danced through the leaves as summer grudgingly loosened her hold and welcomed fall's first visits.

Amanda hugged the older women. "Enjoy yourselves," she said, before turning to hug Sarah. "And you—get rid of those sharp edges and promise me you'll behave."

"I'll hold my tongue if he does. Otherwise, I can't promise anything."

Amanda sighed. "I'll settle for that."

"Here they come," Sarah said, watching Mark and Anthony haul the luggage out the front door. The closer Anthony got, the clearer she could see his irritation.

"What the hell do you have in here?" Anthony asked Sarah, waving the chauffeur away. "Did you bring the kitchen sink?" He heaved her suitcase into the trunk with both hands.

Sarah smiled. "Everything, but."

Anthony pinched the bridge of his nose. "God, what a mouth."

Sarah turned her back on Anthony and hugged Mark, then her sister once more, before climbing into the waiting limousine. She settled into the farthest corner and watched Anthony climb in.

She could endure the drive to the airport, then she'd kiss him goodbye. Figuratively speaking, that is.

It would be easy. She'd keep her cool and wouldn't let him get to her. Bringing her wrist up to check the time, Sarah gasped.

Gone. Her watch had disappeared.

Looking around, she searched the floor of the limousine. "Not again," she muttered, checking out the window just in case it had fallen on the walkway. It was nowhere to be found.

"Is anything the matter dear?" Aunt Lilly asked. "Have you lost something?"

Her mind. "No, everything is perfect." A deep sense of dread settled in the pit of her stomach. Something had disappeared again and she was beginning to suspect why.

The spell.

Her adorable, scatterbrained aunt, like lightning, had struck twice.

Heaven help her.

Sarah sat up straight and checked to see if anything else had disappeared. "Hell."

Her ankle bracket was also missing.

Anything else? She gave herself a once-over. Nope. She exhaled a heartfelt sigh of relief that no other items had decided to vanish while still on her body.

But for how long?

Chapter Two

While her aunt acted like a child let loose in a candy store, Sarah sat as far away from Anthony as she could.

"Isn't this wonderful," Aunt Lilly sighed, smoothing her hand over the supple upholstery of the wraparound seats. "These leather seats are bigger than the sofas we have at home." Aunt Lilly pushed every button she could find as she made an inventory of this unaccustomed luxury.

Distracted, Sarah replied, "That's nice." She took slow shallow breaths to calm her nerves. That didn't help. Her mind was working a mile a minute and Anthony was still too close.

Crossing her legs, Sarah sank deeper into her corner. Like a magnet, her eyes were drawn to the digital clock beside the stereo, reminding her she now had no watch and thirty minutes left of this torturous ride.

She shut out what was going on around her. She'd stay quiet until they reached the airport. Then she'd get the hell out of the damn limousine so she could finally breathe without inhaling Anthony's scent. When she was on the airplane, she'd try to piece together what was happening to her.

Aunt Lilly laughed. "If this car could talk, imagine the naughty stories it could tell."

When neither Anthony nor Sarah answered her, Aunt Lilly glared at them. "What's the matter with you two? For the last ten minutes you haven't said a word."

Sarah forced a smile. "I guess I'm lost for words."

"Must be a change," Anthony said.

"*Basta!* Enough!" Emily said. "If the two of you can't stop acting like children, I'll ask the chauffeur to pull over. Then both of you can get out and finger a ride home."

"*Nonna*, that's *thumb* a ride home," Anthony said.

"Same difference," Lilly chimed in. "Well? Are you going to cooperate?" she asked, shaking her finger at them. "Or do I join forces with your grandmother and kick you out while the car is still moving?"

Anthony pointed to Sarah. "I'll bury the hatchet if she does."

Aunt Lilly folded her arms across her ample chest. "She will if she knows what's good for her. Otherwise, I'll bury a hatchet in both your thick skulls."

Sarah wrapped her hair behind her ear. "She's been watching the *Sopranos* again."

"Well?" he asked.

"Fine." Sarah smiled at the clock—minutes to go. She'd soon be leaving Anthony and some of her troubles behind her.

"Thanks," Anthony said.

"You're welcome," Sarah replied, feeling a bit of her tension ebb away.

Emily looked out the window. "I'm glad we came early, look at this mess."

Sarah stared outside as the chauffeur negotiated the detour redirecting traffic around Toronto's airport as it received a much-needed face-lift and expansion.

"Don't let it fool you. It might look like chaos, but the workers make sure it doesn't interfere with the day-to-day running of the airport," Anthony said.

Sarah narrowed her eyes. "How do you know?"

Anthony shrugged. "It's common knowledge."

"And because his company bid on the carpentry work and won," Emily said.

"Congratulations." Sarah was sure he had worked hard to get the contract. He always worked hard—that was one of the reasons they'd broken up.

When the limousine slowed down in front of sliding glass doors, Sarah exhaled a sigh of relief. Finally.

"Here we are," Anthony said.

"I'm so excited," Aunt Lilly breathed, squeezing Sarah's hand.

Sarah waited while the chauffeur assisted her aunt and Emily out of the car. Anthony gave her a slight bow. "After you."

So that she could be conscious of him eyeing her behind? She didn't think so. "No, after you, I insist."

Anthony laughed. "My pleasure." He exited the car and offered his hand.

Sarah had no choice but to accept. A charge of electricity traveled from her fingertips up her arm. Sarah jumped out of the limo and quickly dropped his hand.

Heaven help her, his touch set alarm bells off in her head. Her body refused to forget Anthony while her mind refused to remember, leaving Sarah precariously balanced on the sharp edge of frustration. Leaning either way would cost her dearly.

Sarah cleared her suddenly dry throat. "Thank you," she offered, easily held captive under Anthony's penetrating stare.

"You're welcome." An unexpected current jumped to his fingertips and up the length of his arm. It had always been like this with Sarah. Narrowing his eyes, he watched her swallow nervously before she looked away.

He felt an invisible barrier come up between them as Sarah straightened to her full height, forcing him to step back. "If you'll excuse me, I'll see if they need my help."

"Go ahead and I'll join you in a second," Anthony said.

"No problem." Sarah quickly followed her aunt inside. Her hair swung from side to side, brushing her faded jean bottom.

He had to hand it to her. No matter what she wore, she always looked good. There was a dignified grace and poise to her movements. With her olive skin, large brown eyes and waist-long black hair, she resembled a modern-day gypsy.

Damned if she hadn't done it again. Every time he glimpsed a softer side to her character, those barriers would come back up. She used that sassy mouth of hers to put him on the defensive.

But he had no intention of doing what she expected.

He understood her distrust. To be honest, in their past relationship he'd been an inconsiderate pig. He'd cancelled dates at the last minute, stood her up because his meetings ran late. And the dates they *did* go on were interrupted by his cell ringing at the most inappropriate times. Anthony cringed at the memories. She'd had every right to walk out on him.

But he resented the fact she'd never understood how important it had been for him to succeed. Swimming with the rest of the industry sharks, he'd had to strike faster and harder or they'd have taken bite after bite out of him, until they drowned his father's company. He would never let that happen.

One minute he was confident she'd always be there and the next she was gone. It had given his inflated ego an overdue lesson. He hadn't realized that he'd begun to rely on Sarah to share each success and failure. When she had left, his victories weren't as sweet. He had tried to get in touch with her but she'd never returned his calls.

Anthony watched the sliding doors close behind Sarah and shook his head. He'd have to tread carefully this time.

"You can run all you want but you won't get far," he said, walking with purpose through the doors toward the women. He was ready for Sarah.

Sarah and Aunt Lilly stepped up to the luggage counter and checked in. Anthony waited for his turn then placed his and his grandmother's suitcases on the conveyor belt. He glanced over his shoulder to make sure Sarah was at a safe distance. She probably thought he was helping his grandmother, and that's exactly what he'd let her think. He needed the element of surprise so she couldn't back out at the last minute.

Over the intercom, passengers were being paged. The air vibrated with excitement and pulsed with the power of nearby airplane engines preparing for takeoff.

And Sarah was finally grinning. He knew exactly what she was thinking. With that relaxed smile of hers, she was counting down the minutes 'til he finally left. Anthony ushered his grandmother in their direction. "Ladies, on to the VIP lounge."

"I'm sure we can find it ourselves," Sarah said. "Besides, you're not allowed through customs, so we'll say our goodbyes so you don't keep the chauffer waiting."

There was that smile again. Anthony pulled out the security badge that he used while working on the job site at the airport. "I can get into most parts of the airport with this baby. And the chauffeur does what he's paid to do." He had already dismissed his driver. Offering his arm to his grandmother, Anthony led the way, ignoring the black looks Sarah shot his way.

Two large, floor-to-ceiling burgundy oak doors greeted them. Anthony pushed them open. "After you," he said to his companions, revealing a sumptuous room.

"*Oh, mamma mia*, look at this," Emily said. "It's wonderful."

His grandmother turned around, taking in the VIP lounge with its polished wood cabinets, upholstered chairs grouped around small tables and smooth granite floors. Businessmen and women relaxed in lounge chairs or chatted on their cell phones.

A hostess greeted them at the door. "Good evening, my name is Claire. Can I offer you anything while you wait? A drink or perhaps something to eat?"

"How does champagne sound?" Anthony asked, taken in by the festive mood.

Aunt Lilly rubbed her hands together. "Bring it on," she said and headed toward the Internet terminals along the wall.

"*Nonna?*"

"*Va bene*, that's fine by me," she said, sitting in a reclining chair and putting her feet up.

"Sarah?" Anthony watched her settle onto a black leather sofa.

Sarah gave an indifferent shrug. "Whatever they want is fine by me."

Sarah grabbed the first magazine she found and absently flipped through it. At the speed she was turning the pages, Anthony wasn't sure she was seeing anything. Only moments after picking up the first magazine, Sarah returned it to the table in front of her and picked up another, repeating the same nervous process.

"What's wrong?" he asked.

"Nothing," she said, not meeting his eyes. "Couldn't be better." Sarah resumed her nervous page flipping.

Could have fooled him. One of her legs was shaking at a fast pace. It reminded him of a nervous twitch. Sitting down beside her, Anthony watched her beneath his lashes. Sarah was on the edge.

"Here you are." The hostess placed a tray holding their drinks and a bottle on the table.

Sarah snatched up one of the glasses as though it were a life preserver and took a large gulp. Anthony stood up to pass

Now You See It...

a glass to his grandmother and walked over to Aunt Lilly at the terminals with another before returning to his seat.

"Thirsty?"

Sarah gulped what was in her mouth too quickly and choked. "Yes," she said, coughing.

"I'd take it easy or you won't make it to the plane."

"I'm fine, perfectly fine."

If that's the case, why is she trying so hard to compose herself? Anthony wondered. Her anxiety was building to the point where she was having difficulty breathing. Surely all the tension wasn't from his presence alone?

From a computer terminal, Aunt Lilly called across the lounge, "Drinking all that champagne won't cure your fear of flying."

Conversations stopped as all eyes in the lounge turned toward Sarah. She blushed in embarrassment at her aunt's loud announcement. "Why don't you just tell the whole damn world while you're at it?" Sarah muttered.

Aunt Lilly smiled at her discomfort as she crossed the room to join them. "Every time we've gone on a trip, Sarah gets a little tipsy so she can relax."

"How frightened of flying are you?" Anthony asked.

"It's not the flying I have a problem with. It's the takeoffs and landings. So now that you know, I'll just pour myself one more glass for the road." She reached for the bottle, but he moved it out of her reach.

"Hey!"

"I want to help."

"I don't remember asking for your assistance. Now hand over the bottle."

Anthony chuckled at the delightful picture Sarah presented. "Aren't you supposed to practice deep breathing and think of a tranquil place?"

"Been there. Done that. I even went to one of those classes that are supposed to help you with your phobias. Nothing's worked." With a resigned sigh, Sarah put her glass back down on the table.

"*Non ti preoccupare,*" Emily said. "Don't worry. My Anthony will sit beside you on the plane."

"That won't be— He'll what?" Sarah's screeched, making some businessmen frown at her. Horrible disbelief radiated through her body. "You can't go on this trip. Who's going to baby-sit your precious company while you're away?"

"I've left it in capable hands. Nothing will happen while I'm away for a week," Anthony smiled. "You wanted to be their chaperone. I'm just coming along for the ride."

"What the hell is a compulsive workaholic supposed to do on holiday?" Sarah pushed her hair over her shoulder.

She did have a point. "Relax."

"You rat." Sarah's eyes narrowed. "You planned this from the very beginning, didn't you? No wonder you caved in so easily." Sarah stood up and grabbed her purse. "Enjoy your trip."

At that moment, their flight was announced. Anthony stood up and blocked Sarah's exit. "Too late. It would cost the airline to search the hold for your luggage, and put them behind schedule."

"Not to mention that it would look suspicious if a passenger wanted to leave at the last moment," Aunt Lilly chimed in. "And because we checked in together, they'd drag our asses to security and we'd all miss our flight."

With dread, Sarah looked out the window at the waiting airplane. "Oh, this is just peachy."

"Let's go." Aunt Lilly took hold of Emily's arm and together they toddled toward the exit.

Anthony picked up his jacket from the sofa and, when he straightened, found Sarah filling her glass again. "None of that," he said, taking the champagne out of her hands before it could reach her mouth and placing it back on the tray. "You won't be needing that."

"Traitor."

Anthony led her out of the lounge. "Trust me," he replied, threading his arm through hers and heading for the plane.

Sarah jerked her arm out of his grasp. "The last time you said that you didn't bother showing up." She marched toward the waiting hostesses.

Ouch. Sarah made a direct hit. He knew the night she was talking about. They had made plans to have dinner together, then after the meal she was going to introduce him to her family. Again, his meeting had run late, and again, he hadn't shown up. That had been the last straw for Sarah.

Once on board, they were directed to their first-class seats. Aunt Lilly and Emily sat together while Anthony and Sarah sat behind them.

Sarah looked apprehensively out the window as passengers continued to board. She jumped when the airplane door shut loudly. "Here goes nothing," she muttered, trying to think happy thoughts, but her muddled mind wouldn't cooperate. Anthony had reentered her life, her jewelry and shoes kept disappearing and she needed a drink.

The plane taxied to its designated takeoff area. Sarah gripped the armrests and squeezed her eyes shut. She took short, quick breaths and hoped the ringing in her ears would stop. A light sheen covered her forehead.

These short moments before takeoff seemed to stretch forever. She knew that once the plane leveled off, her nerves would calm down. For now, she tried to think of something, anything, to distract herself.

Anthony pried her hand off the armrest and cocooned her ice-cold fingers in his warm palms. "Sarah? Look at me."

"Shut up," she replied, refusing to open her eyes while she gripped Anthony's hand. It didn't matter what she clung to, so long as she had a firm grip on something solid.

Anthony pulled his hand out of her tight grip and tapped her earring to gain her attention, making it sway against her neck. "I want you to look at me."

Sarah's eyes popped open. "Can't a person suffer in peace?"

"This is going to be the best takeoff you've ever experienced, I promise," Anthony said, turning sideways in his seat to face her.

"I didn't believe your promises then and I don't believe them now."

Unfolding Sarah's fists, Anthony placed them on his chest. Sarah could feel his heat slowly seep into her cold fingers. The rhythm of his steady heartbeat registered beneath her palms. She couldn't remember if she had turned to him, or if he had pulled her to him.

Sarah's eyes widened. "What are you doing?" She glanced at the seats in front of her, hoping her aunt wouldn't look back to see what was going on.

Anthony rubbed the backs of her hands with his thumbs, sending soothing shivers up her arms. "When I make a promise I keep it," he said, slowly drawing Sarah closer.

Sarah snorted. "Since when?" She watched the determination on Anthony's face as he came nearer. "Anthony, this is not a good idea."

Then why wasn't she pulling harder to be released?

Sarah listened to the engines increase their power. The plane was ready for takeoff.

Without warning, Anthony wrapped her in his arms and brought his mouth down on hers.

Concentrating on the warm, wet pleasure of Anthony's lips, Sarah felt her fear and surroundings slipping away.

Anthony twined his fingers in Sarah's thick, luxurious hair before cupping her cheeks with his palms. This was the best thing he could think of. He had to get her mind off their takeoff.

Well...that was the excuse he was sticking to.

He wasn't sure if he should let go of her anytime soon, in case she slugged him. Gradually, Sarah's eyes drifted shut and her lips softened, the tension draining from her body. Feeling her response, Anthony lessened the pressure of his mouth and enjoyed the fullness of her lower lip. She tasted and felt exactly like he remembered.

He feathered small kisses from her lips to her cheeks, and over her closed eyelids. So soft. Beneath her perfume, her distinct vanilla scent brought back erotic memories. She smelled like his favorite biscotti. If he ever found Sarah in his cookie jar, he wouldn't share.

Anthony trailed kisses along her jaw, up to her ear and licked the spot behind her earlobe. Sarah gasped in surprise and tightened her grip on his shirt. Oh hell. Never mind his grandmother's frosted cookies. Sarah was more addictive.

Pulling back, Anthony could still feel the tilt in his chair as the plane continued to climb. Glancing down into Sarah's face, he watched her open her eyes slowly, her unfocused gaze on him. "How do you feel now?"

In a daze, Sarah said, "Like punching you."

Anthony grinned. "I must need more practice."

A pleasure-pain whimper escaped Sarah as he recaptured her lips. Using his thumbs, he pressed the knots out of her shoulders. Her breathing escalated as they continued to climb. He nearly jumped out of his skin when her tongue tentatively licked the seam of his lips.

Anthony growled his response. What had started off as an exercise in light diversion was quickly turning into one of the most erotic kisses he had ever experienced. Readjusting his legs, he tried to find a more comfortable position. If they didn't slow this down, they'd end up shocking their relatives.

Sarah's head relaxed back, her body turning to liquid in his arms. Her trusting acceptance made her all the more desirable. Beneath his fingers her pulse beat out of control.

His plan of distraction was turning into a test of trust that Anthony had no intention of failing. He would keep her busy until the airplane leveled off and then, he promised himself, he would retreat to a safe distance.

With a low moan, Anthony feasted on her lips and tasted champagne. This was one great way to get drunk. His senses reeled, his rapid breathing matching Sarah's. He wanted to absorb her. Reaching down between the two of them, he pushed the armrest back out of the way and pulled Sarah's soft body closer.

"Much better," Anthony sighed, running his tongue along her teeth to make her open for him.

Their tongues dueled. The motors roared. As the plane continued to climb, so did his temperature.

Heat burned her hands as she slid them over Anthony's chest and wrapped them around his neck to pull him closer. He had to be joking about his expertise. If he was any more proficient, she'd be flying higher than the plane.

"You see, that wasn't so bad." Aunt Lilly's voice spoke through the slight opening between her and Emily's seats. "My, my, my—now *that's* what I call a perfect takeoff."

Reality rudely brought Sarah back to the present. She loosened her grasp and blushed. Pulling back, she nervously pushed her hair behind her ear and straightened her clothes. She was mortified at her own behavior.

Like an idiot, she'd enjoyed every minute of it. Warmth, a sense of security and wanton feelings had flooded her while Anthony had worked his magic.

"You shouldn't have done that," Sarah whispered, despising her body's irritating attraction to Anthony.

For some reason he found her displeasure amusing. "I was only trying to help."

Tried? He'd succeeded with flying colors. "I appreciate your efforts, but next time just let me deal with my phobias in my own way. Okay?" She looked out the window to compose herself, and felt Anthony slowly withdraw his arms from around her waist.

He cleared his throat. "It's your call."

She knew he was waiting for her to turn around. His leg brushed against hers when he shifted in his seat.

She grasped a piece of hair and twirled it around her finger. Her best thinking was done this way. Tightening the tension on the rope of hair, her finger brushed up against her earlobe.

An earlobe that no longer wore an earring.

Oh God oh God! With shaking hands, Sarah touched her other ear and found that it too was bare. They might have fallen off. Leaning over, she scanned the area around her feet.

Nothing.

Dissolving into her seat, she closed her eyes and practiced breathing. This was torture, not knowing when something would disappear off her body. What would vanish next? Her shoes? Her blouse? She could use another drink right about now.

Aunt Lilly called back, "You didn't have to stop on our account, you know. You just go right ahead and do what you were doing and we'll just mind our own business."

Anthony leaned toward her and waved a hand in front of her face. "Are you okay?"

"Couldn't be better," she replied. Her grin felt stiff. "Aunt Lilly's right. That was a perfect takeoff," she said, hiding behind her dry sense of humor.

Caught unaware, Anthony roared with laughter. "Glad I could be of service."

"You'd make a fortune if you bottled what you've got and sold it to female passengers. Come to think of it, even the males," Sarah said, her emotions churning.

"Just think, young man," Aunt Lilly said. "According to my calculations, you have one more takeoff and two landings. I'd say you've got your work cut out for you."

Anthony chuckled. "You won't hear a complaint out of me."

Looking between the seats, Sarah gently reprimanded her aunt. "I thought you said you were going to mind your own business."

"I did. It's just that I get to decide what is or isn't my business," she said before turning forward again.

Once their meals were served, Anthony carefully forked lobster meat from its shell while attempting conversation with Sarah. "Your aunt told me you still do freelance bookkeeping from home."

Sarah's fork slipped across the lobster tail. When had he talked to her aunt about her? "Mm, I like that I can set my own hours." She pulled on a stubborn piece of lobster, trying not to send it flying. "What about you? Last time I knew, you were doing carpentry work in homes, but from what your grandmother said it sounds like you've moved on to industrial contracts."

They sounded like strangers meeting for the first time. Both circling, setting boundaries and making small talk, retrieving information via polite chitchat. Sarah felt silly. After that kiss, what was she supposed to say? *Hey that was some kiss. By the way what have you been up to?*

"That's right, over the last couple of years our company has grown and diversified. When my dad ran it, he only did homes. I took a chance and bid on the larger contracts."

Now You See It…

Sarah watched the movement of his hands as he ate. Smooth, firm, relaxed. He was enjoying his meal, instead of wolfing it down while listening to a business associate on his cell.

"What a difference," she muttered, dropping her lashes and concentrating on the lobster.

"What is?"

"I can't remember a meal without your cell phone."

Anthony grinned sheepishly. "Was I really that bad?"

"Worse," Sarah said, digging at her lobster tail. "Oh, to hell with this, I'm using my hands." She put down her fork, pushed up her sleeves, tucked a napkin in front of her shirt and dug in. "This is more like it."

Sarah tightened her fingers on the meat and pulled it out of the shell. She dipped it into the melted butter and raised it to her mouth, leaning forward to capture the tempting morsel between her lips—melted butter, fingers and all. When her fingers emerged she licked the butter off each tip, conscious of Anthony watching her every move, so engrossed by her actions that he left his fork suspended in midair.

Sarah wiped her mouth to hide her chuckle. She heard him release his breath and inhale oxygen back into his lungs.

"You know, it's much better this way," she said, handing Anthony a napkin. "Put this napkin in front of you for protection and use your hands. It's messier, but this is the only way to eat lobster." Finishing her first tail, she waved an attendant over and asked for another.

When it arrived, Sarah yanked on a stubborn piece of meat and sent it flying toward Anthony's plate. "Oops!" It landed close to his fork.

Anthony stabbed it and brought it close to his mouth. "More for me."

"You wish!" Sarah snatched it off his fork and dropped it into her mouth. "Thank you. That hit the spot."

Anthony pulled a piece of lobster from the tail on his plate and dipped it into the butter. "I don't remember you eating this way on our dates."

Sarah's smile dimmed as she retorted, "Maybe because by the time you showed up I had already lost my appetite."

An uncomfortable silence settled around them. Sarah wiped the rest of the butter off her hands. "Now I'm stuffed," she said, sitting back with a groan.

"You wouldn't happen to know which movie they're showing?" Anthony asked.

"No."

"*What Women Want*, with Mel Gibson," Aunt Lilly said from her seat.

"Your aunt has excellent hearing," whispered Anthony.

"She has what you call 'selective hearing'. She hears only the things she wants to hear."

"My grandmother suffers from the same malady."

"No, I don't," Emily answered.

Anthony grinned affectionately. "See what I mean?"

"You know, I thought only Sarah had a smart mouth, but the two of you could run rings around each other," Aunt Lilly said, one of her eyes peeking through the space between the chairs.

"I may have a sassy mouth, but at least I don't stick my nose where it doesn't belong. Or try to change people's lives by casting spells," Sarah said.

"Speaking of spells," Aunt Lilly paused, "this movie has given me an idea. When we get back home, how about I check to see if there's a spell in my spell book for ESP?"

"And do what with it?" Anthony asked, eyes widening at Aunt Lilly's suggestion.

"Why, cast it. What else would I do with it?"

"For whom would you do this wonderful favor?" Sarah asked.

Aunt Lilly poked her nose between the chairs. "For Anthony, of course. Emily said that he was looking for a nice girl to marry. What better way to find one if he knows what they're thinking? He'd be hitched in no time."

Anthony cleared his throat. "I'd be admitted into an asylum. I have enough trouble keeping my own thoughts in order, let alone having someone else's clogging my mind. Besides, I never mentioned anything to my grandmother about finding someone to settle down with. Women are high-maintenance, you know."

Sarah noticed that the more Anthony nixed the idea of settling down, the faster he tapped his fingers on the serving table. Aunt Lilly must have hit a nerve.

Through the crack in the seats, Sarah could see one of her aunt's eyebrows rise. "Butt out. His answer is no," Sarah said with more force than necessary. "And if I catch you trying anything with that spell book again, I'm going to hide your TV remote." Irritated, she looked out the window.

Women were high-maintenance? That was a laugh. Sarah wondered when was the last time Anthony had done his own laundry or cooked for himself. Sarah bet he even got his secretary to buy presents for his lady friends.

Sarah drummed her fingers on her armrest. There was a prickly sensation at the back of her neck that warned her Anthony was watching.

If he wanted to see a reaction to his words, she wouldn't give him the satisfaction. Besides, his preference didn't bother or concern her one bit. He had nothing that she was looking for in a man.

"Hmm!" huffed Aunt Lilly.

"What did that 'hmm' mean?" Anthony asked.

She turned to him with a blank expression. "That she won't try anything. We wouldn't want to put you in a situation you don't want. And think of the poor women whose minds you'd be reading."

Anthony exhaled a sigh of relief, her sarcasm lost on him. "Thank God for small mercies. Mark told me all about what happened with Amanda. I can honestly say I don't need anything strange happening in my life."

"You and me both."

"So what did she do to you?"

"Nothing much." Sarah crossed her fingers under her table. "Aunt Lilly cast a spell on me, but nothing's happened so far."

Liar. Sarah pulled on her naked earlobe, just in case her earring had come back. Why couldn't her aunt have cast a spell that *gave* her things, instead of taking them away? Her life at this moment was anything but normal. Items vanishing off her person was "nothing much"? What good was a spell if it didn't even work the way she wanted it to?

"I'm just lucky, I guess."

Now You See It…

Chapter Three
☙

The roar of the engines reversing their power and the jarring motion of the tires hitting concrete startled Sarah awake. Clapping and whistles resonated throughout the cabin. Looking up, she found Anthony grinning down at her.

"Good morning. You slept through the movie and even missed the landing," he said.

"You got shortchanged," Aunt Lilly said to Anthony, eavesdropping again.

Sarah combed her fingers through her hair and glanced down at herself. Intact. Thank God nothing had walked off while she slept. Outside, the bright sun reflected off the windows of the airport and heat rose off the tarmac as the plane taxied to a complete stop.

She jumped when one of Anthony's fingers touched her earlobe. "Did you take your earrings off before falling sleep?"

Sarah's hands flew to her ears. "Yes, that's exactly what I did."

She needed to be alone so she could figure out what was happening to her. This situation was quickly spiraling out of control. She wanted her carefree life back, and with Anthony invading her private space and the spell sabotaging her sanity, she was going to go stark raving mad. What she'd like to know is where the hell the missing items *went*.

So immersed in her own thoughts, she was astonished to find Anthony leaning on the armrest and peering out her window. Cornered. Her small sitting space had just gotten smaller. She shifted in her seat and pretended to brush off her jeans.

Aunt Lilly stood up and turned around to kneel in her seat. "What's next?"

Looking closely, Sarah noticed her aunt's eyes were glassy. "Did you sleep?"

"Not a wink," Aunt Lilly proudly stated. "Emily and I have been talking up a storm."

"I'll give them ten minutes into the bus ride before they're out like lights," Sarah whispered to Anthony. She noticed his shaved face and the subtle smell of clean soap. "Did you sleep?"

"I nodded off right after you did, but woke up an hour ago," Anthony said, as the airplane door opened. A rush of heat swirled through the plane.

Grinning, Aunt Lilly hopped off her seat and walked down the aisle. "What are we waiting for?"

"I'm right behind you," Sarah said, standing up. She couldn't give Anthony a bigger hint to hurry up and get off his butt. She was *so* out of there.

"What's your hurry?" Anthony asked, getting up from his seat to stand in the aisle.

"Can't wait to start my holiday," she said, scooting into the aisle in front of him before they both started slowly toward the exit.

Having taken a few moments to gather her things, Emily was now impatient to catch up to Aunt Lilly. "*Andiamo*. Let's go," she said, pushing Anthony right into Sarah.

She stumbled and would have fallen if it weren't for Anthony's quick reflexes. His strong arm embraced her waist, pulling her back against his solid chest. Sarah held on to his hard forearm and felt Anthony's muscles tighten as he supported her.

She closed her eyes, but the shocking feeling of attraction intensified, sending a shiver through her body. Her eyes popped open again. "Thank you," she said. Worried that

Anthony might feel her reaction, she pulled out of his arms and headed off the plane into Spain's hot, blazing sun.

Once on board the bus that would take them to the ship, Sarah sat by a window with Anthony beside her, her aunt and Emily behind them. When the doors closed, Sarah listened with half an ear as the travel rep filled them in on the details for boarding, safety drills and obtaining the key cards to their cabins.

"Did you get all that?" Sarah asked her aunt. The gentle sound of snoring greeted her question.

She glanced behind her and found Aunt Lilly and Emily fast asleep. "That's all right. I'll sign Aunt Lilly up while you look after things for your grandmother."

"Better still, you stay with them while I take care of everything," Anthony said.

Sarah scowled at him. "Thanks for the offer, but we can look after our own documentation."

Anthony returned her glare. "What's with you? Every time I try to help, you go on the defensive."

"It's not the fact that you want to help people that I object to, it's the way you *tell* people what they should do," Sarah answered, watching an angry flush touch Anthony's cheeks.

She wasn't going to budge from her position. Why should she? He'd been unreliable when they had dated and she sure as hell wasn't going to start depending on him now.

Anthony's jaw flexed as he ground his teeth in frustration. "I do no such thing."

"Sure you do," said Sarah. "You're just too stubborn to see it."

A cold silence greeted her words. Dark turbulent eyes met her immovable brown pair. A flush burned her face as she remained under his scrutiny. When Anthony finally spoke, it was with a deep, cold tone that froze Sarah's senses and brought goose bumps to her arms.

"*I'm* stubborn? You are the most maddening woman I've ever had the misfortune to meet. I have no idea what kind of low standards you have for the men you date, but for Italian men, it's genetic to be considerate."

Sarah didn't flinch at his harsh words. It would only make her vulnerable. "'Low standards'? I dated *you*, didn't I?"

Anthony's eyes narrowed. "Next time, I'll make sure not to offer my assistance."

"I'd appreciate that." Sarah turned her attention to the bus window and watched the lush tropical vegetation flash by as they neared the docks.

She clasped her hands tightly to stop them from shaking and counted backward from one hundred. They had said more than enough to each other. She didn't want to say something she would regret later.

They hadn't even boarded the ship and already they weren't speaking to one another. She'd like to know how they would pull off this trip without ruining it for their relatives.

Why couldn't Anthony accept that she didn't want his help? It wasn't personal—she just needed to look after her own things. She didn't want to rely on him for anything. That's just the way she was.

When they arrived at the docks, Amanda roused her aunt.

Lilly groaned. "Oh, I feel like a train hit me. What I need is to take a long nap."

"That makes two of us," Emily said, slowly wobbling along behind them.

Sarah assisted Aunt Lilly off the bus. "Once you get into your cabin, you can sleep as long as you want."

The first sight of the massive, gleaming white hull captivated Sarah. It sat in deep blue water with tiny rippling waves that reflected silver zigzags on the ship's underside. It was one of the newest and largest on the sea. It boasted every amenity a passenger could possibly want, including the very

Now You See It…

latest of technology. The only thing it couldn't do was fly. She guided her aunt to the ship, while a male passenger walking in front of them chatted to the woman beside him.

"Now that's what I call a beauty," he said, gazing at the ship, his voice booming.

"You say that about all your ladies," teased the woman.

The man reached out and hugged the woman. "Nope, only the ones I'm about to board," he said, earning him a light slap on his round stomach.

Sarah and the others approached the check-in counter while a band, dressed in black and gold uniforms, played a lively Spanish melody. A row of impeccably dressed stewards greeted them with sunny smiles.

"Isn't this something else?" asked Aunt Lilly, in awe of their posh surroundings.

Sarah couldn't agree more. The ship looked like a luxurious hotel with its granite floors, gilded mirrors, elegant furniture and marble tables topped with large vases of brilliant red, tropical flowers. Large, oil-painted landscapes of ports they were yet to visit caught the eye.

At check-in, they were given their boarding passes and assigned to cabins.

"Ms. Lilly McCall and Mrs. Emily Mancini, you are on the Promenade Deck in room 700, which is a deluxe cabin. And you, Miss Santorelli and Mr. Mancini, are located in cabins 5078 and 5076, which are side by side, just below on the Cabaret Deck."

Sarah's eyes widened in disbelief. This couldn't possibly be happening to her. Right next to each other? No way. Sarah panicked at the very thought. Every time she walked out of her cabin it would be like she was stepping through a mine field—always on the alert and ready for an explosion.

"Excuse me, but there seems to be a mistake," Sarah said. "We booked our rooms so my aunt and I could stay near each other. It's her first cruise and I'd like to be close to her."

The hostess looked over her reservation. "Well, if there has been a mistake, I can try to arrange another cabin for them on your deck. But they wouldn't be close to you. As it stands, their cabin is above yours, with a staircase just outside their door leading them to you."

"I see no problem with that," conceded Anthony. "And if they need anything, we're just steps away."

"Fine then," agreed Sarah, admitting defeat.

A steward escorted her aunt and Emily to their cabin first. Decorated in blue and rust colors, it contained two single beds and its own sitting area.

"This is just lovely. Now, I have the numbers of your cabins," Aunt Lilly said, shooing Sarah and Anthony out the door. "When we get up, we'll knock on your door or you'll find us relaxing above-deck. Either way, we'll leave you a message."

Sarah kept her distance from Anthony as they followed the steward down to their cabins.

"Here you are, side by side." The steward winked at Anthony. "Lucky guy," he said, unlocking Sarah's door and depositing her luggage in her cabin before leaving.

"See you later," she said and jumped into her room.

"Wait!" Anthony stopped her door from closing with his hand. "What are your plans?"

"Why?"

"If you haven't forgotten, we're in a foreign country. We need to know, at all times, where each one of us is so no one worries."

"You mean so *you* don't worry," Sarah said, stubbornly trying to close the door. She hadn't listened the last time he'd given advice, what made him think she would listen now? Besides, this was her vacation.

Anthony held on to Sarah's door. "I just want to make sure that everyone stays safe and gets home in one piece."

Now You See It…

"Tell you what, I'll have my secretary draw up my itinerary and email it to you." With an insincere smile, Sarah closed the door in Anthony's angry face.

Leaning against her door, Sarah heard Anthony's bang shut. The sound exploded around her, resonating against her frazzled nerves. She slumped as the remainder of her energy drained from her body, leaving her exhausted.

"Damn it," Sarah sighed in frustration.

Sarah spent a few moments looking over her cabin. A round window filled the cabin with bright sunshine and highlighted the cream and blue colors. Even though she had the cabin to herself, she felt trapped.

She'd go crazy if she had to wait in here for the others to wake up. Nor did she want to lounge by the pool after sitting for so long on the plane. "I need to burn off this nervous energy."

Taking a quick shower in the miniscule washroom, Sarah changed into a cream-colored top and a flowing, ankle-length flowered skirt, then slipped on a pair of low, open sandals that matched her top. Strapping a money pouch around her waist, she tossed in her boarding and key cards, a brush and some traveler's checks before heading toward the door, more than ready for some holiday adventure.

As her hand reached for the knob, Sarah heard the sound of Anthony's door opening and closing, followed by the sound of his footsteps walking away.

Interesting. *He can come and go as he pleases, but everyone else has to hand in their agendas.*

Peeking out her door, Sarah checked to see if the coast was clear. "This is ridiculous. I feel like a thief," she muttered.

Angry over her guilty actions, she straightened her shoulders. The ship wouldn't be leaving port for another five hours, so she decided to take a quick look around the ship before heading for the sights in Palma de Mallorca.

On deck, Anthony prowled back and forth to let off steam. With long quick strides, he ate the length of the ship before turning around and heading back, furious. "Her and that damn Irish temper of hers." He was absolutely fuming.

With each step he took, Anthony banged his fist along the railing. "Damn, damn, damn." He received peculiar stares from some of the passengers who stepped out of his way.

Never in his life had he come across such an obstinate woman. Anthony knew the reasons Sarah didn't want his help. One was so that she could remain in control, and two, so that he would keep his distance. He didn't mind the first, but she wasn't getting the second.

Beads of sweat coated his brow and made his clothes cling to his body. Anthony pulled at his red, short-sleeved cotton shirt and fanned it away from his body so the air would cool his heated skin. It didn't help. Dropping his shirt, he wiped his damp palms on his blue safari shorts.

Relaxing cruise? Some tourist he was turning out to be. Sure, he looked the part, right down to the canvas shoes on his bare feet. But relaxed was something he wasn't.

Taking deep breaths, Anthony inhaled the smell of the sea and forced himself to calm down. Looking around, the bright colors of the city and the sounds of the ocean finally registered. Palma de Mallorca, Spain, lay before him in all her splendor.

Leaning against the railing, he watched sea gulls fly above before diving for their food. A fresh breeze ruffled the water, reflecting flashes of silver as the sun glimmered on the surface. Sailboats, yachts, fishing vessels and other cruise liners dotted the port of call. Each rocked gently on calm, undulating waves.

The view of the mountainside was spectacular, with coral-colored homes clinging to its side, adding the perfect touch to the picturesque setting. A cathedral stood proud and tall with its walls shimmering for attention.

Below, Anthony could see the ship being loaded with large boxes of supplies—cases of fruit and vegetables and bottled water passed beneath him.

"Isn't this great?" asked a woman standing close by.

"Yes it is." Anthony glanced at her young, bright smile and blue eyes. She was in her early twenties, still with the blush of youth.

She extended her hand. "I'm Rachael Douglas."

Anthony shook her offered hand. "Anthony Mancini."

"You here by yourself?"

"I'm with family and friends. And you?"

A wistful sadness filled her eyes. "I'm hoping my boyfriend will make the cruise."

"I'm sure he will."

"You have more faith than I do. We had a fight last night and I'm not sure he'll still show up." Rachael touched her flushed cheeks. "Listen to me, unloading on a stranger. You're really easy to talk to."

Anthony watched a small sailboat put up her sails. A little girl waved and Anthony waved right back with a smile. "Not everyone thinks so."

"Thanks for listening," Rachael said, stepping back with a wave. "I'll be seeing you around."

"If you're ever at loose ends, just find me and I'll introduce you to my group," Anthony offered.

"I'll do that." With a final wave she strolled away.

He walked to the other end of the ship and again positioned himself by the railing, where he watched people board and exit.

"The view is quite lovely, isn't it?" A woman walked over and stood too close for Anthony's comfort.

Anthony smiled politely and took a step back, taking in her dark tan, colorful clothes and appraising stare. "Yes."

"But not as spectacular as you," she said boldly, taking a step closer. "If you're free, we could hook up."

He looked around to see if he was the only one being propositioned and noticed for the first time several men and women who seemed to be trawling for partners. Anthony shook his head at the craziness. The woman's bluntness was obviously part of the vacation atmosphere. It made people do and say the most outrageous things. Especially on cruises. "I'm with someone."

"Oh well." The woman shrugged. "Easy come, easy go," she said and walked away.

Close by, an elaborate buffet table was set with a large variety of foods. Picking up a couple of pineapple cubes on toothpicks, Anthony popped the fruit into his mouth and continued to stroll along the deck.

Splashing and screams of victory came from the pool where people played volleyball. It took up a large part of the wider deck below, surrounded by lounge chairs and tables shaded by large umbrellas printed with the swirling wave insignia of the cruise ship. Leaning over the railing to get a better look, Anthony was unprepared when his behind was pinched.

"Hey!" He spun around, rubbing his offended body part, and found an elderly woman sporting a straw hat and grinning at him. For Pete's sake, she was his grandmother's age. Was he the only sane person on the ship?

Anthony narrowed his eyes. "Can I help you?" From her mischievous grin, he figured he had just put his foot in his mouth.

"Well, now that you mention it…" she hinted.

Anthony rubbed his hands over his face. What the hell was he supposed to do? It would be like telling his grandmother to shove off. Making a quick search of the immediate area, he spotted a balding elderly gentleman with a shark tattoo on his arm glaring in his direction.

Now You See It...

Anthony bent and whispered in her ear, "Don't look now, but there's a jealous admirer staring your way."

The woman immediately turned around and headed in the wrong direction. Anthony grabbed her thin shoulders and pointed her toward the man, chuckling. "Happy fishing." The old lady should have been wearing the tattoo.

"Drink?" an accented voice asked.

What the hell? Anthony looked to the heavens for help. Did he have a bull's-eye painted on his back? Or perhaps a sign that said "duck season"? Anthony found a blonde in a next-to-nothing white bikini posing by the railing, holding a tall frosted drink.

"Thanks for the offer, but I'm leaving soon." He was getting tired of smiling at strangers. The shouts of laughter from the pool pulled at his attention. Maybe he would spot Sarah there.

With a nonchalant shrug, the woman walked away. Anthony heaved a sigh of relief. Looking around, he saw that the majority of the passengers were around his age. There were only a few older passengers. He was positive Aunt Lilly and his grandmother had given Sarah the wrong cruise to book. This wasn't the "let's have fun for seniors" ship but the "my room or your room" cruise. If that was the case, how was he to shield his sweet innocent grandmother from the hopping and bopping that would go on?

Irritated and uncomfortable under the hot sun, Anthony almost lost his patience when he was pinched again.

"Now see here—" Anthony started, ready to reprimand the old lady again. Instead, he found a short, red-cheeked gentleman wearing an orange-flowered Hawaiian shirt, sauntering on his way as he blew Anthony a kiss.

Nuts! The people on this ship were certifiable. Even the blonde barracuda was circling again. Her eyes devoured him. Anthony knew exactly what she was thinking. She was hoping to set a trap, using herself as bait.

But Anthony wasn't biting and instead turned back to the railing. Even this blunt gesture didn't stop her from coming over to entice him again.

"Darling, you're still here. Join me for a drink," she said. Her accent sounded heavier this time. He would have to be careful with this one.

"Thanks, but I expect to see my friend any minute now," Anthony replied, watching her pose in her white G-string bikini that showed off a perfect tan and barely hid overflowing curves. He wondered how three little triangles of Lycra could hold so much.

She ran her hands up and down his bare arms and leaned into him so her breasts brushed up against him. "Forget your little friend. Spend some time with Yarmilla instead."

Gently prying her hands from his arms, Anthony took a step back. "Maybe some other time." He hoped she got the hint.

Pouting, she gave it one last shot. "Later then. If you don't find me, I'll find you." She turned away and gave Anthony an eyeful.

He'd had enough. Enough proposals, enough heat and enough bottom pinching. He grabbed a bottle of beer from the bar and prayed Sarah would give up hiding and come out of her room. Knowing her and her bottomless curiosity, he was sure to spot her before long.

Retracing his steps, Anthony glanced over the railing again and caught the split-second image of Sarah's unmistakable long black hair as it swung from side to side. The sight stopped him in his tracks. "That's not Sarah," he said, watching as she chatted with a steward. Her laughter floated up to tease him. "Damn, it is her." With a wave to the steward she disappeared. "And she's going ashore."

He handed his bottle to a stunned passenger, dashed across the deck and down a flight of stairs. He knew he

Now You See It...

shouldn't have trusted her to do the sensible thing and enjoy the ship's pools and activities.

He caught sight of Sarah as he exited the ship. Slowing, he trailed her at a safe distance so she wouldn't know he was following.

Chapter Four

"This is more like it."

Sarah leisurely climbed another narrow cobblestone street. She'd left her tension and Anthony back on the ship, and she was not going to think of him for the next couple of hours. There would be plenty of time for that when she returned.

Pausing under the heavy shade of a palm tree, Sarah caught a glimpse of a tall man dressed in red and blue dashing into a nearby courtyard. She hadn't seen his face but his body was something else.

"Delicious," she chuckled as she resumed her walk. She had heard how friendly the Spanish were. Maybe it was a young man admiring her from afar.

Raising her face to the hot sun, Sarah let the heat melt her body. A breeze soothed her brow and carried the smell of the ocean. She reached the top of the steep hill and turned to admire the view.

"Amazing."

A cathedral's sun-kissed, golden walls towered over terra-cotta roofs. Houses perched against the valley wall, braving the edge of the cliffs to get the best view of the sea, while more dwellings stretched along the basin floor, extending into the embrace of the port.

"This is just what I needed." From her high position, Sarah could see groups of cafés, fishing boats swaying on the gentle sea and busy tourist shops.

The sea air cleared her mind, making it easier for her to think. She needed to remember what she'd been doing when

Now You See It…

her jewelry vanished, so she could figure out exactly what had made each item disappear.

The first part was easy. She'd been arguing with Anthony. Could that be it? What other logical reason could there be for such a coincidence? And how was she going to curb her natural defensive reflexes so she could keep her appearance intact?

If she had to bite her tongue for a week, then so be it. It was either that or return home naked. Sarah shivered—she wouldn't even go there.

Sarah exhaled her confusion and worry and inhaled the heated fragrance of wildflowers before picking up her pace again. Tall, untamed grasses grew along the narrow streets. She peered through wrought iron gates and heavy wooden doors to glimpse patios filled with large pots overflowing with flowers, and vibrant pink begonias clinging to cracks in the walls and balconies.

She felt a silly grin growing. She couldn't believe she was finally in Europe. It was more beautiful than she could have imagined. If she had known it would be so spectacular, she would have made a point of coming sooner. She walked around a group of students carrying knapsacks and continued past a crowded café.

Stone staircases and shaded arcades rose from gardens, where the smell of fresh-grown herbs tickled her nose. Ancient cypress trees graced the sides of stone dwellings and offered a veil of green shelter under their old, twisted branches. Sarah stopped underneath one to catch her breath.

Through the leaves, Sarah caught sight of a familiar red shirt. "Hey, buddy, are you following me?" The red shirt vanished as quickly as it appeared.

"That's strange." Sarah shrugged. "Oh, well," she said and continued her climb. Maybe it wasn't the same person.

Sarah craned her neck to look at the exquisite architecture of the buildings with their ornate scrolls and designs over windows and doors. At street level, her fascination was caught by the pleasing smells of food cooking and the sounds of a dozen international languages as tourists mingled and exchanged stories in broken English or French, using their hands to complete their sentences.

Walking past a butcher's shop, a pungent odor hit her. Looking through the window, she saw sausages and pork hocks hanging from the ceiling.

Two young men on a motor scooter whistled as they zoomed by. "*Hola, signorita!*"

Sarah waved back. "*Hola*, yourself."

The next shop sold cheeses in all shapes and sizes. While Sarah admired the selection in the window, the glass reflected someone in red standing close by.

"Gotcha," Sarah cried, spinning around, only to find an empty wall. This was crazy. Why would anyone follow her? Retracing her steps, she peered around the building and down the same busy street. Nothing.

"Oh, shit." Hearing Sarah's footsteps, Anthony jumped into the first open doorway, interrupting two women arguing. "Sorry, ladies."

Peering around the door, he watched Sarah walk by. "Close call," Anthony exhaled, letting his tension melt into the floor. The silence behind him alerted him to the room's undivided attention.

Turning around, he found a mother and daughter summing him up, while an old woman inched her way toward the door. Gesturing with her hands, the old lady seemed to want him to stay.

"Sorry." Not wasting a moment, Anthony jumped out the door. "Thank you and goodbye."

Now You See It…

"Now that was a *really* close call." He went in search of Sarah at a safer distance. When he emerged into the alleyway there was no sign of her.

Picking up his pace, he checked the little bars that were tucked behind deep doorways. Sarah may have stopped in one to rest or order a drink. Anthony found them tempting. A cold drink would go down easily right about now.

Anthony scanned the area. "Now where the hell did she go?"

Strolling deeper into the old city, Sarah didn't know where she was. But that didn't bother her, since she had plenty of time to retrace her steps. Sarah passed a young couple deep in discussion as they ambled by arm in arm.

A group of old men played cards under a shadowed archway. They stopped speaking when they spotted her and followed her with their eyes. She blew them a kiss and her laughter joined that coming from women dressed in vivid-colored dresses leaning over balconies above.

It seemed that it didn't matter where you went, all men were alike. Always curious to see the goings-on of others. And they said women were bad.

Continuing to stroll along the cobblestone streets, Sarah heard the rapid clicking of needles through an open window. Peeking in, she found an old woman knitting.

"*Hola.*" She gifted Sarah with a toothless smile and resumed her work.

Roaming aimlessly, Sarah turned down another alleyway, eventually slowing her pace. Where the hell was she?

"This is not good."

The homes here were dilapidated, cracked and peeling walls flanking her on the narrow street. A broken gate swayed from side to side, emitting a constant, empty moan, warning her to turn back. Boarded windows stared down at her like unseeing eyes.

"Damn." She suddenly realized there were no people about, either. Retracing her steps, Sarah found herself at a crossroad.

Looking about, she tried to remember which way she had come from. "Now where the hell do I go?" If she couldn't find her way back, she would miss the ship and ruin everyone's holiday.

Again, Sarah felt the tingling sensation down her spine that warned her someone was watching her. Cold apprehension crawled along each nerve ending, urging her to flee.

Breaking into a brisk jog, Sarah searched for a familiar sight to steer her in the right direction. What she glimpsed instead was the sight of a familiar red shirt.

"Hey, you! I know you've been following me," Sarah called, walking to where she had seen the person disappear.

"You might as well come out. I'm lost and I need your help to get back to my ship."

Still no answer.

An eerie silence settled around her. Her breath trapped in her lungs, she listened for movement.

None.

The sun vibrated around her, yet a cold sweat broke on her brow. She needed to get out of here. Fast. Sarah sprinted down the closest alleyway but soon came to an abrupt stop, her way blocked by a foul-smelling bull of a man dressed in a faded red shirt. A cigarette dangled from a set of yellow teeth.

"Move it, buster," Sarah commanded, holding back her fear.

Flicking his cigarette to the ground, the stranger sized her up before speaking in broken English. "You have something I want." With a quick movement, he clasped her shoulder and tried to push her to the ground.

Sarah put her body's full weight into her struggles and watched his eyes fill with anger. Heart pounding, she twisted in every direction, trying to break his hold, making sure she didn't end up on the ground. His face burned with fury.

The thief leered at her and grabbed the pouch at her waist, brutally tugging it toward him. Sarah gasped as the band cut into her back. The pungent smell of the man's unwashed body repulsed her.

Nauseated, Sarah leaned away from him. "You lousy son of a bitch. Let go of me!" She kicked until she successfully connected with his shins and heard a satisfying grunt.

"I want the pouch," the thief growled, eyes glazing over as he continued to pull.

"I'll give it to you if you'll just let go." Sarah tried to pry his fingers off her waist. "Oh God!" Pain shot through her side as thick fingers dug into her flesh. The pain worsened, making stars appear before her eyes.

Sarah pushed at his immovable chest. "I said let go!"

With one sharp tug, the robber ripped the side of her shirt, leering at her exposed skin.

Suffocating, cold fear built behind a wall of anger. *Dear God*, Sarah thought as her strength dwindled, *not this*. Heart pounding, Sarah tensed for his next move. With a rush of adrenaline, she shifted her weight to dodge his fist when it came flying toward her. The swing met empty air, unbalancing the robber. Pivoting, Sarah shoved him hard with all her strength and enjoyed the brief satisfaction of watching him topple over and roll a few feet away from her.

Sarah screamed at the top of her lungs, her body gripped in terror. Before the robber could scramble to his feet, she fled for her life. "Help me!" The scream was ripped from her very soul.

She didn't care where she ran, she just kept running.

A cry of distress sliced through the air, chilling Anthony's blood. He knew that voice.

"Sarah?" He ran in the direction he hoped it had come from.

"Sarah," Anthony cried, frantically searched one deserted alleyway after another. "Answer me."

"Anthony?" He heard her voice, filled with relief. "I'm down here." Anthony strained to hear her next words.

"Follow my voice," Anthony said. The rapid sounds of pounding feet bounced off the walls. "Keep talking, scream—do anything so I can follow your voice."

"Please hurry, he's right behind me!" she yelled.

"Keep running!" His body shook with fear. "Sarah, come to me." *Please, don't let her get hurt.*

"I'm trying!" Her voice was getting closer.

Anthony ran full out. Heart thumping, his shirt clung to his body as he exerted all his strength to reach Sarah's side. His feet pounded on the cobblestones, quickly eating up the distance between them.

Sarah torpedoed into him, knocking the wind out of him. He stumbled with the force of her impact, but quickly steadied them. Holding her back, anger flared to life when he saw her gaping shirt and chalk-white face, eyes huge with unsuppressed despair. Over her shoulder, he saw a man halt abruptly in his tracks.

"You son of a bitch!" Anthony sprang after the thief, whose expression blanched before he scrambled down a steep embankment into an orange grove.

Anthony followed in hot pursuit. "You bastard!"

The robber threw himself down the hill. Breathing heavily, Anthony stopped at the top of the hill and watched his prey escape. A loud yelp sounded when the man's body slammed into a thick, protruding root.

Now You See It...

Anthony glared down at the thief, his fists clenched at his sides. He felt no pity for him, only regret that he had gotten away. He rushed back to Sarah, her body a quivering mass of fear.

Anthony pulled his fingers through his hair. *"Mai in vita mia!"* Never in his life had he felt such numbing fear. Tremors racked his body as the reality of what Sarah had escaped began to sink in.

Raising a shaking hand to ward him off, Sarah pleaded with her eyes. "Anthony."

"Santo cielo," Anthony raged, clasping her hand against his chest. "Is your stubborn pride worth more than your life?"

"Quit yelling at me," Sarah cried, pushing against his chest. "I've gone through enough!"

"Accidente. Damn. You little fool." He grabbed Sarah by the shoulders and brought her body flush with his, wrapping his arms around her. Anthony didn't know who was shaking more—Sarah or himself. "You would have gone through a hell of a lot more if I hadn't been able to reach you."

"Don't you think I know that? I made the mistake of not paying attention to my surroundings. When I finally did, it was too late." Sarah's energy drained from her body. "All I wanted was to walk off some of my frustration."

She had subtracted ten years off his life. Damn her, she was nothing but trouble. Yet, here he was, letting this firecracker of a woman get under his skin.

Anthony pressed Sarah's head against his shoulder and held her tight. His gut twisted when she wrapped her arms around his waist and clung desperately to him. He hated to see her reduced to this. She would have collapsed without his support.

"You have no idea how sorry I am," Sarah mumbled into his chest.

In the distance, a lazy church bell tolled out the hour, while the low hum of vehicles and scooters climbed the sides of the mountain's serpentine roads.

Tenderly taking hold of Sarah's face, Anthony tilted it and stared into a pair of turbulent eyes. "If you ever do anything as stupid as this again, I'm going to kill you," he said and kissed her forehead.

Anthony couldn't understand how he could maintain complete control of a large company that employed hundreds of men and women, yet when it came to Sarah, he had absolutely no power.

Since seeing Sarah again and deciding to go on this trip, his mood had been fluctuating wildly. "God, if anything had..." He left his sentence unfinished. Shaken, he brought his lips firmly down on hers. Just having her in his arms alleviated the fear he had experienced when Sarah's scream had pierced the air. It had sliced through his very soul.

Wetness touched Anthony's lips as Sarah's tears rolled down her cheeks. Anthony feathered gentle kisses over her face, tasting her salty flavor. "Please, Sarah, no more tears," he pleaded, wiping them away.

Running his hands up and down her back, Anthony soothed her until her crying slowed to a hiccup. He lifted her chin to gently wipe her tears.

"If...you...kill me," hiccupped Sarah, "then I won't have to remember this at all." She wiped her tears on his shirt.

"Oh God, Sarah. Have you any idea what I felt when I heard you scream? I didn't know if I would make it to you in time or what I would find. I know you hate taking orders, but just promise me you'll never walk off alone again." Anthony stared into Sarah's eyes, waiting for her promise.

Sarah gave an unsteady nod then reluctantly stepped back. She looked down at the gap in her shirt. With trembling fingers, she tried to tuck the jagged edges back into her skirt.

Now You See It…

Anthony tenderly removed her hands and stroked the dark bruises. Helplessness overwhelmed him. He had failed to protect her. Making sure he didn't hurt her, Anthony carefully straightened her shirt.

He dropped his hands and stepped back. "Where the hell did you get to? One minute you were there and the next I had lost you."

Sarah's head popped up. "You've been following me? Anthony Mancini, you're not only a busybody, you're also a liar." She caressed the side of his face. He trapped her hand and planted a kiss in her palm. "You vowed you wouldn't help me again."

Anthony shrugged. "So I told a little white lie."

"How long were you following me?"

Anthony could see Sarah's shock and fear wearing off, only to be replaced by annoyance. "Take that look off your face," he said before Sarah's Irish temper could rise. "I saw you leave the ship and wanted to make sure you were safe. I kept my promise. Somewhat." So he twisted the truth just a little. If she'd listen to her Italian half, maybe she'd realize how reasonable his logic was.

"Next time let me know you're there," she said before graciously backing down. "Thank you. For once, I'm glad that you're pigheaded. I was really frightened until I heard your voice."

Some thanks. Accepting them with a slow nod, Anthony examined the bruises visible through the gap in her shirt. It wrenched his heart to see Sarah in such a miserable state.

"Let's go," he said, wrapping his arm around her, careful not to hurt her. "We passed a bar earlier, not far from here. You can clean yourself up and rest there." Not waiting for her response, Anthony led them in the direction of laughter and song in the distance.

Entering a small doorway, they found themselves in a crowded, cavernous room. After the intense heat of outside, the room felt cool against Sarah's heated skin as she glanced at the bar's high, white-washed walls and ceiling, and clean, worn out ceramic tiles. Sturdy old wooden tables flanked straw chairs along one wall, while a long glass bar ran along another. This would be a good place to get herself back together.

The hostess that greeted them tsked sympathetically at Sarah's disheveled appearance. *"Venga, venga."* Taking Sarah gently by the elbow, she motioned for her to follow. "Carlos," she shouted at the man behind the bar, "I'll be one minute."

"Si, mi tresor," he said, wiping the glass he was holding.

"Could you show me where the washroom is? *El lavabos?"* Sarah asked, demonstrating that she wanted to wash her hands.

"Si, si, come. I show you while my husband takes care of things in the front." The pleasant woman directed Sarah to a small, clean washroom.

"Thank you." Sarah closed the door and collapsed against it. Wrapping her arms about her, she waited for the aftershocks of fear to subside.

She stared into the small cracked mirror above the sink and didn't recognize the woman with tearstains painted against sun-kissed cheeks. Her nose and shoulders were pink and her hair was a total mess.

Turning on the cold water, Sarah splashed the heated skin of her face and shoulders. "God, that feels good," she sighed. Cupping her hands, she drank until her thirst was quenched.

With the last traces of her tears gone, Sarah turned off the faucet and ran a brush through her hair. A pair of despondent eyes checked her appearance and stared back at her. She might feel violated and gutted at the moment but her stomach reminded her that she was very much alive. Resolutely turning away, Sarah opened the door and returned to their table.

Now You See It…

Sarah looked around and took better notice of the lay of the room. Under the glass bar, a cornucopia of food was displayed in large, deep ceramic plates, and hanging above the bar were enormous legs of air-dried ham. The jovial bartender and his wife were a whirl of activity, meeting the demands of their customers.

With shoulders slumped, Anthony rested his elbows on the table and held his head in his hands. With a hesitant touch, Sarah placed her hand on his shoulder. "Are you okay?"

Confused, tired eyes returned her stare. Without saying a word, Anthony stood up and guided Sarah to her chair.

His weary expression only made Sarah feel worse. She was responsible for putting it there, and hated that fact. She wished she could erase his pain.

"You have to promise me that if you wander off again you'll either have someone accompany you or you'll join a group," Anthony started, tapping his finger against the tabletop to stress his point. "Otherwise, I'll have to handcuff you to me. That way I know you're safe."

This little thing she could agree upon. Sarah extended her hand across the small table. "I promise," she said, watching his smile return.

Anthony shook her hand then pointed to the small plates filled with delicacies in the center of the table. "Eat," he said and poured her a glass of wine from a carafe.

He took a dark piece of bread from a basket, then dug his fork into the melted Camembert and twirled the hot stringy cheese around his fork. Dropping the melted cheese on a corner of the bread, he bit into it.

Not needing a second invitation, Sarah followed Anthony's example and bit into her own morsel of heaven. "Oh, this is good," she said, realizing how hungry she was.

"There's bacon rolls stuffed with dates, little sausages—or *chorizos,* as the natives call them. Then there are *gambas,* which are prawns. We've got mushrooms and olives in oil and pickled artichoke hearts."

"This is amazing," Sarah said, trying another delicacy. "That woman must get up at dawn to prepare all this." She savored a mushroom and artichoke together. "This is good, too."

"She also said that if you wanted some, there was *lechona*, which is suckling pig."

"Oh, no. This is more than enough." Sarah continued to sample from the different dishes.

"She called these *tapas*," Anthony explained, reaching for another piece of bread.

Wiping her hands on her apron, the proprietress rushed by. "Okay?"

Sarah smiled back. "Yes, okay." She watched the woman scramble off again. "Isn't it funny that no matter where you travel, 'okay' is recognized?"

"I know. I can hear French, Norwegian, Italian and German, but they all understand that simple word. Watch..." Anthony raised his glass and cheered, "Okay?"

He received a resounding, "Okay!" followed by laughter as others raised their glasses filled with wine to salute him back.

Sarah laughed at the exuberance of the other patrons. She knew exactly what Anthony was trying to do. He was distracting her, trying to take her mind off what had happened. A thin layer of protection that surrounded her heart melted.

Sarah looked down at her empty dish and pushed it away. "I sure polished that off. I guess I was hungrier than I thought."

"Did you want to order anything else?"

Now You See It...

"No, thank you." Sarah pulled his arm toward her and looked at his watch. "Besides, we should be going or the ship will leave without us."

Anthony glanced at her wrist. "What happened to your watch? You kept checking the time when we were waiting at your house, so I know you had one. Did that guy take it?" he asked, his face clouding with anger again.

"No, no, it's nothing like that." The lines around his mouth and eyes relaxed. "I just seemed to have misplaced it."

Anthony motioned for the bill and the barman's wife quickly presented herself at their table. "Thank you," she said as she gathered the notes Anthony handed her.

Rising from her seat, Sarah waved at the happy bartender and patrons on her way out. "Smart woman," she said as she began walking in the direction of the port.

"Why do you say that?"

"She may have prepared all those dishes but she was also the one to collect the money. That cookie knows what goes in and out of that place. Her husband was happy to serve behind the counter and mingle with his friends and customers. She even laughed when he flirted with that group of young French women."

Anthony chuckled. "That old guy was harmless."

"There is no such thing as a harmless man." Sarah smirked at Anthony's comical indignant expression. "Unless he's dead, of course."

They made it back to the ship on time. "Come on," Sarah said, grasping Anthony's hand, only to feel him tug in the opposite direction.

"Where do you think you're going?" he asked.

"To find my aunt and your grandmother."

Anthony stared pointedly at her ruined shirt. "Don't you think you should change first?"

"Oh God, you're right. I wouldn't hear the end of it if Aunt Lilly found out." What was she thinking? She must be more shook up than she realized. Sarah was conscious of the passengers staring at her. She drew closer to Anthony to hide her appearance.

With a smooth movement, Anthony wrapped his arm around her waist and drew her close to his side. Sarah appreciated his smooth maneuver as he whisked her away from prying eyes.

Sarah hugged Anthony's waist to hide the side of her shirt and climbed the steps leading to their deck. "Let's see if my aunt attached a note to our cabin door like she said they would."

"Here it is." Sarah opened a piece of paper attached to her door and read it aloud. "It says, 'at the shuffleboard, see you there'. Give me a moment to change," Sarah said, opening her cabin door.

Sarah was conscious of Anthony as she threw off her sandals, grabbed a change of clothes and rushed into the bathroom.

Quickly stripping, she slipped on a white, short-sleeved cotton top, a red miniskirt and a pair of red sandals with laces that crisscrossed around her ankles.

She gave herself a once-over in the mirror. Not a trace of her ordeal remained, unless you looked closely into her still wounded eyes.

Plastering on a wide grin she didn't feel, Sarah stepped out of the washroom. "Ready." She found Anthony leaning against her open doorway, patiently waiting. "Better?"

Dark hooded eyes traveled over her body, leaving a trail of heat behind. "Perfect." His voice sounded like the deep purr of a tiger.

"Then let's go." Before she could take a step, one of the sandal's straps unraveled. "Nuts." Sarah tied the laces again and double-knotted them as a precaution. "Now I'm ready."

Now You See It…

That's when the other strap decided that it, too, wanted freedom. Her grin was starting to hurt. "One more time."

It was a losing battle. As soon as she retied the sandal, the laces of the other unraveled again. "Of all the no good, lousy, stinking luck."

"Need a hand?"

Red in the face, Sarah straightened and threw off her sandals. "They're defective." She found the ones she had worn earlier and jammed her feet back in them. "And stay on," she muttered.

She was totally confused. This time she hadn't been arguing with Anthony when things started to happen with her clothes. So what could it be that triggered the spell?

"Who are you talking to? You remind me of your aunt," Anthony said, his eyes dancing with suppressed laughter.

"Myself." Sarah ushered him out the room and closed the door behind them.

The spell was picking up speed.

Chapter Five

Aunt Lilly nudged Emily. "You see what I see?" she asked, watching Sarah and Anthony walk toward them.

"They're holding hands," Emily responded excitedly, squeezing Lilly's hand.

"Isn't this wonderful?"

"I know. *Che bello*, it's lovely," said Emily, covertly watching them approach.

"You think we're smart enough to plan a double wedding?" asked Aunt Lilly.

"I think we are brilliant. If we play our cards right we make it a double wedding no problem."

Aunt Lilly patted Emily's hand. "Oh, I love the way you think. Now, no more—they're coming."

Anthony spotted Aunt Lilly and Emily sitting under an umbrella nursing two frosted drinks, while watching a lively game of shuffleboard. With Sarah's hand in his, they made their way toward his grandmother and Lilly. Thank God he wouldn't have to worry about those two—Sarah was more than he could handle.

All around, a festive mood prevailed. Teams played volleyball in the pool, a band played in a shaded corner of the deck while people sampled from a lavish buffet, and a waiter circulated with a tray full of drinks.

Anthony, on the other hand, felt anything but festive. His stomach still churned with the unsettling thought that he might not have been able to rescue Sarah in time. Seeing her concerned expression, he gave her hand a reassuring squeeze and plastered on a smile he didn't feel.

Passengers gazed at the city from the railings of the ship while others slept in lounge chairs. After long flights, a few drinks and the hot sun, many of their fellow vacationers were comatose.

"I see that you're finally getting along," Aunt Lilly commented, pointedly staring at their joined hands.

Anthony noticed Lilly and Emily's not-so-innocent smiles as he pulled out a chair for Sarah. "You both look relaxed. I'm glad you stayed on board and took it easy," he said, bending over to kiss his grandmother's cheek. "You even have a bit of a tan."

"Ha." Aunt Lilly banged her hand on the table. "We got our tans on the beach that our taxi drove us to."

"You what?" The blood drained from Anthony's face. Horrified, he dropped into his chair. He was not having a good day. "What do you mean on a beach? I thought we agreed that you would stay on board and rest." He looked from his grandmother, to Aunt Lilly and back again. The mischievous gleams in their eyes didn't bode well for him.

"We did take a nap," said Aunt Lilly. "But when we woke up we were restless, so we decided not to waste the first day of our vacation."

"So what did you do?" Sarah asked.

"We hired a taxi and told him to drive along the coast until we spotted a beach we liked," Aunt Lilly said.

Anthony relaxed back into his chair. That didn't sound so bad. Hopefully they had gone to a place filled with people. "Where did you end up going?"

"To a secluded beach called Playa Mago." Aunt Lilly looked at Emily and together they burst into fits of laughter. Anthony wondered what the inside joke was.

Sarah gasped. "Isn't that a nudist beach?"

"A nudist beach?" roared Anthony. People around them stopped what they were doing and glanced toward their table. Anthony lowered his voice and whispered through clenched teeth, "Tell me you didn't."

"We sure did," Aunt Lilly chuckled. "The beach was so small that some people had to sun themselves on the rocks. We sat under a palm umbrella outside at the restaurant that overlooked the beach."

Anthony rubbed the tense muscles at the back of his neck. What was wrong with the women in this family? "When you got out of the taxi and saw it was a nudist beach, why didn't you get back into the taxi and drive off?" Was he the only reasonable person here?

"We didn't realize it was a nudist beach until we were seated at the restaurant," Aunt Lilly said.

"How could that be?" Sarah asked.

"Quite simple, really," Aunt Lilly said. "We had our eyeglasses on in the taxi when we counted out our fare. But when we got out, we took them off and threw them into our beach bag so we could put on our sunglasses."

Emily smiled. "But we couldn't find the sunglasses because they were at the bottom of Lilly's bag. Instead of searching in the hot sun, we sat down first."

The three of them were going to kill him before this trip was over. "That's when you noticed it was a nudist beach?"

"No, not yet. We still hadn't found our sunglasses," Aunt Lilly said. "While I searched my purse, Emily glanced over at the sun worshipers and commented that some of the people had forgotten to iron their T-shirts. When we finally put on our sunglasses, that's when we realized it was a nudist beach."

"Please tell me that's when you left?" Anthony pleaded.

"Oh no dear, we didn't leave then either," Emily explained, still laughing. "You see, the wrinkled T-shirts turned out to be a group of seniors. By then we were so weak from laughing that even if we wanted to get up, we couldn't."

Now You See It...

Aunt Lilly leaned against Emily and through her mirth finished, "They reminded us of a bunch of walruses."

Sarah covered her mouth to hide her smile, but her eyes were mischievous.

Anthony was not amused. "I can't believe this. I leave you on board for a couple of hours and you wander off. You could have gotten hurt." He made eye contact with Sarah.

"Oh, fiddlesticks," Aunt Lilly exclaimed, waving away his concern. "Your grandmother and I sat under the shade and stuffed ourselves. So stop your worrying."

"Someone might have approached you," said Anthony.

Aunt Lilly chortled. "And done what?"

Sarah smirked. "Anthony, they do have a point. Where would a nudist hide a weapon?"

Aunt Lilly wiped her eyes beneath her glasses. "Believe me, the only guns we saw weren't loaded," she said, sending Sarah and Emily into renewed gales of laughter.

Anthony felt his face burn. "I don't find this funny," he said sternly. Didn't they know how serious this was?

Aunt Lilly chuckled. "Guns," she said, sighing. "I think we picked the perfect holiday."

Anthony glared at Sarah. "Your aunt is a terrible influence on my grandmother," he said, leaning back in his seat. "All of you are going to give me gray hairs by the time this cruise is over."

That sobered Sarah quickly. "No one twisted your grandmother's arm. She knew what she was doing."

He knew she was right. His grandmother was old enough to take responsibility for her own actions.

"Antonio, Lilly didn't make me do anything I didn't want to do," Emily assured, patting his arm. "Besides, Italy is filled with statues of naked men."

"And you know the saying, once you've seen one, you've seen them all," Aunt Lilly said.

"Aunt Lilly, keep your voice down." Sarah looked around to see if anyone was listening. "Statues are totally different from what you saw."

"No, they're not." Aunt Lilly leaned her ample bosom against the table. "The statues imitate life. In this case, life wasn't as solid."

"That's enough! I get the picture," Anthony said. Everyone kept a straight face. Seeing their not-so-innocent expressions, Anthony threw his hands in the air. "I surrender. There's no winning with the three of you. Waiter!" he yelled, gesturing to a steward, "Jack Daniel's, and make it a double. Sarah?"

"A hot-fudge sundae. Extra chocolate sauce and peanuts, please." Sarah looked at Anthony. "Relax, we'll make this vacation more interesting for you," she said then smiled at the waiter. "I changed my mind—can I have the triple-chocolate brownie delight instead?"

"Do you want one or two spoons with that?" the steward asked.

"One."

"I don't think I can take much more of this type of excitement. I just hope this is the last time you three ladies go wandering. Tomorrow, I'll book a tour for us in Bizerte, Tunisia. If you're not with me, then you'd better be on this ship or with another tour group." Anthony made eye contact with each one of them. *"Avete capito?"*

"Va bene, fine Antonio," Emily said, nudging Aunt Lilly with her elbow.

Aunt Lilly took a large sip of her drink. "So long as there's food, I'm game."

"Sarah?" Anthony raised his eyebrow. If she had no intention of coming, he was going to look for a pair of damn handcuffs.

"Count me in. It should be fun."

Now You See It...

"Finally," Anthony sighed. He'd have all three where he could keep an eye on them.

"Speaking of fun—has the spell started working yet?" Aunt Lilly asked.

"No!" Sarah's face turned red with her abrupt response. Her laugh sounded forced when she said, "I'm happy to say that it backfired." As soon as the waiter placed the brownie delight in front of her, she dove in.

"Damn." Under her breath, Aunt Lilly mumbled into her glass, "Under layers you will find, a special person with a mind."

Anthony shook his head. The old lady never gave up. "What are you doing?"

"Nothing, absolutely nothing."

The rumble of the large diesel engines starting seemed to turn on an electric switch among the passengers.

"This is it," Aunt Lilly exclaimed, pushing herself away from the table. "Let's get a bird's eye view as the ship sets sail."

Anthony wasn't quick enough to assist his grandmother and watched her toddle toward the railing. "I've never seen her walk that fast before," he said, following at a more leisurely pace beside Sarah.

Below them, large iron chains were being pulled in from their moorings, releasing the ship. Like a graceful swan, the ship glided forward. The wind picked up, making the flags, pennants and burgees flap noisily.

The breeze swirled Sarah's hair around her face. Without thinking, Anthony wrapped a strand behind her ear, making her jump. Her smile dimmed only to valiantly return. From her confused expression, his caress had taken her by surprise.

The ship sliced through white foamy waves. "Look back there," Anthony said, pointing to the wake of the ship. It trailed behind like a white lace bridal veil.

Sarah's face lit with excitement and her cheeks flushed from the sun's heat. "This is the life." Closing her eyes, she raised her face to the wind.

Standing elbow to elbow, Anthony enjoyed this simple pleasure with Sarah, not surprised by how much he wanted to share more of these experiences with her.

The city grew smaller as the ship distanced itself from port. "Now, that was lovely," Aunt Lilly said, moving away from the railing. "I'm off to get ready for dinner. I can't wait to taste all that good food. Why don't we meet in the lounge at eight o'clock?"

"You can wait that late for your meal?" asked Anthony, he and Sarah following behind them as the old ladies made their way to their room.

"I'm stuffed." Aunt Lilly rubbed her stomach and grimaced. "I think I might have overdone it a bit on the sweets at the open buffet," Aunt Lilly admitted as she inserted her card in her door.

"We'll see you then," Sarah said.

Leaving Aunt Lilly and his grandmother at their door, Anthony walked beside Sarah to their cabins, conscious of her body whenever it brushed up against his.

"What if I come by in an hour so we can go together?" Anthony asked.

"I'll see you then."

"Yes, Anthony. Of course, Anthony. Anything you say, Anthony."

A knock sounded on Sarah's door. "Coming," she called out, then practiced her responses one more time. "Yes, Anthony. Of course, Anthony. Anything you say, Anthony." She had to remember to keep cool, otherwise who knew what would vanish next.

Now You See It...

Taking one last look in the mirror, Sarah pointed her red-painted toes that peeked through black stiletto evening sandals, making her long, black skirt open, exposing a long slender leg up to her thigh. She adjusted the flaring, black chiffon sleeves on her V-neck top.

A light dusting of blush, mascara and gloss and a gold necklace finished the picture. Tossing her loose, shining hair behind her shoulder, she opened the door. "Perfect timing," Sarah said, stepping into the corridor and giving Anthony's appearance a quick once-over.

Dressed casually in a taupe-colored suit, an open cream-colored shirt and expensive brown leather shoes, he was the picture of casual success. His hair glistened from his shower and was tied at the back of his neck. His skin was so smooth from his recent shave that she wanted to reach out and test its softness. She needed to move her butt before she really did something stupid. "Let's go."

With a sharp intake of breath, Anthony blocked her way. "What are you doing?" he asked, incredulous. His expression of surprised delight quickly deteriorated into embarrassed astonishment.

"Anthony—"

Before she could utter another word, Anthony pushed her back into her cabin and slammed the door in her face. She snapped her mouth shut, stunned by his abrupt behavior.

"Have you lost your mind?" Sarah shouted, pounding on her door.

"I haven't, but you have. God!" It sounded like Anthony was pounding his forehead against the door. "Why me? Only me."

"What the hell are you talking about?" Sarah pulled at the doorknob, but it wouldn't budge. "Anthony, this is not funny." She'd walked out of her cabin prepared to be the most agreeable companion, only to have her own door slammed in her face. This time it was Anthony who was acting strange.

"If you still want to open the door after what I have to say, then it's your business. Okay?"

She stopped rattling the doorknob. "This better be good Mancini, and it better make up for the abominable way you're behaving," Sarah replied, placing her hands on her hips and tapping her foot furiously.

"Oh, it will. Sarah—look down."

She did. And screamed.

"Why the hell didn't you tell me my top was gone?" The shock of what she saw hit her full force. She crossed her arms over her black, lacy pushup bra and began to pace her cabin. "But that can't be possible. I didn't disagree with anything you said this time," she said.

"This time? Sarah what are you talking about?" Anthony sounded concerned.

Sarah pulled her fingers through her hair. "I know I had a top on when I opened the door."

"Wrap yourself in a towel so I can come in," Anthony said. "I can't help you from this side of the door."

"No one can help me," Sarah mumbled.

"Sarah?" Anthony knocked on her door. "Can I come in?"

What was the use? "Slowly count to ten then come in." She opened her door just a little and rushed to the bathroom to wrap a towel around herself. "Oh dear God." She wasn't going crazy. She was positive she had opened the door fully dressed. "This is great, just great. What the hell am I supposed to do now?"

"...ten." The door slowly opened and Anthony peeked into the cabin, his expression guarded.

Sarah felt the room start to spin. Her legs were about to collapse beneath her. "I don't feel that great."

"Sit down," he said, taking her arm. "I'm sure we can figure this out."

Now You See It…

Sarah thankfully sank onto one of the small beds. Staring blankly at a spot on the carpet, she rocked herself back and forth. An overwhelming fear gripped her body. "There's nothing to figure out. It's that damn spell. It's finally kicked in with a vengeance."

"I knew I should have called a doctor after this afternoon's incident," Anthony said, picking up her phone and beginning to dial.

Sarah grabbed it out of his hand and slammed it back into its cradle. "You aren't listening," she yelled. "Things have been disappearing on me the whole damn trip."

"From the start?"

"Well, if you want to get technical, it started the day you walked into my kitchen. What you witnessed were not the remains of a food fight but the catastrophic ruins of a spell my aunt had just cast on me."

She felt miserable and Anthony's disbelief wasn't helping any. "Believe me, if I hadn't seen it with my own eyes, I wouldn't believe me either." Sarah frantically moved her hands to emphasis her words. "The hors d'oeuvres exploded, the wieners did a striptease and the champagne cork took a shot at me."

"I can't believe that." Anthony recaptured her hands and placed them on her lap. "When your aunt asked you if the spell had started working you told us it hadn't."

"I lied." Boy, had she ever.

"There has to be a logical explanation for what's happening."

"Logical?" She laughed hysterically. "Oh, for Pete's sake, sit down," Sarah pulled at his arm, "my neck is starting to hurt."

Anthony sat on the other bed, faced her and clasped one of her hands. His heat penetrated her numb fingers. "Maybe with everything that happened today, you weren't thinking straight and forgot to put on your top. Let's go over what you did before you opened the door."

"There's really nothing to explain. I got ready, Aunt Lilly and Emily came by to say they would meet us in the dining lounge and then I waited for you. And that's it."

Sarah was miserable. There was no logical reason why her top had disappeared. "And take that look off your face. I'm not crazy. Wait 'til I get a hold of my aunt. It's that damn spell she cast that's making my clothes disappear."

"When Aunt Lilly came by, did anything happen? I mean, did you have your top on when you opened the door?"

"Yes."

"How do you know?"

"Please!" Sarah snorted. It was her turn to look at Anthony as though he was crazy. She might be a little off-kilter at the moment, but she had all her screws in tight. "If I had opened my door half-dressed, I would have shocked your grandmother while my aunt would have asked if I was making a fashion statement."

"You have a point there," Anthony sighed, rubbing his face.

"Why, just look at the lovely reception I got from you. You liked what you saw so much you slammed the door in my face." Sarah wanted to wipe the smirk off his face.

"It was either that or let you give a free show to the rest of the passengers and crew."

With her nerves short-circuited, she slumped in defeat. "Now what?"

"Where do you think your top went to?" Anthony asked.

"How the hell should I know?" Sarah yelled, her voice rising a decibel as she became more distraught. "When I dressed, I pulled my top out of this drawer," she explained, getting up and pulling open the drawer she had taken her top from.

Now You See It...

She stilled.

"Holy crap...but it can't be." Her hands trembled as she pulled out the top to show Anthony.

Anthony came to stand next to her. "Is that the one you were wearing?"

She slowly nodded and swallowed past the lump in her throat. "Yes." She was having a difficult time accepting what was happening to her.

"Let's experiment. You slip your top back on and we'll see if anything happens," Anthony suggested, turning his back to her.

Sarah was so desperate she'd try anything.

"Ready?"

"Yes." Sarah clasped and unclasped her hands, her body stiff as she held her breath.

Turning, Anthony met her stare—then looked down to her shirt. A grin lit his face. "It's still there."

Sarah released the breath she was holding. Her body shook with relief. "Thank God." She gave Anthony a weak smile.

"Oh, shit!" His grin dissolved into amazement.

In a blink of an eye, the top had disappeared again. "Oh hell!" she exclaimed. One second she'd been wearing it and the next it was gone. Like a magician—now you see it, now you don't.

Mortified, Sarah snatched the towel off the floor and wrapped it around herself again. "You see, I'm not going crazy." She looked in the same drawer and found the top again. "See what I mean!" she yelled, waving the garment in Anthony's face.

"Take it easy." With shaking hands, Anthony took the top from her. She was glad she wasn't the only one losing it. "Maybe it's only this top. Try another one. With all the clothes you brought, maybe one of them will stay on."

Sarah marched to the open suitcase that lay on one of the beds. "Of all the times for the spell to kick in, this is the most inconvenient, the most disastrous, the most—everything." With her back to Anthony, she dropped her towel and snatched the first thing that came to her hands. This time she put on a flowered top.

"Here goes nothing," Sarah said, turning around and facing Anthony.

"Well?" With the cool draft from the air-conditioner on her bare skin, she already had her answer.

Anthony cleared his throat. "I think you should look for yourself."

"Damn!" She turned to her suitcase and found the top back in its place. All neat and tidy, the complete opposite of her life.

She should have put two and two together when she'd found her sandals back in her closet. At least she now knew that her watch and earrings were back home in their original spots.

"What the hell am I supposed to do?" she wailed, wrapping the towel around her tightly and flopping onto the bed. Grabbing her hair, Sarah pulled to relieve some of the tension in her temples. She could feel a headache coming on.

"I know what I'll do—I'll leave. I'll go back home."

Anthony shook his head. "What about Aunt Lilly and Emily? That will make them miserable."

"Oh God, you're right. I couldn't do that to them." Sarah wrapped her arms around her waist and rocked herself. "Then *you* leave. Every time we're in the same room, things vanish. If you go, then this will stop happening to me."

"I'm not going anywhere."

Why did he look so offended? "Sure you can. Tell them your office called with an emergency and you had to leave. They'll think it's perfectly normal for you."

His eyes darkened with anger. "I'm not leaving. There has to be a solution. You wouldn't happen to have the spell with you?"

"Yes."

"Maybe there's some kind of escape clause that will make the spell disappear."

"We're talking about a spell my dear absentminded aunt conjured up, not a legal document. How rational do you think it's going to be?"

"Good point. Still, we have to start somewhere."

Sarah nodded toward her suitcase. "It's in the side flap. Read it, but it's not going to do you any good."

Flipping the suitcase shut, Anthony unzipped the outer compartment and pulled out a rolled piece of paper. Sitting down beside her, he looked over the spell then glanced at Sarah with determination.

"Under layers you will find, a special person with a mind. Keep on peeling one by one, for your journey has just begun." Anthony gave a long whistle of disbelief. "I think you're going to lose all your clothes."

"I already figured that one out for myself, Einstein. What I want to know is what I'm supposed to do to stop it from happening?"

"I think I might have a solution. The first sentence said, 'under layers you will find', but it didn't specifically say *whose* layers. You understand?"

Sarah crossed her fingers. "What you're saying is that my clothes may be disappearing, but if I wear someone else's, like yours, nothing will happen?"

"Exactly. It's worth a shot." Anthony rushed out the door and quickly returned with a shirt in hand. "Try this on."

Standing up, Sarah slipped a hand through the sleeve of a black silk shirt, while the other hand held onto the towel. With trembling fingers, she attempted to button up the front.

"Let me," Anthony said, completing the task so she could pull the towel from beneath the shirt.

Sarah held her breath and waited. She stared at her chest, trying not to blink. Seconds ticked by and nothing happened. Finally, Sarah released a heartfelt sigh.

Anthony chuckled. "I knew it would work. At least it's still on. That's a good sign."

As far as Sarah could see, there was nothing to be happy about here. "Why are you taking this so well?" she asked, rolling up her sleeves. She took a hair clip from her drawer and pinned up her hair, then fanned herself. She was an absolute nervous wreck.

Anthony shrugged. "What else am I supposed to do? I suspected something crazy would happen after what Mark went through with your sister." He shook his head. "Your aunt has outdone herself this time."

"Tell me about it."

"So we'll keep our eyes open in case the rest of your clothes disappear and be prepared."

"We? That's very magnanimous of you," she said, her voice heavy with sarcasm. "You get to keep your eyes on my body and I have to stay alert so I can keep one step ahead of you."

"It's the least I can do."

Now You See It...

Chapter Six

ɞ

Sarah's glanced from the couples dancing to a Latin beat, to the passengers serving themselves at the scrumptious buffet, to the sparkling crystal chandelier. White dots of light painted the room, turning it into a floating fairyland.

At a table near the dance floor, she spotted Emily and her aunt with a female passenger who couldn't seem to take her eyes off Anthony. "Over there," Sarah said, pointing in their direction. "So who's the blonde beside your grandmother? She doesn't look too happy to see us. Or more precisely, me."

Anthony groaned. "Not her again."

"You know her?" Sarah laughed to cover her annoyance. "Boy, you sure work fast." The woman's face lit with excitement the closer they got to the table. "Are you sure we're not cramping your style?" She saw his jaw clench as he ground his teeth.

"I don't work fast, that woman does. I didn't pick her up. She kept offering me drinks and wouldn't leave me alone while I kept my eyes open trying to find you. If it was up to me I'd give her the shove off, but I don't want anything upsetting my grandmother or your aunt. Do me a favor and follow my lead," Anthony said, wrapping his arm around Sarah's waist to pull her close to his side.

Sarah pointed at the blonde. "You think an arm around my waist is going to stop someone like that?"

"That's what I'm hoping. Any suggestions?"

She had plenty. "Leave it to me and you'll see how fast your problems disappear." Hell, if she had clothes vanishing into thin air, getting rid of a person should be a piece of cake.

"Darling," gushed the blonde, with a pronounced Swedish accent, "I've been waiting for you." She smiled at Anthony and ignored Sarah.

In front of everyone, Anthony kissed Sarah's forehead. "Sweetheart, I'd like you to meet Yarmilla. I told you about her today."

"You're the one who kindly offered Anthony a drink. That was very thoughtful of you," she drawled, finding it difficult to be polite to a woman who didn't acknowledge her. If Yarmilla continued to pout at Anthony like that, Sarah was going to be sick.

Finally, the blonde turned to stare coldly at Sarah. "And your name?"

Sarah clasped her hand to her chest. "Oh, how rude of me. I'm Sarah, and I'm sure you've already met Aunt Lilly and Emily."

Yarmilla grimaced. "We've met," she said, turning her attention back to Anthony.

Before the barracuda could open that artfully painted mouth of hers, Sarah cut in, "Sweetheart, why don't you get us some food while we chitchat." Sarah caressed Anthony's chest and innocently grinned. "You know—girl talk."

"Ladies, if you'll excuse me."

With a quick kiss to her cheek, Anthony hurried away. Sarah noticed Aunt Lilly and Emily's antennae had gone up and now they were waiting to see what she was up to.

Pulling out a chair, Sarah strategically sat across from the woman and began her campaign. "I'm sorry. I didn't catch your full name."

Yarmilla sat up straight, making her cosmetically enhanced breasts stretch the gold material of her dress even more. In a voice filled with self-importance, she proudly announced to their table and those surrounding them, "I'm Yarmilla Vanda Trava."

Now You See It…

"Such fascinating names," Sarah said. "I wonder if they have a meaning." Sarah was astonished by the immediate change in the woman's demeanor. She must be one of those people who loved to talk about themselves.

"But of course," Yarmilla said haughtily, throwing her bottle-blonde hair over her shoulder with a long red nail. "'Yarmilla' means 'she who sells at market'."

Aunt Lilly snorted. "Sweetie, we already *know* what you're selling."

Sarah gave her aunt a warning frown, while Emily grinned at her outspokenness.

"And Vanda?" Sarah needed time to think of something that would get rid of this woman.

Yarmilla looked in Anthony's direction before answering. "'Vanda' means 'seeker'."

"Oh, how nice. You must do a lot of traveling," Sarah complimented with a double-edged sword.

"Oh, I've done my fair share with my first and second husbands," Yamilla boasted.

"Where are your husbands now?" Aunt Lilly asked.

Yarmilla shrugged. "Dead. You see, they were much older than me. You could say I was just too much woman for them," she said, grinning at her insensitive joke.

"Oh dear, how terrible," said Emily.

"Not really." Yarmilla fingered her ten-carat, square-cut diamond ring. "I'm doing just fine."

"I wasn't talking about you." Emily glared at Yarmilla. "I meant your husbands. What did you do, give them the evil eye?"

Seeing a fight brewing, Sarah diverted Yarmilla's attention. "What does your last name mean?" she asked the blonde, thinking of something that just might get rid of her.

Yarmilla heaved an impatient sigh. "It means 'fresh grasses'."

Aunt Lilly wiped her mouth on her napkin. "Oh hell, now I've heard everything. Sweetie, I've got news for you—"

Sarah gave her aunt a light kick under the table. "No wonder Anthony found you so interesting." Sarah watched the predator's gleam return. "He was saying how nice it was to meet such a worldly person. You see," Sarah leaned forward and dropped her voice to a conspirator's whisper, "he's a carpenter who's been working hard for the last couple years to put a down payment on a small home so he can finally move out of his grandmother's house."

Sarah kept a straight face as the lady paled. Now all she had to do was go in for the kill. "We felt so sorry for the poor dear because he never gets to travel, so we all pitched in for this cruise." From the disappointed look on Yarmilla's face, Sarah had succeeded in her mission.

Yarmilla sat up in her seat. "Let me get this straight," she said, all evidence of an accent vanished. "Anthony's a carpenter and he lives with his grandmother?"

All three women nodded sympathetically.

Yarmilla abruptly stood up. "What the hell am I doing wasting my time here?"

"What's the rush?" asked Aunt Lilly. "Stick around. Maybe after dinner we could do something exciting like play bridge or take in a movie?"

Sarah gleefully watched a look of horror enter Yarmilla's eyes. "Later girlfriend," she replied, heading in the direction of the next unsuspecting male.

"Now that was fun," Sarah said as Anthony returned to their table.

"What took so long?" Anthony offered a full plate of food to Sarah. "It looked like she was glued to the damn chair. Where'd she go?"

Sarah took the plate out of Anthony's hands. "Let's just say she went to mow her grasses," she said, then imitated

Yarmilla's accent while batting her lashes at him. "Here darling, sit beside me. I vant to know all about you."

Anthony sat down. "How did you get rid of her?"

"Easy, she's looking for husband number three. Someone rich enough to keep her in the lifestyle she's accustomed to."

Anthony frowned. "So what did you say, that I was poorer that a church mouse?"

"Basically, that you were a low-paid carpenter who still lived with his grandmother because you couldn't afford a place of your own. She hasn't got a clue how well the trades get paid nowadays," said Sarah. *Or how fine Anthony looks when he works under the hot sun, bronzing his wide shoulders and hard biceps into an even sweat-soaked tan, his jeans riding low on his lean hips as he carries planks of wood over his shoulders.* God, how she remembered.

Anthony chuckled. "Jeez, you made me sound like a loser. She was no match for the three of you. Remind me never to cross you as a group, I don't think I'd come out of it the same."

The force of the memory made Sarah squirm in her seat. Determined to put Anthony out of her mind, she focused on cutting into a tender piece of chicken. "So what's on the agenda for tomorrow?" She leaned over her plate to take a bite and her hair fell into her food.

"Oh, crap!" Now what? She felt behind her head for her clip and found it missing. She looked around and under her chair, hoping to find it. Nothing. Her eyes pleaded with Anthony for help as her complexion paled under the soft lights. Why now? Why here? That's all she needed—to have her clothes disappear in a room full of passengers. Sarah sank lower in her chair.

Just the thought of that happening horrified her. The thought of having to hide under the table, naked, mortified her.

Without missing a beat, Anthony pulled the elastic out of his hair and offered it to her. "Tomorrow we dock in Tunisia, Africa. How about we join a tour group and travel to one of their beaches?" Anthony asked, squeezing Sarah's knee under the table.

"No problem." Sarah pulled her hair back and secured it with the elastic, giving Anthony a weak smile of thanks. "Does that sound fine with the two of you?"

"Absolutely," Aunt Lilly said.

"*Nonna?*"

"*Va bene,*" Emily replied.

"That's settled then."

Anthony relaxed and enjoyed his meal and the entertainment, but kept a close eye on Sarah's face and hands as she ate. She gripped her cutlery hard to keep her hands from shaking.

One minute she felt as cool as the perfectly starched, white tablecloth, and the next, color heated her cheeks as thoughts of disappearing clothes kept popping into her head. The worried and inquisitive looks Anthony kept sending her didn't help, either. She bet he could only image the thoughts running through her head.

On top of everything, throughout the meal and then their desserts, her aunt kept giving her suspicious looks. Sarah figured it was only a matter of time before she stuck her nose where it wasn't wanted.

"Here, have another cream puff," Sarah said, serving Aunt Lilly her fourth helping in the hope that it would take her attention off her and back on her plate.

"By the way, what happened to the pretty top you were wearing when we came by your cabin?" Aunt Lilly asked.

Sarah's hand jerked, making a piece of her cherry cheesecake shoot across the table and splatter red sauce on the white cloth. "Sorry about that," she said, gingerly putting her fork down. She stirred her coffee instead of finishing her dessert.

"Anthony lent me one of his because my shoulders were sunburned and it was more comfortable," she hedged. The cool fabric on her hot skin was a constant reminder of Anthony.

"That was generous of him," Aunt Lilly said.

More than generous, if you asked Sarah. If he'd listened to her and left on an emergency call, she'd still be wearing her top and enjoying the remainder of the cruise knowing her clothes would stay on. Instead, she was short-circuiting from his encouraging touches and the shirt's soft caresses every time she shifted in her seat.

A wide yawn surprised Aunt Lilly before she could cover her mouth. "Oh dear, excuse me. Today has been a day of overindulging. And I really overdid it on the sweets and sun. I think it's time for this old bird to nestle in for the night."

Sarah listened to her aunt grunt and exaggerate her fatigue as she stood up. Smooth was something her aunt wasn't.

"Em, aren't you tired yet?" Aunt Lilly nodded her head in the direction of the dining room exit.

Emily quickly stood up. "Oh? Oh...yes. You young ones enjoy yourselves. Take a stroll on deck or go dancing."

Arm in arm, they left the table.

Sarah blushed. "They're not very subtle, are they?"

Anthony's eyes filled with amusement. "As delicate as a herd of elephants," he agreed, pushing his chair back and extending his hand. "But you won't hear a complaint out of me."

Sarah looked at his hand, dreading his touch. She needed to gather her strength and courage because she could feel herself slipping into those same old warm feelings again. She'd clamp her heart behind a steel vault and throw away the key.

In her opinion, fate had a sick sense of humor. She had promised herself that she would keep her distance. Now she had no choice but to stay close to Anthony.

"Scared?" he asked.

"Not in the least," she lied, placing her hand in his. What was she worried about? It was only a dance on a crowded dance floor. "You don't have to do this, you know."

Even with the dining room's soft lighting, Sarah could see Anthony's eyes darken.

"I'm following orders. We're to dance and stroll," he said, drawing Sarah onto the floor and into his arms. The instant their bodies touched, Sarah knew she'd made a big mistake.

Like chocolate left under the hot sun, her curves melted against solid muscle. Time ceased to exist as they danced to the sultry, hot music of the Latin band, the spicy notes surrounding her. What started as one dance drifted into another and then another.

Energy vibrated off the dancers as pleasure built. Couples kept pace to the strong beats. Swaying and twirling, Sarah did the same and stayed in sync with Anthony. Each step, each movement was made as one.

Beneath the palm of her hand, Anthony's strong heart beat a steady caress. A light sheen covered their flushed bodies. Clothes clung. Bodies fused.

Anthony bent her over his arm, her hair brushing the floor, before guiding her back up to bring them chest to chest, her pliant body liquefying into his.

Cradled against Anthony's strong legs, her pelvis tingled with every shift of his muscles. Heat radiated off his body, scorching her. Perfume and cologne mingled as their temperatures climbed. Sarah didn't know where she ended and he began.

Staring into his hypnotic eyes, Sarah felt Anthony's commanding pull. Lights and people faded, leaving Sarah dizzy in a world where only the two of them existed. Hungry intent strengthened his face. Licking her suddenly dry lips, Sarah felt Anthony's chest rise on a hoarse gasp.

"Do that again," Anthony commanded, tightening his hold, molding Sarah's body against his. Transfixed, he followed the tip of her tongue as it moistened her lips again. Anthony craved the scent and taste of this woman.

Seizing the moment, Anthony savored Sarah's lips with slow thoroughness. Her heart pounded erratically against his. He'd missed the feel of Sarah in his arms. The tiny pleasure noises she made increased his satisfaction and need to please her more.

He missed their talks, her sassy mouth and gentle teasing. Anthony wished for a more private spot, somewhere he could enjoy Sarah at his leisure instead of center stage among strangers.

Raising his head, Anthony waited for Sarah to open her eyes. "Follow me," he said, and keeping her body against his, he led her away from the crowds and into the clear night.

Emerging on deck, they were surrounded by a refreshing breeze. It cooled Anthony's skin and fanned shivers up his spine. A quiver shook Sarah's body and vibrated against him, teasing his heightened senses.

Waves crashed against the ship's hull as it sliced through dark waters. Above, heaven opened her arms, displaying a glorious show of twinkling bright lights.

He guided Sarah behind a secluded set of stairs and drew her back into his arms. Like a whisper of air, he brushed her lips. It was a fleeting touch, yet her responding soft moan encouraged him forward.

More. He needed more. He wanted the same simmering feeling they'd experienced on the dance floor. Tightening his hold, Anthony traced his tongue along lips that opened and invited him in. Shocking pleasure rushed through his body.

The abrupt sound of his cell phone jolted his senses. Damn, not now. He pulled it out of his pocket. "Yes?" he barked, his voice sharp and concise.

"Anthony? I know you said not to call unless it was an emergency, but we have one on our hands," said his VP.

"Then take care of it." A cold knot formed in his stomach.

"I'm giving you a heads-up that word on the street is, Carmichael's is getting ready to make a hostile takeover."

"Keep your ears to the ground so we know what those sons of bitches intend to do and keep me posted." He rang off. This cruise couldn't have come at a worse time.

He grimaced when Sarah stared at him with reproach. The phone call had taken just seconds, yet the damage was done. "Sarah, take that look off your face."

Her condemning eyes judged him. The reach for his cell had been an automatic reflex, one that could cost him dearly.

She wrapped her arms about herself. "Things never change, do they?"

"You don't understand—that call was very important."

Her hollow laugh mocked him. "They always are." She took a step away from him. "It's late. If we want to make the half-day tour, we'd better get a couple hours of sleep."

Escorting Sarah to her room was the last thing Anthony wanted to do, but he knew that stubborn look on her face. He waved her forward. "After you."

Thick silence surrounded them as they made their way down to their cabins. "Good night," Sarah said, inserting her key card into the slot before opening the door and stepping inside.

"Good night," Anthony replied.

With a quick nod, Sarah closed the door, leaving him standing in the silent hall.

Sarah leaned her head against the cold steel of the door and moaned. What a fool! What a stupid, stupid fool! The cruise atmosphere had carried her along and made her forget the real Anthony. In the end she'd nearly served herself on a platter.

He hasn't changed. Not one damn bit. He was the same self-absorbed workaholic that measured success by monetary value. The romantic nuances and kind gestures had been an act. He was passing the time 'til he returned to his life. Once again, she was just a convenience.

"I'm such an idiot," she groaned, pushing away from the door and noticed that her bed had been turned down and a chocolate lay on her pillow. A small light had been left on to softly illuminate the cabin, softening her image in the mirror.

She didn't recognize the person staring back at her with hollowed eyed and a dejected stance. But she *did* notice her necklace was missing. She rushed over to her suitcase and opened the side pocket she had taken it from, reached in and pulled it out.

It must have vanished either on the dance floor or when they had been kissing under the stars. Either way, she hadn't noticed its disappearance 'til now. "I give up," she sighed, dropping it back into the pocket before zipping it up.

Quickly stripping, Sarah jumped into the shower and scrubbed the scent of Anthony's cologne from her body. Its fragrance brought back vivid images of them entwined on the dance floor.

"Stupid, stupid, stupid," she berated herself. When would she ever learn?

After drying off, she donned a rose-colored nightgown with spaghetti straps, then blow-dried her hair and brushed its length 'til it shone.

Turning off the lights, Sarah slid under clean crisp sheets. With a tired sigh she relaxed her head into her soft pillow and felt the small bump of the forgotten chocolate.

Reaching behind her head, Sarah grasped the chocolate, unwrapped it and popped it into her mouth. Rolling onto her side, she hugged the pillow for comfort.

She had to remind herself Anthony wasn't what she wanted. She needed a man who was reliable. Someone solid she could depend on. Sarah punched her pillow. Her standards sounded dull, but at least they were safe. Why couldn't she find excitement and passion and trustworthiness in one man?

Tomorrow, she'd tell Anthony that what happened on the dance floor had been a mistake. It scared her how quickly she could lose herself in his embrace, in his kisses. He'd always had that effect on her. But at the end of this cruise, Anthony would resume his life as if nothing had happened, and she'd end up with another broken heart.

This time, Sarah wasn't sure if she could mend all the pieces. With a heavy sigh, she sank further into her pillow. She needed to protect herself.

It was her last thought as she drifted off.

Sinking deeper into the warmth of her bed, she tried to get back to sleep but someone was pounding on a door.

"Sarah? Are you up?"

Her eyes popped open. "Anthony?" she called. Throwing off her covers, she stumbled out of bed and nearly tripped. Opening the door, Sarah peeked through the tiny opening. "Good morning," she said and smoothed her hair away from her face.

"Good morning." Anthony's appreciative glance traveled over her disheveled appearance.

She ducked behind the door. With her flushed cheeks and tousled hair, she bet she looked like a woman who had spent the night making love, while Anthony was freshly shaven, his hair still wet and tied back. He wore khaki shorts, a cream polo top and sandals on bare feet. He was carrying a T-shirt. "I thought you might need this," he grinned.

The thin spaghetti strap of her nightgown slipped off her shoulder. Self-conscious of her appearance, Sarah slid the strap back into place. His eyes followed her hand up to her shoulder and lingered on the tender space at the base of her neck.

Sarah held out her hand for the T-shirt. "Give me five minutes."

Anthony cleared his throat and handed the shirt over.

"About last night…" They both began at the same time.

Silence.

"Ladies first."

"I wanted to apologize for last night. I don't know why we got carried away like that. You're not my type anymore, and I'm sure I'm not yours. We can both blame our irrational actions to the party atmosphere on the ship."

"Is that what you want?" he asked.

"Yes. My life is already complicated enough with this spell, so I don't need to make it more difficult. Look, let's be honest here, we've been thrown together because of my aunt and your grandmother, otherwise our paths would never have crossed again."

"I see," Anthony said, taking a step back, his eyes guarded. "I understand."

Sarah smiled. "I'm glad that's settled," she lied, surprised at how easily he had agreed. "So, for the rest of the trip we'll be buddies."

"Sure," Anthony said with an indifferent shrug. "Buddies."

"Give me five minutes and we'll go to my aunt's cabin."

"I'll give you ten and meet you there."

Sarah shut her door, her grin dissolving. "Yeah right. Buddies."

Not willing to dwell on her traitorous feelings, Sarah sprang into action. Whipping off her nightgown, she jumped into the shower for a quick rinse. Leaving her hair loose and wet, she tied a bandana over it, making a knot behind her head. She slipped on a black bikini, a pair of black shorts and Anthony's white T-shirt.

Looking into a mirror, she chuckled. The T-shirt covered her shorts completely and looked more like pajamas. Rummaging through her suitcase's side pocket, she pulled out another ankle bracelet. "Ha! I have more than one ankle bracelet you know. And there're a lot more where this came from. Let's see if this doesn't stay on," she said, strapping it to her ankle.

Putting on a pair of comfortable walking sandals, she placed her sunglasses on her head, snatched a bag and a large straw hat and left.

Nearing her aunt's cabin, Sarah could hear men's voices in deep discussion. Pushing the door open, she found Anthony leaning against a wall with his arms folded over his chest, listening carefully to a man in uniform.

"What's going on?"

"The ship's doctor is examining your aunt," Anthony said.

A middle-aged gentleman smiled down at Aunt Lilly, who sat up in bed with her housecoat on. Emily sat on the other bed silently.

"Aunt Lilly?" Sarah looked her over but couldn't see what the problem was. "Is it your heart?"

"No dear, I'm just fine. Anthony wouldn't listen to me and insisted on calling the doctor," Aunt Lilly said, glowering at him.

Sarah sat on the end of her aunt's bed. "Will someone please tell me what's wrong then?"

"My feet and ankles have swollen," Aunt Lilly explained, lifting her gown to show her. "And it's quite uncomfortable."

"Did you trip and hurt yourself?" Sarah asked, tenderly touching her aunt's puffy ankles.

"I was explaining to your aunt that she overindulged yesterday," the doctor said, chuckling at Aunt Lilly's guilty expression. "For the next couple of days, she needs to eliminate all drinks and desserts that contain refined sugar. She should also watch the amount of coffee she drinks. She's overburdened her kidneys and needs to flush them out. She needs to drink plenty of water and take it easy. By tomorrow, she'll feel a lot better and the swelling should have gone down." He turned to Lilly. "Remember to stay off your feet for today."

Sarah still wasn't satisfied. "So I shouldn't worry?"

"That's correct," the doctor said, patting her aunt on the shoulder. "I see this a lot. Especially with the older passengers, who tend to go overboard on the goodies their first day." He snapped his medical bag shut and lifted it off the bed. "Ladies, Anthony." He shook hands with Sarah and Anthony and left.

Anthony closed the door behind the doctor. "So what's the verdict?"

Sarah took control of the situation. "I'll call room service so Aunt Lilly can have breakfast in bed," she said, getting up from the bed. "Once she's eaten, we'll spend a day on deck around the pool."

"You'll do no such thing. Wasting a positively good day babysitting an old woman," Aunt Lilly said.

"You two go," Emily said, waving Sarah and Anthony away. "I'll keep Lilly company, and we'll even promise to stay on board."

Sarah shook her head. "I'd prefer to stay, in case you need my help."

"I don't want your help," Aunt Lilly declared, glaring at Sarah. "I have the ship's crew at my disposal. What do I have to do to get rid of you? Throw you overboard?"

Anthony chuckled. "She's got a point."

"It's settled then," Aunt Lilly said, giving Emily a nod. "Kick these two out of our cabin."

"*Va bene.*" Emily escorted them to the door.

"And I don't expect to see your ugly faces until late afternoon," Aunt Lilly commanded from her bed as Emily closed the door in their stunned faces.

"You heard the woman," Anthony said, leading Sarah up to the deck, where a magnificent breakfast buffet was set under a clear, blue African sky.

"How about breakfast?" she asked.

"I've already had mine. You go ahead while I arrange a day with my buddy," he said and strolled away.

She frowned at Anthony's retreating back. Was he being facetious or sarcastic? With a shrug, Sarah filled a plate with fresh tropical fruits and a pile of fluffy pancakes, which she smothered in syrup before sitting at a table in the sunshine. She leisurely watched people while she enjoyed her breakfast.

"Coffee?"

Sarah smiled at the steward. "Yes, please," she said, enjoying the activity going on around her.

Passengers tossed towels onto lounge chairs to stake their claim before heading for the buffet table. She figured they had a long strenuous day of sunbathing ahead of them. A couple of women in skimpy bathing suits were oiling up, while a matronly couple wearing identical flowered shirts and straw hats had white sunscreen plastered on their noses.

Sarah grinned. "Talk about extremes."

"Ready?"

Sarah hadn't noticed Anthony's approach. "Yes," she said, wiping her mouth and standing up.

At street level, Anthony went in one direction while Sarah strolled toward a group of buses. "Anthony, this way," she called.

"Follow me. We're not going on the buses."

Sarah retraced her steps and frowned at the bright yellow jeep. "I thought we were going to a beach?" She had hoped they would spend the day surrounded by noisy tourists. Now she grew tense.

"We *are* going to a beach. It's just that I have no intention of boarding a bus like a bunch of cattle and being herded around Tunisia."

Sarah sighed, some of her tension melting away.

Opening the door, Anthony took hold of Sarah's hand. "Madam, your chariot awaits," he said, helping her in before closing the door.

If this was her chariot, then why did she feel like she was boarding a runaway train?

Chapter Seven

Sarah slipped on her sunglasses. Trapped. She watched Anthony circle the front of the jeep and climb in. "So, where exactly are we going?" she asked after he'd closed his door. It felt like the interior had shrunk.

"Tabarka." He slid on his sunglasses and started the jeep. As he shifted into first gear, Anthony's knuckles brushed her leg.

Sarah jerked away in surprise. Hell, it was tight in here. She held her breath and hoped that she could control her body's reaction. "Where and what is Tabarka?"

"It's a beach about a couple hours' drive along the African coastline from Bizerte," Anthony explained, changing gears and bumping into her thigh again.

Sarah tried to make herself smaller by shrinking into her seat as they merged into heavy traffic. This was terrible. It was bumper to bumper, the stop-and-go motion causing Anthony to continuously change gears, driving her up a wall.

Each accidental touch singed her nerve endings, making it difficult for her to sit still. And the slight breeze coming through the open windows wasn't cooling her off. If she had to put up with the brush of Anthony's hand every time he accelerated or slowed down, she'd go crazy.

Anthony glanced over and smiled. "Enjoying yourself?"

"Couldn't be better," she lied. Shifting her legs toward the door, Sarah leaned her elbow out the window and feigned interest in the passing scenery. She must look like a damn dog with her hair flapping behind her.

Forget about Anthony, think reliable. Dependable. She tried to remember men she'd dated in the past who had these qualities, but Anthony's face kept popping into her mind. "Bother," Sarah said, swatting her flying hair away from her face.

She reached for the bandana's knot at the back of her head to tighten it, and came up empty. "Hell. This is just great."

"What is?" Anthony glanced at her as he drove, then did a double-take and chuckled. "Your bandana has vanished. If you want, you'll find another one in the bag in the back."

No, I didn't want. What she really wanted was to wipe the smirk off Anthony's face. "I'm fine," she replied. Her fingers rapidly braided her hair then rummaged through her purse, finding the elastic Anthony had given her the night before. She tied the braid's end so it wouldn't unravel again. "There, problem solved."

Her problems were far from solved. Her life was slowly disintegrating in front of her very eyes. The trouble was, it was coming undone in front of Anthony, too.

Thank goodness they'd soon be surrounded by vacationers. Noisy, crowded beaches, shops and restaurants filled to overflowing with tourists were the cure.

Nonchalantly, she crossed her legs and noticed that her ankle bracelet was missing. Another point scored by the spell. She chewed on her lower lip and glanced at Anthony, her heart turning over in response. She had to remind herself that he wasn't what she wanted, what she needed. *Reliable, reliable, reliable,* she chanted in her mind. God, how she resented this spell and the predicament it placed her in.

She shifted so her back was against the door. This, too, was a big mistake. Now she could look at Anthony all she wanted. She needed a distraction.

In the backseat, Sarah saw a large cooler, snorkeling gear and an athletic bag. "You've thought of everything," she remarked.

"I asked one the chefs on the ship to pack us a lunch and I brought extra bottles of water, just in case," Anthony shrugged. "You can never be too prepared."

She could cross crowded restaurants off her list. Anthony shifted in his seat and sighed. The dry wind seemed to relax him, while it only made Sarah grow more rigid— each breeze teased her senses with the scent of Anthony's cologne. Oh hell—she knew climbing into this tin can had been a mistake.

He drove with confidence, his movements smooth, precise, his attention carelessly focused. His thigh muscles flexed each time he changed gears.

Sarah looked away, gritting her teeth. If he could relax, then so could she. She'd show him it didn't bother her having him near. Leaning her head back, Sarah enjoyed a warm calming breeze. They were just buddies, after all.

Along the coast, Sarah caught tantalizing glimpses of sparkling blue waters and little towns tucked in sheltered coves, with brightly colored boats anchored close by. Sheep grazed on hillsides, while men sat under trees to escape the heat.

"Look over there," Anthony said, pointing at intermingled traces of ruins on the sides of a jagged mountain. Its sharp outline cut into the cloudless blue sky.

Anthony smiled. "Keep your eyes open for a small dirt road to your right. One of the stewards on the ship said that just before we reach the strip of hotels we'd find a beach used by the locals."

Oh the horizon, Sarah spotted the outline of buildings before barely catching a quick glimpse of an opening between tall shrubs. "Ah, I think you just missed it."

Anthony geared down and quickly pulled onto the shoulder of the road. Turning toward Sarah, he placed his arm

Now You See It...

along the back of her seat and reversed. The hair on his arm brushed against her neck, sending shivers down her spine. She kept her posture stiff and leaned forward, pretending to watch the scenery.

Reaching the hidden opening, Anthony steered the jeep into the tall vegetation. Sarah sighed with relief and relaxed back. Soon, she'd be able to get out of this metal contraption of torture and mingle with the natives.

The rocky decline led to an absolutely captivating sheltered bay. Anthony brought the jeep to a stop. "Welcome to our own piece of paradise." He took off his sunglasses and threw them on the dashboard.

Not wasting a moment, Sarah jumped out onto soft, white spotless sand, her feet sinking into its welcoming warmth. At last, the distance she needed.

She marveled at the beauty of the clear water that mirrored the brilliance of the sky. The sea lapped against the shore, forming never-ending ripples in the sand, while a seagull waddled by, pecking for food. Tall grasses swayed with the gentle touch of the breeze.

And not a damn human being in sight.

Apprehension captured her frantic heart. Sarah scanned the beach. No one. Dread raced up her spine. Only Anthony and herself. Hidden from passing cars, away from curious tourists.

Taking deep breaths, Sarah tried to stay calm. There was nothing to it. Really. She ignored the rapid beat of her heart. All she had to do was keep a safe distance from Anthony. With a bay at her disposal, she couldn't be safer.

Anthony walked by carrying the cooler. "If you grab the snorkeling gear, I'll bring the rest of our things."

"No problem," Sarah said, turning back to the jeep.

Reaching between the seats, she grabbed the flippers and masks in one hand and the large nylon athletic bag in the other—and backed into Anthony's hot chest.

"Steady." Firm fingers grasped her waist.

She took a quick, sharp breath. "Always am."

Steady? There was nothing steady or secure about her life. Disappearing clothes, a reappearing ex-boyfriend and a secluded beach. She'd hoped to blend into a background of tourists, not audition for an X-rated movie.

"Take this." Sarah handed Anthony the bag so he wouldn't feel her body's reaction to his. "Thanks."

Side by side, they strolled to the spot where he had left the cooler. "Would you like to snorkel first and then have lunch?" Anthony asked as Sarah dropped the flippers and masks onto the sand.

"Good idea." A swim would cool her off.

Anthony opened the bag and spread a towel on the sand, while Sarah slipped off her sandals and shimmied out of her shorts. About to pull off her T-shirt, she stilled. "Forget that."

Anthony looked up from what he was doing. "Did you say something?"

Sarah smiled innocently. "Not a thing."

With a shrug, Anthony laid out a second towel.

She wasn't taking any chances that her bikini would disappear on her. That's all she needed. Being exposed to Anthony's eyes on a deserted beach was a combustible combination.

Sarah positioned her mask on her head and blew into her air tube. Glancing over to see how Anthony was doing, she tried to swallow. *Oh yes, he was doing just fine.*

He'd already discarded his top and shorts and was standing in a tight pair of blue Lycra swimming trunks. They embraced his narrow waist and hugged his muscular thighs. The shorts hid everything and left little to the imagination.

Bronze skin glistened over sinew and sculpted muscles. A dusting of fine hair covered his chest and tapered down over his flat stomach to disappear from sight.

His biceps bunched as he adjusted his mask onto his head. Each movement emphasized the lean perfection of his body. Sarah felt hot. Burning hot. She fanned her T-shirt away from her body. Her eyes unwillingly strayed back to Anthony's tempting physique. His controlled power jumped across the sand, overwhelming her. Sarah felt herself falling apart.

Stepping back, she distanced herself from Anthony and the feelings that churned within her, fisting her hands by her sides. "You've got to be out of your mind to think what you're thinking," she mumbled. He was more than she remembered. More energy, more temptation, more man. He was just too much.

She needed to cool off. Regain control. Inhaling deeply, Sarah slowly released her breath, calming her frazzled nerves. She made herself remember all the times he'd stood her up. All the missed dinners and interrupted lunches spent picking at her food while listening to him on his cell.

Looking up, Anthony grinned devilishly. "Ready?"

"Sure," she replied, throwing her sunglasses onto a towel.

Picking up her fins, Sarah strolled to the water's edge and slipped them on. Delicious coolness kissed her feet as the water rushed between her toes in the fins. Across the bay, the water reflected different shades of blue with an occasional white shimmer, and a single lonely cloud floated by.

The waves grew choppier as she waded farther in, pushing and pulling on her legs and body. Curls of white foam swirled around her as the waves reached her chest. Eager to dive into the azure swells, she moved forward and felt the ground descend sharply. Adjusting her mask over her eyes and placing the snorkel in her mouth, Sarah dove.

She submerged into a crystal clear underwater world. Unspoiled beauty unfolded around her. Surrounded by serene silence, Sarah watched the bubbles from her snorkel as they floated lazily upward. Swimming to the surface, she inhaled and dove again. Anthony never left her side.

A tiny school of colorful fish escorted her on her descent before quickly darting away. Sarah nonchalantly tried to drift away from Anthony, heading for the waving sea fans, plants and clams that clung to an outcrop of rocks, only to find him quickly changing his direction and, with firm strokes of his fins, headed toward her again. With a light caress, Anthony caught her attention and pointed to a small gray shark, its shadowy shape fading as it swam farther out to sea.

Sarah nodded. The harder she tried to distance herself, the more she found herself trapped by Anthony. She'd turned to the sea for its space, only to submerge herself in feelings she'd rather not think about. If watching Anthony undress on shore had staggered her, seeing him glide through the water was delicious torture.

A memory flashed through her mind of their hands entwined over her head, his body gliding against hers, each pleasuring the other to unbearable heights before finally crashing in one another's arms.

Large bubbles rippled into the water with an acquiescent sigh. Drifting upward, she replenished her air at the surface and, with a hard kick, descended again.

Drawing near, Anthony guided Sarah past another large outcrop of rocks. A steep underwater cliff appeared, below it a blazing underwater fire of red coral stretching up from the sea bottom.

Anthony squeezed her hand to express his pleasure. Through the glass of his mask his eyes reflected his enjoyment. Sarah nodded and quickly withdrew her hand.

She didn't know if she could trust this Anthony. Attentive, gentle, totally focused on enjoying the moment. If she compared the workaholic from the past to the man swimming beside her, she'd swear they were two separate people.

She reined in any feelings of tenderness that slipped through the cracks of her protective exterior. Wary, her instincts warned her not to believe this mirage.

Anthony waved for her attention then pointed to the surface, indicating that their time was up. Taking a final look around her, Sarah floated upwards.

Surfacing, Sarah lifted her mask to the top of her head and let her mouthpiece dangle. "That was lovely," she said, letting the current carry her away from Anthony, away from temptation.

Anthony leisurely glided backward toward shore, finally standing when he could touch the bay floor. "Come on, I'm starved."

"You go ahead." She wasn't ready to get out yet. Sarah continued to body surf on each passing swell. She closed her eyes against the glare of the sun and floated.

"I'll wait for you," Anthony called back, walking out of the water and dropping his gear. Crossing his arms over his chest, he watched her.

Sarah straightened and touched the solid sandy bottom. She'd stay at a safe distance and compose herself. "It's too lovely to come out yet, you go ahead and eat."

If she convinced herself that she felt nothing, then perhaps her body would stop double-crossing her. Never mind her two-timing clothes. Under the water, she could see the T-shirt still plastered over her black bikini. Good, everything was still in place.

The trouble was, Sarah could feel her swollen nipples pressing against the black fabric of her bikini.

"Come on, Santorelli," Anthony called, taking a threatening step toward her. "Are you coming out or do I have to come in and get you?"

"What's the rush?" Her lips thinned in irritation.

He was magnificent standing under the hot glaring sun. His hair glistened while water droplets clung greedily to his body, and little rivulets sketched over his chest. Beneath Anthony's stare, Sarah could feel goose bumps rise on her arms.

"I thought that after we've eaten we'd visit the hotel strip."

And where there were hotels, there were tourists. And crowds. Pretending to enjoy the sun's reflections, she bent her head back and hid from his scrutiny. "You're right. Let's hurry and eat so that we can do some sightseeing."

Sarah's evasive maneuvers didn't fool him one bit. She was running scared. Thrilled by her hungry perusal one minute and the way she hid her reactions the next, Anthony grew all the more determined to chip away at her crumbling wall of reserve.

She was stalling. Up 'til now he'd used the strategy of retreat, then attack. He'd pretended to accept her ridiculous suggestion of being buddies because it suited his purpose. Taking advantage of the small space of the jeep, he'd purposely touched her leg every chance he got, forcing Sarah to mask her awareness, keeping her unbalanced.

Anthony chuckled. So he was a bastard, but he was playing for keeps. With only one week to prove his worthiness and ignite Sarah's trust, he was fast running out of time. He needed to show her that he had changed and that she should give him a second chance.

Today was for them. To remind Sarah how good they were together. And Anthony just prayed the cell phone he'd hidden in the gym bag wouldn't ring, otherwise he'd have two strikes against him. He'd brought it only because of the rising trouble back in Toronto.

Since they'd arrived, he'd kept his distance, kept his expressions closed, hoping that she would melt and become the woman he once knew. Instead, she'd retreated. The only choice he'd had was to advance again. To keep her unbalanced and tuned to her buried emotions.

"That's it, time's up." Anthony walked back into the water. Sarah's head snapped up at his announcement. The closer he got, the rounder her eyes became.

Stopping in front of her, he lifted the mask off her head. "Just moving things along." A charge of electricity surged between them.

Ensnared. Her rapt expression didn't lie.

He purposely glided a hand over her shoulder then gently caressed the side of her face. Sarah lowered her lashes and looked away, exposing the pulse that frantically beat at the base of her neck.

He lowered his eyes to veil his intentions, returned to shore and dropped Sarah's equipment. "Come on, Santorelli. If you stay out there long enough you'll end up as shark bait."

"Don't push it, Mancini." Straightening her shoulders, she slowly waded to shore.

She reminded him of a water nymph as she emerged. Tall and sleek, water trailing over one shoulder where her braid lay. His transparent T-shirt clung to her body, outlining her curved shape and her unbound breasts—

His breath caught. He stood there—blank, amazed and very shaken. Her bikini top had disappeared. Sarah had kept his T-shirt on for protection and now the cotton was plastered to her breasts, exposing her sinewy body.

Anthony fisted his hands and groaned as she waded into shallow water that now reached her waist. She was stunning. The sea air hardened her dusk-colored nipples. His gaze lowered, traveling over her flat stomach and noting the black bikini bottom that still covered her. Down long shapely legs and back up again. He returned to a pair of hooded eyes. Anthony wasn't going to give her a chance to retreat.

Reentering the sea, Anthony quickly ate the distance between them. Her stare became defensive the closer he got.

She tried to skirt around him. "I thought you were hungry?"

He blocked her. "I am."

Reaching out, Anthony molded Sarah's body to his. They fit perfectly. A moan filled with pleasure and pain escaped his lips.

"Oh, God, you're—*we're* making a big mistake." She gave a token push against his chest while her eyes told a different story.

He weaved his fingers through her hair, tilted her face and brought his mouth down. The biggest mistake he'd ever made was letting her go. His lips pried hers open and, with skilled insistence, melted her resistance. With a whimper, her body relaxed. A sigh of yearning escaped her lips and vibrated through his body. Her fingers curled in his damp hair, pulling him closer.

She tasted the same. Sweet. Addictive. Anthony wanted more. He needed Sarah to disintegrate. To feel the same untamable urgency he felt. To rattle her into giving more of herself so that he could do the same.

With shaking fingers, Anthony traced the indentation of her waist and grasped the curve of her hip, pulling her against his arousal.

He was going up in flames. Bright, hot flames. They consumed him from the inside out. Sarah licked the salty water off his neck before gently biting his earlobe. His deep growl answered her. She rubbed her breasts against his chest, her nipples giving indescribable pleasure.

She braced her hands on his shoulders, letting the receding waves tease her away from him, only to return and connect them again. Like a temptress, the flowing sea titillating his senses with its to and fro movements.

Sarah was pure liquid. Anthony was certain that her grasp and the buoyancy of the water were the only things keeping her up. Her almond-shaped eyes melted, going from rich brown to midnight black.

"You take my breath away," he sighed, tracing her lips with his fingertip.

She bit the end of his finger, licking a droplet of water that clung there. Anthony groaned. Beneath the water he cupped her bottom with one hand, pressing her lower body into his. Flowing with the rhythm of the sea, Anthony swayed back and forth. Sarah's body arched, begging to blend with his.

Satisfaction built to triumph. He'd always had this effect on her. He wanted her to enjoy just a little more of this madness before he pulled away. To show her how good they still were together. Attack and retreat.

But the problem was his brain was melting down and his body was burning up. The more aroused Sarah became, the less he was able to pull back. His well-planned tactic was ambushing him.

She opened her mouth, taking his fingertip into its warm wet recesses and sucking. Anthony tilted his head back as pleasure filled him. His neck and shoulder muscles tightened as he emitted a low deep growl.

He lifted her into his arms. "*Cara*, you drive me crazy." He walked out of the water and, with quick strides, carried her to their towels.

Sitting with his legs stretched out before him, Anthony pulled Sarah down to straddle him. Whipping off her T-shirt, he kissed the tops of her soft, full breasts. An answering hiss and the tightening of her fingers in his hair were his rewards. How he'd missed her body's responses.

Anthony gently arched Sarah back over his arm and captured a nipple. He laved the tip thoroughly before finally bringing it into his mouth.

Beneath his tongue, her body stiffened. "Anthony, stop!" she cried, grasping his hair and pulling his head up.

"Easy," Anthony groaned, prying her fingers from his scalp.

"My bikini top is gone!" Sarah frantically covered her breasts with her hands and checked to see if the rest of her bikini was still in place.

"I know."

"You knew?!"

Anthony stroked her arms. "*Si.*"

Heat traveled up her neck and filled her cheeks. Outrage mixed with vulnerability as the meaning of his words sank in.

"You louse!" Squirming, Sarah tried to lean away. Her frantic actions rubbed her hot center against his arousal. "I need to put my T-shirt back on." She frantically looked around and spotted it lying on the ground, covered in sand. "Damn."

Anthony continued to nibble her neck. "Wouldn't have done you any good," he cajoled. He needed to get her angry. At her most volatile was when Sarah let slip her true emotions.

"Why not?" she demanded, shaking with a mixture of suppressed anger and desire. Still she kept her breasts covered.

Anthony swirled his tongue around the shell of her ear. Delicious shivers shook Sarah's body. She groaned and swayed closer to his chest.

"It's transparent. Besides," he leaned away from Sarah so that he could meet her eyes, "I'm not going to let you retreat behind that wall of yours."

Sarah's anger solidified, replacing her desire. In a cold low voice, she repeated, "You're not going to *let me*?" She tried to get off his lap without using her hands and stumbled right back into his lap. "You can at least give me a hand."

"No." Anthony caressed the bottoms of her breasts with the sides of his thumbs.

"No?!" she exclaimed.

Now You See It...

His calm reply infuriated her. An angry flush now covered her body. She tried to hide her vulnerability beneath her determined aggression.

"This," Sarah's body shook, "is another thing I hated about our relationship. You always imposed your choices over mine. I was scared that I would get used to it and lose myself."

The blood drained away from his face. It felt like she had hit him in the stomach. Scared? His mind couldn't grasp the idea. He hadn't viewed his desire to help and make life easier as controlling. But she obviously did.

Disgusted at his own insensitivity, he immediately lifted her off his lap.

He had done what he thought was right for her, only to realize now that he had selfishly manipulated each situation to suit his own needs.

With abrupt movements he pulled an extra T-shirt out of his athletic bag, dropped it next to Sarah and then carried the flippers and masks back to the jeep, giving her a moment of privacy to get dressed. When he returned they stared at each other like two opponents.

With a sigh of defeat, Anthony dropped onto the towel next her and tried to hold her hands, only to have Sarah jerk away.

"People change," he said. He saw uncertainty in her eyes, and felt terrible that he had put it there. "I've changed."

His cell phone rang, contradicting his words.

Sarah's dry bark of laughter was scornful. "Aren't you going to answer that?"

Torn between the women he loved and a business that was his life, Anthony wavered. "Sarah—"

The phone continued to ring.

"Oh, for crying out loud, just answer the damn thing."

Reaching into the bag, Anthony flipped it open with the snap of his wrist and growled into it, "What?"

"Carmichael's made their move and have been snapping up shares all morning."

"How many?" Anthony listened intently.

"They're up to thirty percent of the company's voting stock, compared to your fifty-one percent. At the rate they're buying, they'll have quite a few seats on the board and could sway the remaining shareholders on future decisions."

He wanted to crush the cell in his bare hands. "Start buying," he snapped, turning his cell off and throwing it onto the bag. Once this little bump was over he'd turn around and buy out Carmichael's. He hadn't known the sons of bitches had the balls. They'd shown *him*.

"Sarah, I can explain."

She lifted her chin and boldly met his eyes. "Oh, I can see how much you've changed."

He pulled his fingers through his hair. His hands were tied concerning his company. But that didn't mean he couldn't work on his relationship while he waited for news. She was retreating behind her protective wall and nothing but the truth would set them on a road to trust and healing.

"It wasn't your fault our relationship ended. I was running a tight schedule and you weren't my top priority." Anthony saw Sarah jerk from the sting of his words before looking away.

Sarah gazed out over the bay, refusing to meet his stare. "Why are you telling me this now? It doesn't matter anymore," she said, twirling her hair around her finger.

Dread sank in the pit of his stomach. Placing a finger under her chin, Anthony gently turned her toward him. "Because I never got the chance to apologize. Never had the opportunity to make things right."

Sarah pulled her chin away. "So I could hear what? That I'd become a convenient inconvenience? Don't worry, I got the picture. Thanks, but no thanks."

Frustrated, Anthony rubbed his hands over his face. "That's not how it was at all. I was trying to make a success of the company. Between the pressures at work, trying to stay one step ahead of the bank, two steps ahead of a hostile takeover and a whopping jump ahead of your hints about wanting to meet my family, I felt trapped."

"Well, no one's holding you down now."

"After you'd left I kept telling myself the same thing. That I was free and should be glad about it. Then one day my dear grandmother had had enough of my foul moods."

"What did she do?" Curious, Sarah finally faced him.

"She told me that I should be pleased with myself that I had gotten exactly what I wanted. Since I hadn't spent much time with you, I really didn't know you. So no great loss."

"And you agreed?"

"Hell, no. I got angry. I told her that I knew you better than anyone else. The way you twirl your hair around your finger when something is bothering you." Sarah dropped her hand onto her lap and gave him an angry stare. "What your favorite foods are. How you love autumn and Halloween. And how you secretly carry romance novels in your purse."

She shrugged. "So you noticed a couple of my quirks while I was with you, no big deal." Sarah threw a stone toward the water. "So what are you saying? That you want to try again or that you're sorry that it ended so poorly."

"Both."

"Forget it. There's no way I'd go through that again."

She didn't trust him not to abandon her again. He had his work cut out for him this time. "Let me prove myself."

"What's the use, you'll eventually revert back to your old habits again," Sarah said, pointedly staring at his discarded cell phone.

Anthony pulled his fingers through his hair. "Then test me."

Sarah laughed. "Oh that's just great. Give me one good reason why I should accept your challenge?"

They'd get a second chance at love. "Because we'd both win," he said, holding his breath.

Sarah's eyes reflected her thoughts as they formed, separated, then came back to take root. "Here's the deal. For the remainder of this trip you get to learn who I am all over again," she said.

Anthony's eyes cleared as a large grin erupted.

Sarah raised her hand to stall his reaction. "Not so fast. There will be no work and no interruptions. You invest in quality time or I'm cashing in my accumulated points and walking away free and clear. Otherwise, I'm not promising anything and I'm certainly not investing anymore of my time on you."

He knew she was skeptical. He would prove his sincerity. "Deal. You drive a hard bargain."

Sarah reached into the cooler and handed Anthony a sandwich. "I learned from the best."

Now You See It…

Chapter Eight

What had she just done?

Even worse, how could she do this to herself again? Where Anthony was concerned, she was a glutton for punishment. Sarah's lingering feelings of anger drained away, leaving confusion and doubt. What if he hadn't changed? The more important question was—what if he had? A small flicker of hope grew. She could give him one more chance.

Maybe he *had* changed. She knew she wasn't the same woman she'd been two years ago. But one thing was for sure—she didn't want to see his highhanded, Italian attitude getting in the way.

If he could put aside his tendency to manipulate then she could store away her Irish temperament. She could.

"A word of advice," she told him sternly. "I'd ease up on your pushing if I were you."

"If I hadn't pushed I would have taken off the first time you opened that beautiful mouth of yours and dug into me."

"If I remember correctly, I dug into you each time you stood me up. You deserved what you got."

Anthony raised his hands in surrender. *"Va bene."*

"Still doing that, I see. You used to revert to Italian whenever you were anger or—" Sarah closed her mouth and blushed.

"Or when I made love," Anthony finished, his eyes catching and holding hers.

"I'd forgotten," Sarah lied.

"Really? Do you know that I can sense your mood changes? Your uncertainty? That's the trouble with the men in my family. We're cursed. When it comes to the women we care about, we seem to be attuned to them."

Sarah's defenses rose. "I'm glad you're already cursed. It saves me the trouble of hexing you myself."

"I'm serious. Every time the women in my family get sick, the men get it worse. I have an uncle in Italy who, every time my aunt got pregnant, gained more weight than she did. They stopped at three kids. He said he couldn't take it."

Sarah chuckled. "You're just making that up."

"I wish." Anthony rubbed a cold water bottle against his forehead. "And don't even mention the word contractions."

"How come you never told me this when we were going out?"

Anthony shrugged. "We never got around to it."

They hadn't shared a lot of things. She had spent more time waiting for him than learning about him. Their history together had consisted of missed meals and hot sex. And neither of those pastimes had been conducive to talking. There was no use regretting a time that couldn't be recaptured.

Anthony fell silent. She wasn't sure if he was giving her time to regroup or if he was planning his next move. It made her antsy. Either way, she intended to keep him unbalanced. His innocent expression gave her every reason not to trust him. "I'm keeping my eyes on you."

Anthony chuckled. "You'll have to stay close to me to do that."

Sarah tore off a piece of her sandwich and threw it to a seagull. "Do you always have to have the last word?"

"Only when I'm right."

"You're not right." Sarah took a gulp from her water bottle. "You're tenacious."

Now You See It...

"And maybe you recognize this headstrong trait because you have it yourself," Anthony replied, following Sarah's example and throwing the rest of his meal to another seagull.

Having had her fill, Sarah knelt over the cooler and tossed all her garbage inside. She was tired of this tug-of-war. "Let me know when you're finished eating."

Sarah looked out over the bay and practiced slow breathing. It was times like these when she felt like strangling Anthony. Each time she felt comfortable enough to let down her guard a bit, he would push the limit further.

Placing her hands behind her on the sand, Sarah leaned back and inhaled the sea air deeply. To relieve some of her tension, she rotated her head in a circular motion. Her feet tunneled channels into the sand while her mind furiously dissected the events leading to her bikini top taking a hike.

She'd spent a glorious hour enjoying the beauty of the sea and hadn't argued with Anthony once. Emerging from the water, she'd felt a pull of attraction, had enjoyed her body's reaction to Anthony as he stood under the hot sun.

Oh, God. *Was that it?* Sarah covered her mouth and stared across the water. She was finally starting to understand. Her heart pounded a steady beat in her ears, tolling her fate. It wasn't the arguing that made her clothes disappear—it was her attraction to Anthony that made the spell kick in.

"What would you like to do next?" Anthony asked, interrupting her thoughts.

Run and hide. Glancing over her shoulder, Sarah found Anthony packing their cooler. He had already slipped his shorts and shirt back on. *Don't look, don't look,* she chanted in her head. It was frightening to think that she would expose herself every time she fantasizes about him.

Stupid spell. If he had this effect on her then she wasn't going to suffer alone. The one thing she could do was use his attraction against him.

If he was waiting to see what she would do next, she'd just have to surprise him. She'd keep him so unhinged that the poor dear wouldn't know if he was coming or going.

Sarah stood up and wiped the sand off of her. "What if we drive toward Tabarka? You said there were hotels and shops there. I thought I'd pick up a piece of coral jewelry for Amanda."

As Anthony packed everything back into the jeep, Sarah slipped her feet into her sandals and jumped into the driver's seat. "My turn to drive. You can relax," she said, putting on her sunglasses.

Anthony settled himself in the passenger seat and passed her the keys. "I didn't know you could drive a stick-shift."

Sarah turned on the ignition. "Something else you didn't know about me," she retorted. From the corner of her eye she saw him shake his head, perplexed at her attitude.

Sarah pressed the gas pedal, spraying sand behind them. Anthony quickly grabbed the door handle for leverage as the jeep rocked wildly from side to side. Sarah looked over and chuckled. Looking in both directions, she steered onto the road and accelerated, her knuckles brushing against Anthony's leg as she switched gears. He jumped and squeezed his legs closer together. She bit her lip so she wouldn't laugh.

They quickly came across a row of luxury hotels that bordered the beachfront, kissing sparkling clear waters. As soon as she parked, Anthony jumped out of the jeep.

"What's the rush?" She may have been over the speed limit a tad—and entering the path of oncoming traffic to surpass a slow vehicle before changing back at the last moment may have been a bad idea—but they had still arrived in one piece.

Sarah joined him on the cobblestone boulevard. She could feel its scorching heat beneath her sandals. "Didn't like my driving?" she asked nonchalantly.

Now You See It…

With a shrug, Anthony pulled her along. "Actually, you drive like an Italian."

Grass beach umbrellas flapped as light gusts of wind caressed tanned sun worshipers shaded from the afternoon heat. "Look over there," Sarah exclaimed, pointing to the marina filled with sailboats and yachts undulating on gentle sea swells. Speedboats flew by towing parasailors. Further out, Sea-Doos zigzagged back and forth. "This is fantastic."

The enchanting white and blue Tunisian-style village captivated Sarah. Strolling in amicable silence, they passed open-air restaurants and cafés. Cutlery and glasses clinked over the relaxed conversation of vacationers. Beaded curtains jingled as visitors exited and entered shops.

Chimes played against the door as Sarah entered a coral shop. "Shopping," she sighed. "What a girl does best." Corals from pale peach to vibrant red drew her eyes, while displays of custom-made jewelry under glass counters tempted her further.

She selected a peach coral ring set in gold for her sister, while Anthony made a few purchases of his own.

"Sarah, I'll wait for you outside," he said, the chimes on the door ringing as he walked out into the sunlight.

Exiting the store a few moments later, Sarah eyed Anthony's purchases. "You didn't do so badly either. Most men I know would have waited impatiently outside while I browsed."

"I'm not like most men."

He could say that again. From the very first, Sarah had known he was different. Each time he'd walked into a room women devoured him with their eyes, while the men envied him.

And she hadn't been any better, addicted to the euphoric high she got each time they made love, only to crash to an emotional low when he hadn't bothered to show up for one of their dates.

That roller-coaster ride had cost them their relationship and taken a toll on her well-being. There was no way in hell she was willing to board that same runaway train under the same circumstances. Things had to change. *He* had to change. He said he had, but Sarah still couldn't trust his words. Now she was in the present and she'd focus on the moment.

"Where to next?" Sarah asked, admiring the passing shop windows.

Anthony glanced at his watch. "Unfortunately, we're running out of time and we still have to return the jeep."

"We still have time to buy a drink and dessert for the ride back." She took Anthony's hand and led him to a café. "Come on."

They ordered two freshly squeezed lemonades and two generous portions of baklava for their trip back. The flaky, honey-soaked pastry was filled with hazelnuts and crumbled easily. "Here, you hold this," she said, holding out the desserts as they reached the jeep.

"I have a better idea," Anthony said, taking the keys out of her hands and ignoring the offered package, he slipped into the driver's seat and turned on the motor. "I'll drive this time. It seems that the passenger seat is smaller than the driver's."

Sure it was. Once clear of the hustle and bustle of the busy hotel strip, Sarah handed Anthony his baklava. "You're in for a treat," she said, watching him take his first bite. Just as she expected, the honey trickled onto his chin and dripped under his collar.

"Damn." Anthony tried to capture the honey while driving, which only made it worse. "Do you have anything in that bag I could use?" he asked as he continued to drive.

Sarah lifted her sunglasses to the top of her head. "I'll take care of it," she said, unfastening her seat belt and leaning over to lick the drop of honey from Anthony's chin.

His body jerked. The jeep swerved. Wide incredulous eyes stared at Sarah. Her devilish grin grew. Placing her finger

Now You See It...

under his chin, Sarah brought Anthony's attention back to his driving. He needed to focus on keeping on the right side of the road.

This little game of control was costing her dearly. Remaining detached while touching Anthony's skin and absorbing his drugging heat was an option that was quickly fading. She felt herself melting, wanting to lean closer and touch him in places she knew would give him pleasure.

No. Sarah took a deep breath to steady her nerves. Her reaction to him was getting in the way of what she'd set out to do. She counted backwards to distract her mind from her body's reaction.

She concentrated on finishing the job. Control and showing Anthony that she was no longer susceptible to him were her goals.

"What do you think you're doing?"

Sarah leaned over again and purposely smacked her lips. With the tip of her tongue, she traced the honey that was still on Anthony's neck and the top of his collar. "I'm cleaning up."

She'd felt Anthony's reaction the first time she touched him, enjoying it when he tensed more with each passing lick. A small vein danced on the side of his neck as he withstood her playful torture.

She savored the last drops of honey and calmly sat back to nibble on her own pastry. She'd done it. Her heart pounded and her body was hot with suppressed arousal, but she'd done it. She'd held everything back with superhuman strength and beat the spell. One point for Sarah.

"Finished?" Anthony's nerves were on high-alert, clamoring for a taste of Sarah's sweetness.

Sarah smiled. "All done," she said, taking another bite of her baklava. "Mmm, I knew it would taste good." She licked drops of honey from her fingers.

Anthony's eyes followed Sarah's movements before returning to the road. "You're getting back at me, aren't you?"

"I have no idea what you're talking about."

Anthony raised his eyebrow. "Really?"

Sarah's expression remained serious. "Positive. Would I do that to you?"

"Hmm." Anthony let that soft remark float between them. Damned if he wasn't uncomfortable. And the little minx had enjoyed torturing him. Looking at him, Sarah lapped away at a drop of honey on her finger while wearing a triumphant grin.

With a serpent's speed, Anthony dropped his baklava back into the bag and clasped Sarah's wrist.

"What are you doing?"

Anthony smiled at Sarah's astonished expression. "Cleaning." Pulling a finger into his mouth, he sucked the sweetness away.

Sarah gasped when his tongue wrapped itself around her finger. Anthony could hear Sarah's labored breathing. A soft moan escaped her lips as he paid close attention to her next finger. His tongue thoroughly polished each and every fingertip.

He had to remember to breathe while his heart ran a quick mile. Sarah looked away and squirmed in her seat. A light dusting of goose bumps covered her arms. Through her T-shirt, Anthony could see the outline of her nipples. Reaching her pinky, Anthony ended her torture.

"All done." Anthony placed her hand back onto her lap. "Would you like me to start on the other?" he asked. Taking his eyes off the road for a second, he observed her blush before looking forward again.

"No...no," Sarah replied, readjusting herself in her seat. She dropped the rest of her sweet back into the bag and sat back, annoyed. "If you're still hungry..." She took his hand off

Now You See It...

the steering wheel and dropped his piece of baklava into it. "You can keep your mouth and hands busy with this."

Anthony threw his head back and laughed. Sarah clenched her fists. Anthony tensed for a playful punch that never came. She was beautiful.

"Ha, ha, yourself," she said, bringing her hand up to grab her sunglasses off her head and instead grasping air. "Shit."

His chuckle dissolved into a gasp. "Holy crap."

"Of all the—" Sarah jerked in her seat and banged her head against the door. "Ouch, ouch, ouch." She rubbed the spot that hurt. "I can't take much more of this."

"You aren't going to let a small thing like a spell get you down? All we have to do is stay one step ahead of it." Anthony reached into the backseat with one hand and pulled out a brand-new pair of sunglasses with the tag still attached. "Here. Problem solved."

Sarah snatched the sunglasses out of his hand. "Small? At this moment, there's nothing I'd like better than to kick someone," she raged, ripping the tag from the sunglasses and throwing it on the jeep's floor. "This absolutely burns me up." She pushed the glasses onto her nose and crossed her arms over her chest.

"Relax. Getting upset isn't going to solve anything."

"That's easy for you to say. You're not the one who's cursed." Anthony's soft chuckle grated on her nerves. "You keep that up and I'll help Aunt Lilly with her next spell."

"No you wouldn't."

"So now you're a mind reader? Maybe you'd like the ESP spell she offered?" Or maybe she could find a spell to shrink his penis into oblivion. Sarah smirked. That would shut him up quick.

They returned the jeep and boarded the ship in good time. As soon as they set foot on deck, Sarah spotted Yarmilla.

It looked like she had been waiting for Anthony. Wearing a miniscule gold bikini, she weaved her way toward them.

Sarah was amazed at the woman's audacity. "Don't look now but you're being used for target practice. Mind if I do some shooting of my own?"

"Be my guest," Anthony chuckled.

Yarmilla latched onto Anthony and pouted. "Darling, I've been looking for you."

"You don't give up easily, do you?" Sarah shook her head in disgust. "I have to hand it to you—you sure have a one-track mind. I figured once you found out he didn't have the kind of money you needed to maintain your lifestyle you'd have gone on to greener pastures."

"I changed my mind," Yarmilla said, rudely blocking Sarah with her back. "Darling, send your little friend away. I have a proposition that would be beneficial to both of us."

Smiling coldly, Sarah dislodged Yarmilla's claws and moved in. "Whatever you wish to say can be said in front of me. We don't keep secrets, do we sweetheart?" She wrapped a stray lock of hair behind his ear. "Besides," she turned her attention back to Yarmilla, "you may think you're my competition, but I don't think you can top my offer."

Yarmilla's eyes traveled disdainfully over Sarah's rumpled outfit with contempt. "Why would he settle for a small-town girl like you when he can have a woman like me?" Yarmilla turned toward Anthony, "You never did mention what your relationship is with this person."

"I intend to make her my wife," Anthony stated boldly.

Yarmilla dropped her hands as though burned. Narrowing her eyes, she stared coldly at Sarah.

Smirking, Anthony placed a finger under Sarah's chin and closed her mouth for her.

His words pierced her heart, chipping away at her protective armor. This was news to her. But of course he wasn't serious. Anthony was just playing along. Sarah leaned against Anthony and shrank half an inch when her sandals disappeared from her feet. She wiggled her toes against the warmth of the ship's deck. He gave her an inquisitive stare that asked what just happened, but she shrugged it away.

He had to be joking. Sarah quickly recovered and played along.

She hugged Anthony's waist and laid her head against his chest. "As to your other question, that's easy. This little gal's daddy owns a teeny-tiny construction company worth millions. He promised to hand it over to Anthony lock, stock and barrel when he marries me."

Yarmilla's mouth opened and closed like a fish out of water. Fierce eyes glared at Sarah then Anthony, and back again.

"If you have a better proposition, I'm all ears." Sarah leaned over to peck Anthony on his cheek. "But be forewarned, he doesn't come cheap." She could feel his body shaking with suppressed laughter.

Yarmilla shot daggers. "You bitch. You're worse than I am!"

Sarah felt Anthony's arm tighten on her side. It was time for Sarah to put an end to this nonsense. "And that's saying quite a bit, coming from someone like you. If you're in the market for a gigolo, I know a couple who are looking for a good lay."

"I do my own fishing."

"If I were you I'd check your tackle. You've been using low-grade bait." Sarah watched Yarmilla's face burn with anger before she stalked off.

Anthony's body shook harder. "You were brilliant."

"You weren't too shabby yourself. You shocked me with that whopper of a lie about us getting married." Sarah's chuckle died on her lips when his expression darkened.

Anthony remained silent, his smile looking strained as his expression turned guarded. Tension wrapped around Sarah, making it hard for her to breathe.

His jaw clenched. "You thought I was lying?"

Sarah hadn't seen his lips move, yet each softly spoken word sounded like a loud bell tolling within her head. They vibrated down her spine, sending nervous shivers throughout her body.

"Of course," Sarah laughed, the sound brittle to her ears as the broken notes fell around them. "You played your part perfectly. I don't think she'll bother you for the rest of the cruise."

"Antonio?"

Sarah stepped back, relieved for the interruption. She watched Anthony's grandmother barrel toward them.

Scowling at Anthony, Emily demanded, "What did that *vipera,* that snake want? I thought we had gotten rid of her."

Sarah cleared her throat. From Anthony's determined look, she knew they weren't finished with their discussion. She needed to divert his attention. Smiling, Sarah said, "That snake wanted to proposition Anthony. She was offering cash for services rendered."

Emily turned an angry shade of red. "I fix her." Waving a fist, Emily turned to charge after the gold bikini. "*Stronza! Idiota.* My grandson is not for sale."

Anthony pulled his grandmother back, kissed the top of her head and calmly drew her to his side. Sarah didn't like the gleam in his eyes. "*Nonna,* calm down. You don't have to worry about anything. Sarah told her she was marrying me to keep me out of trouble."

Emily threw her hands in the air. "*Finalmente!*" She embraced Sarah in a tight hug. Grasping her face, she kissed both of Sarah's cheeks. "I go back to the cabin and tell your aunt the good news."

Sarah was relieved her aunt was better, but Anthony wasn't going to get away with this. The rat! He had turned the tables on her. Sarah held tightly to Emily's hands. This is the thanks she got for covering his back. Next time she'd let him get rid of his own messes.

"No wait! I never said that!" Sarah held her breath, horrified that Anthony could stand there looking so smug. "Mancini, you better fix this or there's going to be a man overboard." Sarah kindly patted Emily's hands so she would listen. It broke her heart that she was about to hurt this dear woman. "I'm sorry, but your grandson is teasing you."

The jubilant light left her eyes. "Antonio, is true?"

Anthony drew his grandmother back to his side and bent over to whisper in her ear. Sarah watched suspiciously as Emily's frown cleared to a small tentative smile. She began to nod slowly and her smile grew to a gleeful grin. Then her headshake escalated to a fast up and down movement.

Seemingly satisfied, Emily patted Anthony's cheek and toddled as fast as her old body would take her down the ship's deck.

Sarah fisted her hands against her hips. "Now what did you say?" Sarah didn't trust the look on his face.

"I told her the truth. That you hadn't proposed to me." Anthony guided Sarah to the buffet by the pool and pushed a glass of fresh lemonade into her hands.

She took a large gulp, letting its tangy sweetness flow down her dry throat. "What else? It took you that long to say such a short sentence?"

Anthony idly swirled the ice in his glass with the tip of his finger. "And I promised my grandmother that I'd be on my best behavior and I'd do what was right."

And pigs would fly. The weasel had taken control of the scene and twisted it to his liking. And now she found herself in need of fixing the situation, without hurting or alienating anyone. "Here," she said, thrusting her drink into his hand.

"Hey! Where are you going?" Anthony shouted at Sarah's retreating back. "And where are your sandals?"

"My cabin, and none of your damn business." Each quick step across the deck reminded Sarah that she wasn't wearing a bikini top or her sandals. From the appreciative stares some of the male passengers were giving her, they didn't seem to mind.

Slowing her pace, Sarah smoothed her walk to reduce the bounce of her chest. At the same time she hopped from one shady spot to the next. *Hot, hot, hot. Ouch, Ouch, Ouch.* Damn, her feet burned.

She knew she'd find the damn bikini top, sunglasses and stupid sandals in her room. "You want my sandals?" she asked aloud. "Then you can have them. I brought more than one damn pair of shoes on this stupid cruise." Some passengers gave her a wide berth as she grumbled her way to her cabin.

One step forward, two steps back. "Next time, I'll write my own freaking spell. 'Under layers you will find, a special person with a mind.' Blah, blah, blah." Grumbling, Sarah opened the door leading to the interior of the ship and finally stepped on cool tile. "Aunt Lilly could have turned me into a genius—instead I'm a flasher."

The hex had pounced on her life and tossed it right out the window.

Now You See It…

Chapter Nine

Sarah slammed the cabin door behind her. It felt good, but it still didn't relieve the tension churning inside of her. Like a caged lioness, she prowled her tiny room. "Stupid, stupid spell." Sarah looked pleadingly at the ceiling. "Can you cut me some slack here?" She was confused enough by the day's events without Anthony contributing further.

She stripped out of her clothes and tossed them to the foot of her bed. Entering the bathroom, she turned the shower on full blast. The water rinsed away the sea salt along with her tension, sapping her body of energy. A day in the sun had finally caught up with her. She was drained physically and mentally.

She wasn't any better at manipulating Anthony than she was with the spell.

Sarah grudgingly admitted that his quick wit could surprise and delight her. Yet his obstinate stubbornness and immovable opinions angered her. He needed to learn how to bend.

On top of everything, she had to think of what to wear to the Captain's Welcome Dinner that wouldn't disappear halfway through the meal.

She wrapped her hair in a towel, grabbed her body lotion off the counter and sat on her bed. Pouring a large dollop in her hand, Sarah methodically spread the vanilla-scented cream over her body 'til her skin was supple and perfumed.

Drizzling cool drops of lotion across the sun-heated skin of her breasts and stomach, she watched the rich liquid slide over her skin. Its creamy moisture traced delicious shivers wherever it slid.

Putting the bottle down, Sarah flattened her palms against her abdomen, capturing the droplets of lotion in both hands. With circular motions she caressed her stomach and the underside of her breasts. With widening strokes, she spread the cream up her sides and down her waist. Back and forth, teasing herself by moving closer and closer to her breasts. On the last pass, she cupped them in her hands.

"Oh God." Sensations flooded her body. Opening her hands, she brushed her nipples with the centers of her palms. Around and around she rotated her nipples, sending vibrations trailing straight to her inner thighs. Sarah closed her eyes and groaned.

Anthony's touch had whet her appetite and left her hungry. He'd given her a tiny glimpse of what she had been missing since he'd left and now she wanted more. She was a fool, existing behind a false sense of security, believing that she controlled her emotions. That was a laugh. Her emotions controlled her. She was left with no power over her reactions to Anthony.

And to top it all off, this spell was acting against her. She didn't even want to think what it meant or where it would lead.

Feeling claustrophobic, Sarah decided to take a stroll on deck before dinner to clear her mind. She grabbed a tiger-striped bra and underwear set from the dresser and noticed the black bikini top she'd worn that morning innocently sitting in its original spot.

"Traitor," she said, and with shaking fingers she touched it. Dry. Like she had never worn it.

"To hell with it." Sarah tossed the striped bra back into the drawer and slammed it shut. She was sure it would only disappear and end up in the same place. It didn't matter that she wore no bra. A little jiggle never hurt anyone.

Now You See It…

She thrust her feet through her thong then selected a pair of black silk pants, with four-inch slits up each side.

Since she couldn't wear any of her tops, she threw Anthony's T-shirt back on. She hadn't wanted to see him until it was necessary, but she had no choice. She had to borrow another shirt or else she would be the only casually dressed passenger at tonight's formal dinner.

"Nuts." Chewing her bottom lip, she looked around her cabin to see if there was a solution. Zilch. If she wore her own clothes they would disappear, and she couldn't use the drapes or the bedspread.

Hearing noise in the hallway, Sarah opened her door a sliver, peeked out and gasped. Maybe her luck had changed.

A steward was coming toward her, pushing a rack of clean and pressed clothes. Sarah rubbed her hands together. This just might work.

Sarah figured if the clothes weren't hers, they wouldn't vanish. By the end of this cruise she would be known as the clothes bandit. *But look on the bright side*, Sarah thought, *if I can get my hands on a shirt, I won't have to ask Anthony for one.*

The steward stopped a short distance from her door. Sarah waited for him to step to knock on a door across the hall. As soon as she heard talking, Sarah opened her door, grabbed the first shirt that came to her hand and accidentally unhooked a pair of pants, making both garments fall to the floor.

As inconspicuous as she possibly could, Sarah bent to retrieve the shirt. All she needed to do was retreat into her cabin and no one would be the—

"Hi there," the steward said.

Sarah's head popped up. "Um, hi." She plastered a smile on her face and straightened. "When I opened my door I found this on the floor," she lied, passing the confiscated shirt back and smiling at the steward. "I was just about to pick up the pants for you."

"Thanks." The steward re-hung the shirt and plucked the pants off the floor. "I'd get in big trouble if anything went missing. You wouldn't believe the things some passengers do to get their hands on other people's clothing."

Sarah pressed her hands to her chest and feigned shock. "You don't say."

"Honest. Thanks again." With a nod, the steward pushed the trolley down the hallway.

Sarah watched her chance roll away. "Damn."

Closing the door, Sarah grabbed her brush from the dresser and pulled it through her hair. She'd bide her time. Maybe Anthony wasn't even in his cabin. Perhaps he was up on deck having a good time, sunning that body of his.

On the next stroke Sarah rapped the top of her head with her knuckles. "Hey!" No brush. "Now what the hell is happening?" She had assumed that things would vanish only if Anthony was around. This just proved her wrong again.

"This is not good, not good at all," she muttered, spotting the brush back on the dresser. She wasn't even safe in her own cabin, alone and with the door locked.

Picking it up, Sarah blocked any thoughts of Anthony and continued to brush her hair to see if anything happened. When the brush remained, some of her tension ebbed. Maybe it was a one-shot deal.

She took a deep breath and exhaled. It was time for her to knock on Anthony's door. What if he was asleep? Sprawled on the bed the way he used to do. Hogging all the pillows. Sarah remembered one night after they had made love her pillow had been pulled right from under her head. She smiled at the memory. Half-asleep, Anthony had apologized and pulled her back into his arms.

Lost in the past, the brush disappeared from her hand again and reappeared in its spot on the dresser. Sarah jumped and gasped at the sight of her empty hand.

Fine. If the spell wanted her possessions then she'd be prepared. She marched to her suitcase and put on a pair of gold earrings, a necklace to match and a dozen bangles on her wrist. "You want war? I'll show you what a first-born Italian female can do."

What next? She tapped her finger on her lips. Ah, rings. She put two on each hand. Large suckers, heirlooms that weighed her hands down. This was one battle she intended to fight every step of the way.

"Next." She spotted a large hair clip next to her bed. Swirling her hair up, she pinned it in place. "I can do this." Her eyes fell on a vibrant fire-colored shawl. Why not? She folded it diagonally, making a large triangle that she tied around her hips. "Now I'm ready."

Squaring her shoulders, Sarah walked out of her cabin and firmly knocked on Anthony's door.

Anthony flung the door open, still dressed in his shorts, his hair disheveled. It looked like he had just woken up, his eyes still slumberous.

She cleared her throat and clasped her hands together to stop herself from reaching out—and realized that something was already amiss.

Pretending to play with her necklace, Sarah peeked at her hands and found them bare. Her heart did a quick gallop. She needed to do a quick inventory without tipping Anthony off.

Anthony ran his fingers through his hair. "You're ready?" His glance traveled over her tailored pants and his T-shirt. "My shirt looks good on you," he said with an appreciative smile.

"Speaking of shirts…" Sarah pulled on her ears. Good, still there. "I've come to bum my daily supply." She patted her hair. Intact. "That is, if you don't mind." She placed her hands on her hips and felt the shawl beneath her fingers.

Anthony cleared his throat and looked away. "Of course I don't mind," he said, standing aside so she could enter. Opening his closet, he waved her forward. "Take your pick."

He pointed toward the spare bed. "There's a pile of clean T-shirts you can help yourself to. Give me a minute while I just jump in and out of the shower and we'll go down to dinner together." Not waiting for a reply, Anthony dashed into the bathroom.

Was he nuts? Sarah didn't waste a moment. Selecting a black silk shirt from the closet and two T-shirts, she quietly left his cabin, making sure the door didn't bang behind her.

Back in her own cabin, she threw the T-shirts on top of her suitcase, took off the one she was wearing and slipped on Anthony's black silk shirt. About to tuck it into her pants, Sarah changed her mind. "You can forget that," she muttered, removing the shawl and tying it again, this time on top of Anthony's shirt. If her pants disappeared when she was at dinner — or worse, on the dance floor — at least she'd be partially covered.

Putting on her black stiletto sandals, she dropped her key into her pocket and was out the door as though the hounds of hell were chasing her.

The decks were softly lit for the evening. Passengers who had eaten an earlier meal were leisurely strolling arm in arm, enjoying the evening. Sarah followed behind a group of men in tuxedos and women in designer evening gowns as they headed for one of the attractions on board.

When she reached the stern of the ship, she stood at the railing, admiring the wake as it trailed behind the magnificent vessel. Voices dwindled and faded, leaving her to dig through her churning emotions, all boiling together, foaming to the surface, ready to overflow.

Sarah closed her eyes, letting the evening breeze and the sound of the sea soothe her. She didn't know what she felt anymore. Her confusion and vulnerability left her on the defense, always waiting for Anthony's next move, while anticipation and excitement encouraged her to be a devil and go for it.

"You're not planning on jumping, are you?" a concerned male voice asked.

Startled out of her reflections, Sarah tightened her grasp on the railing and turned. A short, plump old man, with a crown of white curly hair and white bushy eyebrows, stared at her inquisitively. He reminded Sarah of a senior elf.

She smiled. "No, just relaxing."

"Might you be Sarah?" he asked.

Her eyes widened. "How did you know?"

"I saw you talking to Emily earlier this evening and deduced that the tall gentleman was Anthony, and assumed you were Lilly's niece. I spent a large part of the day playing poker with the ladies."

"So, did my aunt talk your ear off?"

He shook his head and chuckled. "I heard all about you and your sister Amanda today. Pleased to meet you," he extended his hand, "I'm Albert. Your aunt is a lovely woman. Cheats at cards though."

"That's my aunt all right. Pleased to meet you," Sarah said, accepting his handshake. "Are you alone?"

Sadness filled Albert's eyes. "'Fraid so. For ten years my wife and I had taken this cruise. Two years ago she passed away from cancer, but before she died she made me promise I'd continue our tradition." Albert desolately shook his head. "Said it was one way to relive the good times and at the same time heal the pain."

Sarah smiled gently at Albert's poignant display of emotions. "Your wife sounds like she was a lovely and smart woman."

"She was that and more," he agreed, looking away.

What this man needed was a strong dose of Aunt Lilly and Emily to cheer him up. "Well, let's get this show on the road so you can do what your wife asked of you," Sarah said, hooking her arm through his and leading the way to the dining hall. "Do you dance?"

Albert chuckled, his good humor quickly returning. "You bet."

"Well then, let's have a spin on the dance floor."

Albert opened the door and escorted Sarah in. "I'm at your service."

The sound of a five-piece band playing a lively tango greeted them. "I must warn you, Margaret and I took dance lessons, so hang onto your hat young lady," Albert said before twirling Sarah onto the dance floor.

Albert was a combination of Old World charm and delightful humor. She really liked the guy. He hadn't been lying about his dancing ability either.

Maybe he could sweep Aunt Lilly off her feet and keep her out of trouble. From his ever-present mischievous grin, Sarah bet he'd be up to the challenge. Perhaps she'd do a little matchmaking of her own.

During another spin, Sarah spotted her aunt, Emily and Anthony sitting close to the large windows that looked out on the clear night.

When the song ended, Sarah fanned her hot face. "That was wonderful," she grinned, slipping her hand through Albert's and waiting for him to catch his breath before tugging him toward her aunt's table. "Come and say hello to everyone. I spotted my aunt as we danced."

"I believe you know each other," Sarah said to Lilly when they approached the table. She watched her aunt blush for the first time. Why, the little devil. If she didn't know better, Sarah would swear her aunt was smitten.

Aunt Lilly introduced the others. "Albert, you know Emily and this is Anthony, her grandson."

Now You See It...

Anthony stood up and shook hands with the older gentleman. "Pleased to meet you."

Sarah's eyes traveled over Anthony. He wore a black suit and shirt and a tie that had a gold clip attached. His dark look made his aura all the more powerful. Her cold fingers held onto Albert's sleeve. "Would you care to join us?"

"That's kind of you but I promised another friend that I would join him." He lifted Sarah's hand off his jacket sleeve. "But I'd like to have the privilege of asking these two women for a poker rematch?"

"You're on," Aunt Lilly said, nudging Emily. "And bring your money, I feel lucky tonight."

"Anthony, it was a pleasure meeting you. Sarah, thank you for the dance." With a wave, Albert left.

"Isn't he charming?" Sarah asked as she sat in the chair Anthony pulled out for her, watching her aunt concentrate on meticulously folding her napkin.

Aunt Lilly gave an indifferent shrug. "Mm, he seems like a nice man."

She didn't fool Sarah one bit.

Anthony handed her a menu and sat back down. "Where did you run off to? When I came out of the shower you were gone."

Sarah felt her face heat up. "What kind of thing is that to say in front of these two busybodies?" Judging from Aunt Lilly and Emily's sly grins, they had already come to their own conclusions.

"Oh?" Aunt Lilly leaned forward. "Is there something you want to share?"

"I borrowed another shirt," she explained, pinching Anthony's thigh under the table. He'd better stop making these types of comments or she'd be asking for another table.

Aunt Lilly's face dropped in disgusted disappointment. "You're the only woman I know who borrows clothes from a good-looking man instead of taking advantage of his body."

"At least with the clothes I can always discard them whenever I want."

Aunt Lilly gave a resigned sigh. "You don't take after my side of the family, that's for sure. Well, let's order. I don't know about you, but we've got a big night planned." Aunt Lilly leaned over to Emily and said in a not-so-quiet whisper, "Stubborn jackasses. The faster we leave these two alone, the better."

Sarah took a sip of her ice water and watched Emily nod.

"Come on, Em, you heard the gentleman. We have a date." Lilly waved for a waiter so they could place their order. Aunt Lilly and Emily ordered fettuccini Alfredo while she and Anthony chose the surf and turf platter. When the waiter departed, they sat back and enjoyed the music, watched the elegantly dressed dancers as they spun past.

A wine porter stopped at their table and Anthony chose a chardonnay from the wine list. "Since these two spring chickens are deserting us, what are your plans for the evening?" Anthony asked, sipping his glass of wine.

Sarah leaned back in her seat to let their waiter place her food in front of her. When she spoke, she included the others just in case she could change their minds. "The daily bulletin said this evening we could use a Mantic Message Mat."

"What's that?" Aunt Lilly asked.

"Aunt Lilly, you'd love it, it's something like a Ouija board." Sarah bit into a garlic-flavored Parisienne potato. "You can watch more magic happen."

"Na," Aunt Lilly said, twirling her fettuccini with her fork. "I've met my quota for the week."

Sarah shrugged and turned toward Anthony. "That means it's just you and me." She kept her expression bored. "I'm sure it's not something you would be interested in."

"Not so," Anthony said.

After everything she'd been hit with today—the overactive spell, her body's traitorous responses to Anthony's closeness and his proposition—she just wanted some time alone to regroup.

Sarah tightened her hold on her utensils and stabbed her meat. "Why don't you try your luck at the casino tables? I'm sure it would be more to your liking."

"I think I'll stick around." Anthony bit into one of his grilled prawns. "Unless that bothers you?"

Yes, it did. "Me?" Sarah stabbed a carrot and popped it into her mouth. "Why should anything you do bother me?" She wasn't going to get the breathing space she needed.

"Good." Anthony settled back in his chair with a satisfied grin. "It's settled then."

"*Dio, dammi pazienza!*" Emily shook her finger at Anthony. "You are pigheaded just like your grandfather used to be."

Sarah placed her elbows on the table, cupped her chin and smiled. She was going to enjoy this.

"His grandfather was the same. He liked to have things his own way. While you—" Emily turned her attention to Sarah.

"Hey, wait a minute," Sarah interrupted, straightening in her seat. "You haven't finished dissecting Anthony yet."

"*Per piacere*, please, you remind me of me at your age." A far-off look entered Emily's eyes, her smile reminiscent. "Like you, no one was going to tell me what to do. Especially not an opinionated rooster who thought all the women loved him." She shook her head and laughed. "And they did."

"What about you?" Sarah asked, pushing her peas around her plate.

"I was cautious, like you are with my Antonio." Emily patted Anthony's hand. "You need to be patient with this one. Like his grandfather, the women like too much, give too much." Emily tapped the top of her head. "He has a *testa dura*—a hard head. You just knock harder and maybe he listens."

"I thought I was the only one who thought he was a pain in the butt," Sarah said, leaning forward and twirling a sample of her aunt's fettuccini onto her fork.

Anthony leaned closer and growled into Sarah's ear, "Keep it up, Santorelli, and I'll deal with you after your reinforcements have left."

Sarah raised an eyebrow and returned the challenge.

"I am to blame that he is so spoiled," Emily said. "Now he's out of control. Don't let him get to you. You let him know what you want, and if he doesn't listen you tell him to go ride a bike."

Anthony's indignant frown grew darker. "You mean 'go take a hike'."

"*Si*. You will see tomorrow when we land in Rome. I have a cousin meeting us at the docks. All the men on that side of the family have the same *male vizio*, same bad habit," said Emily.

"So what do the women do?" Sarah picked at her food, more interested in what Emily had to say.

"*Facile*—easy, the women in my family say yes a lot then do what they want. I used to do the same thing with his *nonno*." Emily chuckled. "After a while, he got the hint."

"Now I'll never hear the end of it," Anthony said.

All three women grinned at him.

After coffee, Albert came to pick up his dates. "Ladies?" He hooked their arms through his.

"Don't wait up for us." Aunt Lilly waved on their way out.

Soon after the lights dimmed, announcing the entertainment was about to start. Through the darkness,

Now You See It...

Anthony's deep voice whispered, "What's so special about this board?"

His velvety tone caressed Sarah's skin. It pulled her toward him. Taking a deep breath, she drew herself up. "It tells your fortune. It's blue, with a round surface that has symbols that attract loving spirits. In addition to the alphabet, it has frequently used words and even some sentences so it answers your questions faster than a Ouija board."

The hostess drew the audience's attention to the dance floor where she had set up the board on a pedestal. "Does anyone want to start the evening with a question?"

"Ah, I don't believe in that garbage," came a woman's belligerent voice in the darkness. It sounded like Yarmilla.

The hostess smiled. "Then you've got nothing to lose. Ask a question that only you would know."

Silence. Stillness. An occasional cough was heard while everyone held their breath and waited for a question.

With a cynical laugh, the woman finally spoke. Sarah could hear the confidence in her voice. "Here's a question for that damn thing. Ask it what my second husband liked to eat every night just before he went to bed."

Sarah held her breath. There were goose bumps on her arms. The hostess watched as the board began to spell out the words.

"A whiskey on the rocks and a peanut butter and crushed potato chip sandwich."

A loud gasp had the audience sitting up in their chairs.

"Son of a—"

"Did it answer correctly?" the hostess asked.

"On the nose," the passenger replied.

A collective gasp spread through the room. No one was laughing now. Questions erupted from everywhere. Each time the board came back with the correct answer, the crowd grew more excited. The questions came fast and furious.

All during the questions, Sarah tried to conceal her eagerness. She was dying to ask the board about her future, but she didn't dare. She pensively chewed her bottom lip. Taking a deep breath, she cautiously raised her hand. Anthony had an unholy gleam in his eyes that ate at her small store of courage. Chickening out, Sarah dropped her hand back down.

"Go ahead." Anthony knew Sarah was hesitating because he was around.

She was a distraction. Too tempting for her own good, sitting there with her long glossy hair pulled up, emphasizing her cheekbones, and those soulful eyes taking everything in.

Sarah stubbornly shook her head. "Nope, I don't need to know anything."

Little liar. From the longing glances she sent the board Anthony knew better. He understood her more than she thought. Like when he had opened his door to give her his shirt. He hadn't been sure at first if she had been giving him baseball signals or doing the Macarena. He'd bit the inside of his cheek when he'd realized that she was inconspicuously trying to take inventory of her clothes and jewelry.

He shrugged. "Fine. If you don't want to ask a question, then I will." He raised his arm to get the hostess's attention.

"What do you think you're doing?" Sarah grasped his arm and pulled it back down.

Anthony gently pried Sarah's fingers away. "Finding out what I want to know." He raised his arm again.

"You don't need to know anything," Sarah said, desperately hanging on to his raised arm. "What could you possibly ask when you already know everything?"

"Not everything." Anthony raised his voice to gain the hostess's attention. "I have a question."

Sarah released his arm and nervously fidgeted in her seat. She looked from one end of the room to the other, and

Anthony was positive she was planning her escape. "You're the one who wanted to see this show."

She looked like someone who was cornered. Anthony was sure the only reason she was acting this way was because she knew exactly what he was about to say.

Anthony raised his voice and asked, "Is there a special woman in my life?"

Before the hostesses could answer, a female heckler replied, "Sweetie, if you need someone, come to mama."

The audience chuckled.

When the room quieted down, the hostess read his answer. "It says she's not sure yet."

Sarah's hair unraveled from her knot and fell in front of her eyes. The clip holding it had vanished. In a jerking motion, she threw her hair over her shoulder. "Anthony, you have no idea what you're dealing with."

More teasing snickers sounded, among the women's longing sighs.

"Will she ever be sure?" Anthony felt a shiver of dread slither down his spine. Gently drawing Sarah's hands in his, he looked into her eyes.

"Only time will tell," the hostess said.

Her earrings and necklace popped away in a blink of an eye. Sarah touched her ears and neck. "Anthony, if you know what's good for you, you'll stop right now."

"What must I do?" Anthony asked, exhaling a breath he hadn't known he was holding. He felt a cold mist form on his upper lip. Sarah's hands shook in his palms. He held tightly to reassure her that everything would turn out fine. Who was he kidding? He was hanging on to Sarah for himself.

"Hey buddy, you in a rush?" yelled a male voice from the audience.

Another man answered, "If I had her, I'd be in a rush to."

Sarah pulled her hands away and clutched her pants in a death grip.

When the room finally quieted down their hostess said, "Wait, it's spelling out something. It says there are more layers to peel away, but your journey's end is near." The hostess looked toward Anthony with a quizzical stare. "Do you know what that means?"

The spell—Anthony realized the spell was for him. He could kiss Aunt Lilly for casting it, now that he finally knew what it meant. The deeper Sarah fell in love with him again, the quicker her clothes would vanish. It was only a matter of time before Sarah figured it out and put them both out of their misery.

Anthony felt the room's eyes search for him in the pale darkness. He cleared his throat. "Yes, I do." He caught Sarah in his penetrating glance and watched her withdraw behind her anger.

"You don't believe what that board said, do you?" Sarah asked, wrapping her arms protectively around her waist. "It was only for the entertainment of the passengers and shouldn't be taken seriously."

Anthony crossed his arms over his chest. "I believe in that board, just as much as I believe in crazy aunts who cast spells on their nieces and make their clothes disappear."

"That's what I was afraid of," Sarah replied, a shadow of alarm touching her face.

Now You See It…

Chapter Ten

ಶ

"Speaking of aunts," Anthony stood up and extended his hand, "let's find them."

Sarah pushed her chair back and scooted around the table. Anthony's smile dimmed at her attempt to put distance between them. Worry brushed against his heart, filling it with heaviness. He only had the cruise to prove himself. Once they returned home, his chances would be next to nil.

"Let's take a stroll before we head for the casino." He placed his hand on the base of her spine and felt Sarah stiffen. Opening the door, he ushered her through then dropped his hand. His attempts to get close were failing. Butting his head against Sarah's was only making matters worse.

Anthony breathed in the ocean air and glanced at the heavens. Like diamonds on black velvet. "Isn't the evening sky amazing?" he asked, strolling toward the railing and leaning against it.

Alone. Surrounded by passengers who freely dished out advice and women who encouraged his attention, he still felt isolated. Anthony breathed in the sea's peacefulness and tried to calm his frantic heart.

"Yes, it is," Sarah agreed, stepping away from the railing. "Shouldn't we be looking for our respective relatives?" Her hands fidgeted with the knot of her shawl on her hip.

"What's your hurry? We're in the middle of the ocean, it's not like they can go far."

With a resigned sigh, Sarah drew closer. His senses responded to her nearness. He gripped the railing to give him strength. "Look at the reflection of the stars on the sea. Funny, no matter how far apart two objects are they can affect each other. It's like that for people sometimes."

The way Sarah's eyes widened, Anthony knew she had understood his deeper message. "As long as you've been touched, you'll carry a special feeling inside of you forever. Always connecting you to that special person or moment."

"Like Albert. He's been reliving memories of his wife so he can heal his pain and move on with his life."

"Exactly," Anthony replied, struggling to keep his grin in place. "That's the whole idea, to go forward. If Albert locked his memories away, it would be as if his wife never existed. But when he shares them, he relives their love and learns to live through the telling."

What about you? he wanted to ask. *When will you live through your past and allow yourself to forgive?*

Sarah shifted uneasily on her feet. He'd have to wait and see if she had the courage for that final step. To finally move on.

What preoccupied him most was wondering which direction she'd take. She could move toward him or walk away.

At this point, they were both possibilities.

A light breeze swirled around Sarah, making her shiver. She wrapped her arms around herself and rubbed the goose bumps on her arms. Anthony draped his jacket over her shoulders then slipped his hands into his pants pockets.

The warmth of his jacket seeped into her body, dispelling the chills from the cool night air. All that remained were the quiet shivers of anxiety as her head fought with her heart. If she did what her heart told her to do, Sarah would take what Anthony offered. If, however, she listened to her head, she would keep her distance and lose this chance.

Now You See It...

And still Anthony watched her, analyzed her. If she was honest with herself, she'd made a few observations of her own. Like a movie, pictures of Anthony flashed through her mind — standing bare-chested under the sun, sharing a sandwich together or arguing. She liked all the different sides to him, she just didn't trust how she felt.

Like now — after giving her something more to think about, he'd backed away. Yet he remained close enough to remind her of what she could have.

Sarah watched the material on the front of his pants stretch as he fisted his hands in the pockets. Anthony hadn't a clue how devastating he looked. The wind caressed his shirt, while the dim light transformed him into a living shadow.

But if she stepped into that shadow, would she lose herself?

She needed a clear head and being so close to Anthony wasn't helping. If she could only clear her mind she was sure her traitorous body would follow. Damn it, she could do this. She'd do a word association. Sarah closed her eyes and willed herself to focus.

Cruise – sea.

Sea – pirate.

Pirate – Anthony.

"Oh brother." Sarah opened her eyes and found Anthony staring at her.

With his hair severely tied back and his body held by invisible restraints, he radiated a contained power that simmered just below his skin. He exerted the same control in his work, on his life.

To hell with it. If the spell was trying to push her in Anthony's direction then just this once she'd be spontaneous.

Impulsively, Sarah moved closer and undid the tie in his hair. Running her fingers through it, she enjoyed its thickness and fresh clean smell.

His body shuddered beneath her touch but he remained immobile. Under his watchful stare, Sarah surrendered to her wishes and played with the thickness of his hair. "Amanda was right. You do look like a pirate." She wrapped his hair behind his ear and tweaked the diamond in his earlobe. She trailed a finger along the shape of his face, tracing his jaw.

Anthony emitted a low moan that vibrated in his chest. Moisture coated his upper lip as the exertion of keeping his emotions in check took its toll. Sarah leaned closer and thrilled at the powerful effect she had on him.

Embracing his neck, Sarah melted into his chest, making his body jerk. Like a spring that has snapped he clasped her to him and held her tight. He brushed a kiss on the crown of her head then rested his cheek there. Tremors shook his body as though a powerful force had been unleashed.

It felt wonderful to be clasped in a pair of strong arms. She could easily get used to the security that radiated from Anthony, enveloping her. She felt cherished.

A tug-of-war pulled between her heart and mind. A sense of finally belonging blossomed in her chest, pushing back her fear of abandonment.

Anthony rested his forehead on hers. "You're killing me."

"I know, but I still need more time to think. I don't want to rush into anything, only to regret it later." She felt out of her depths. Something was holding her back, yet this wonderful man continued to wait. Sarah cupped Anthony's cheek and he cupped his hand over hers. "Thank you," she said, glimpsing sorrow and understanding in his eyes.

A cool breeze caressed her legs as Anthony reluctantly pulled away. Sarah found it *too* breezy. Looking down, she gasped at what she saw. Or what she didn't see.

"Oh, my God!" Pulling Anthony by his shirt, she flattened his body against hers, her back to the railing. "I desperately need your help." This time the spell had gone too far.

Anthony looked down at her bare legs. "Your pants decided to take a walk?" His chuckle dissolved into unmasked hunger when he noticed that the shawl she wore barely covered her. "You're wearing animal striped underwear?" he asked in a voice loud with surprise.

"Why don't you just announce it over the loudspeakers so the whole ship will know?" Sarah peeked around Anthony and spotted passengers relaxing on lounges close by. "You want them to see me like this?" She pulled his jacket tightly around her.

Anthony blocked her in by putting his hands on the railing. "Take off the shawl."

"Have you lost your mind? I'm trying to figure out how to outwit the spell and keep my clothes on, not voluntarily take them off."

"You'll still be covered by my jacket."

"This is all your fault," Sarah said, feeling for the knot on the shawl. "If you'd stop popping into my head, my clothes would stop popping off," she griped as she handed over the shawl.

An insufferable grin lit Anthony's face. "I'm in your head? That's a start," he said, taking the garment out of her hands. "This can easily wrap around your waist." He opened up the shawl and slipped his hands under the jacket, tied it at her waist and smiled at his design. "Now you're covered almost to your ankles."

"What about this?" Sarah took a step, making the shawl gape up to her thigh.

"We improvise," Anthony said, unhooking his cufflinks. "Now, don't think about me while I do this or we're right back where we started."

Sarah closed her eyes and chanted, "Don't think, don't think, don't think," while Anthony pulled the shawl together and secured it with his cufflinks.

"How's that?"

Sarah opened her eyes and found Anthony rolling up his sleeves. Taking a few tentative steps, Sarah felt the scarf gape to just above her knee. "Perfect," she smiled, walking back to Anthony.

Anthony leaned forward and tweaked the fabric so it fell better, then wrapped his body against hers to keep her out of sight of the passengers' curious glances. She could just imagine what they looked like, wrapped tight as a Christmas gift with their hands locked around each other.

"Hey, Buddy! Can't find your cabin?" An older gentleman wearing a tuxedo with the tie undone grinned at them from his spot further along the railing.

Looking up, Sarah laughed at the man's comical expression. "What about you? Can't find yours either?"

"Sure I can. But my missus is in it."

Sarah gasped.

The man raised his hands. "Don't get me wrong. I love the little lady. But we had an argument, so I'm walking off some steam." He scratched his head and grimaced. "You could say I'm in the doghouse right now."

"You could always take her dancing or to the movies to make up," Sarah said.

He hit his forehead with the palm of his hand. "Why didn't I think of that? Thanks! You know, you're one of the nicest couples I've met on this crazy ship."

"We're not a couple," Sarah and Anthony said in unison.

The man scratched his head again. "Anyone with half a brain can tell you're mad for each other." Frowning at Anthony, he asked, "What's the matter with you, boy? She's a hot number if there ever was one."

"Oh, it's not me. The lady here is cautious."

He gave Sarah the once-over. "Missy, there's slow and then there's *slow*. Give the poor guy a break and put him out of his misery. Women! I've been married to my missus for thirty

Now You See It...

years and I still haven't figured her out." He mumbled as he walked away, "And they say men are complicated."

Anthony chuckled at the man's retreating back. "Do you think he gets into trouble every time he sticks his nose where it doesn't belong?"

Sarah crossed her arms over her chest and pointedly stared at him. "No, you think?"

"I'm not going there." Anthony pulled her arm through his. "Let's go check the casino for Aunt Lilly and my grandmother."

Over the clinking sounds of gambling chips and the spin of the roulette wheel, they heard Aunt Lilly yelling, "Show me the money. Come on girl, be good to me."

Anthony ushered Sarah ahead of him. "Sounds like we found them."

Seated at the slot machines were Albert, Aunt Lilly and Emily, happily dropping coins into the machines as they drank cocktails.

From their flushed faces, Sarah bet they were drunk. "Hi, everyone." Three pairs of glassy eyes turned to her.

"Sarah dear, we've been having a wonderful time with Albert," Lilly said, wobbling on her stool. Anthony quickly grabbed her shoulders and straightened her back onto the seat. She squinted her eyes and tried to focus on Sarah. "My, did you change again?" She shrugged and continued. "Doesn't matter. I love your new skirt, but I'll have to take in your jacket."

Her aunt was really sloshed. "Um, Aunt Lilly, don't you think you've had enough?"

Her aunt stuck her tongue out as she squinted at the machine and clumsily put money into the slot.

"Nonsense. I've only had one drink. I must say, though, it must be bottomless, 'cause I never seem to be able to finish it." Aunt Lilly raised a small glass and took a sip.

Anthony shook his head. "Your drinks are refilled for free if you play at the slots."

Aunt Lilly giggled. "Is that what they've been doing?" she slurred. "They have such lovely service and manners on this ship, don't they my dears?"

Albert and Emily nodded their agreement.

Albert raised his glass in the air. "A toast. To the finest ladies on this ship. If my Margaret were here, she'd have had a royal time."

Sarah took her aunt's glass away from her. "Why don't we call it quits? Tomorrow you can try your luck again," Sarah said, trying to draw her aunt away from the machine.

Aunt Lilly refused to budge. "I still feel lucky. Do you know that I beat Albert and Em at poker?"

"Because you cheated," Emily said.

"If you don't mind," Aunt Lilly jabbed her money in the general direction of the slot, "I'll just put one more dollar in the machine for old times' sake."

Anthony guided her hand so she could drop the money in the slot. Aunt Lilly patted him on his cheek. "You are such a lovely boy."

"And then we go," Emily said, hanging on to the side of the slot machine for support. "Tomorrow in Roma we have fun with my *famiglia*."

Sarah watched the slot machine's three rows of fruits and figures spin. Each slot clicked into place.

Seven, seven, seven.

"I don't believe it," Sarah gasped. Lights flashed. Bells rang. No one could be more astonished than herself that Aunt Lilly had won.

Now You See It…

"Would you look at that?" Aunt Lilly squeezed Sarah's hand.

"How much did you win?" Sarah asked.

"Approximately five thousand dollars," replied the smiling officer in uniform who had come up behind them. "It was time for this baby to pay out." He opened the machine and turned off the light and bells before resetting it. He wrote up a coupon for the amount won and handed it over to Aunt Lilly. "If you'll follow me, you can cash that in."

By the time they finished at the cashier's wicket and made it to Lilly and Emily's cabin, it was the early hours of the morning. Anthony opened their cabin door and waited for them to enter.

"May I ask what you intend to do with all that money?" Albert politely asked Aunt Lilly.

Aunt Lilly winked at Emily. "I think I'll save it for a special occasion."

Albert weaved from side to side, still unsteady on his feet. "Ladies, it's been a pleasure. What time do you wish me to meet you for breakfast?"

"Between nine and ten o'clock," Emily said. "Tomorrow, my cousins will take us on a tour of Rome, Italian style."

Albert bowed. "Good night, then." Holding onto the wall, he wobbled away with as much dignity as he could muster.

Anthony and Sarah helped the women to their beds. Sarah took off their shoes and left the bathroom light on. Anthony kissed both ladies on the cheek. "Good night Lilly, *nonna*."

"Tired?" Anthony asked when they reached their cabins.

Sarah handed his jacket back and unlocked her door. "I'm bushed."

"I'll see you tomorrow. I mean today. And remember, if you need anything…"

"Just knock on the wall and you'll come running," Sarah finished.

Anthony placed a swift kiss on Sarah's surprised lips. "That guy was right, you are a hot number." He ushered her through the door and closed it on her pleased expression.

Grinning happily, Sarah undressed and was about to put on one of Anthony's clean T-shirts when a loud pounding sounded at her door.

"Dolly, sweetheart, open this door. I know you're in there. I lost my key again."

Sarah gripped the T-shirt against her body. If she didn't answer, maybe he'd realize his mistake and leave. From the way he stumbled over his words, Sarah could tell he was drunk.

"Ah darlin', don't be like that. I know I shouldn't have left you to go gambling. If you open this door, I promise I'll make it up to you tomorrow."

Loud suspended silence filled the cabin. Sarah inched closer to the door and listened. Maybe he'd finally figured that he had the wrong room. Sarah jumped back when the doorknob rattled.

"Dolly!" His voice was louder now as he pounded on her door again. "I'm losing my patience."

That sounded like one very determined husband or boyfriend. She wasn't taking any chances of making him angry. She waited breathlessly, in the hope he would give up and leave.

His fist landed on the door, shaking it on its hinges. "I've had enough." The voice seemed to catch its breath. "You want to be like this? Fine, I'm breaking down the door."

"No wait!" Sarah jumped on top of the spare bed and banged on the wall. "You have the wrong cabin. I'm sure you'll find your Dolly in your cabin," she yelled, banging on the connecting wall with her fist. Where the hell was Anthony?

Now You See It…

Anthony's door banged open.

"Who the hell are you?" the astonished man asked from the other side of the door. "And what have you done with my Dolly? I want my Dolly."

Sarah covered her mouth to smother her laughter. The man sounded ridiculous.

"Can I help you?" Sarah could hear the dark menacing tone of Anthony's voice.

"This is none of your business."

Sarah stepped off the bed and listened at her door.

"It is when you're barking up the wrong tree." Anthony's tone had deepened to a low growl.

The man started to stutter. "L-look, all I want to know is what the l-lady did with my Dolly."

"Your what?"

"My wife, Dolly."

Pulling on the T-shirt, Sarah quietly opened her door and peered outside. She saw the back view of a very wide, short man facing Anthony, who, at that moment, happened to be dripping water on the floor with only a towel wrapped around his waist as he glared down at the intruder.

Sarah's eyes skimmed over his still wet shoulders and down his chest. With his arms crossed and his wide-legged stance, he was magnificent. The other man clasped and unclasped his hands as he shrank in size against Anthony's anger.

Opening her door wider, Sarah confronted the gentleman. "Look, you've made a mistake. There's no Dolly here."

Sarah didn't know if the man was going to plow past her or if his mistake would sink in upon seeing a strange woman. Either way, Anthony stepped in front of her to keep her out of harm's way.

The red-faced man tried to see past Anthony. When he saw Sarah, he took a step back. "I'm so sorry—I think I've got the wrong cabin."

The guy's expression was priceless. Sarah skirted around Anthony. "You do."

"What was I thinking? If Dolly hears I went pounding on a stranger's door in the early morning hours, she's going to kill me." The man edged away from them. "Is there anything I can do to make it up to you?"

"How about letting us get some sleep?" grumbled Anthony.

"You got it."

God this was hilarious. Sarah watched the man plow down the hallway.

"You okay?" Anthony hugged her to his chest, his heart pounding against her ear.

"Yes, I'm fine." Sarah wrapped her arms around his waist and muffled her laughter against his chest. Anthony tightened his hold as her body's shaking increased.

"Hey, it's over, the guy's gone."

This only made her shake harder.

"Sarah?" Tilting her head, Anthony looked into eyes filled with laughter.

"Dolly? He wanted his Dolly?" She shook harder.

This was the Sarah he remembered. Anthony rested his forehead on hers and smiled. He didn't care that they were standing in the hallway, both half dressed. What mattered was that Sarah was finally opening up again.

"You know, you almost have it right. But you're supposed to be on the other side of the door."

Anthony jumped back to face the man who had been strolling on deck earlier. He assumed the petite, red-haired

Now You See It...

woman wearing dark-framed glasses and a flowered sarong was his wife. The man and his wife avidly observed their semi-undress.

"Um, we were just going to bed," stuttered Sarah and flushed when the woman giggled.

The man looked up to the ceiling, as if asking the almighty for help before looking back at them. "You should do yourselves a favor and get married already."

"Roy, there you go again sticking your nose where it doesn't belong." His wife shook her head at her husband before adding her own two cents' worth. "He's right, though. Your girlfriend here is what my husband likes to call a hot number."

"Come on, pumpkin, let's go *inside* our cabin. We'll leave these two to figure it out for themselves." Roy guided his wife away. "You should try it some time," he called over his shoulder, "it's quite comfortable."

"He seems to catch us at the most inopportune moments," Sarah yawned. "Now, this is really good night. I'll see you in a couple hours." With a wave, Sarah closed the door behind her.

What a night. With a tired sigh Anthony turned the knob of his door and found it locked. Closing his eyes, he leaned his forehead against it. "Give me a break," he said and pushed off the door.

Anthony looked up and down the hallway and thankfully found it deserted. A shiver shook his body, reminding him of his lack of clothes. Grinding his teeth in frustration, he shook the door handle again. Useless. He tightened his towel and knocked on Sarah's door. "Sarah? Open up."

He could hear the sound of her feet dragging before the door opened. "What?" Sarah leaned against the doorframe for support.

"I'm locked out of my cabin and need to get one of the pursers to open it," Anthony said.

"Fine." She gave a tired sigh. "You better come in and use the phone."

"Thanks." The click of the lock sounded behind him as the door closed. He pulled his fingers through his hair. "I'll only be a moment."

He dialed the purser and listened to ringing. "No one's answering." He dropped the phone back on its cradle.

Sarah motioned to the spare bed and yawned. "You can sleep there. Tomorrow, or rather today, you can call someone to open your door."

"Are you sure?" Tired and irritated, he rubbed the goose bumps on his arms.

"Positive. Just take my suitcase off the bed and it's yours for the night." With a tired wave she crawled back into bad. "Now this is *really* good night because I can't stay awake any longer." Rolling over to face the wall, Sarah hugged her pillow and snuggled under the covers. Within minutes her breathing slowed down, letting Anthony know she'd fallen asleep.

Anthony looked down at Sarah's body. The pillow could have been him. He lifted her bag off the bed. "Some cruise this is. I'm finally in Sarah's cabin and she's asleep. To top things off, I'm *giving* her clothes instead of taking them off."

Swearing under his breath, Anthony turned off the light and dropped his towel before crawling into bed. Putting his hands behind his head, he stared at the ceiling and listened to the hum of the engines.

He closed his eyes and gave a tired sigh. Another day had come and gone. Each second that ticked by either cemented a new beginning for them or finished them off for good. Icy fear twisted his heart at the very thought.

He refused to think that way. He looked over at Sarah as she sighed in her sleep. He couldn't lose her. She'd given him a second chance and he'd make sure they were still together when the ship docked at its final port.

Now You See It…

As he tried to calm his mind enough to sleep, he heard the sound of intimate laughter as a couple passed his door. Didn't people sleep on this damn ship?

"Oh hell." Anthony rolled onto his stomach and covered his head with the pillow.

His body and soul weary, Anthony finally drifted off.

Chapter Eleven

Sarah woke to a brightly lit cabin and stretched lazily. Turning over to check what time it was, she spotted Anthony sprawled on the next bed. She immediately recalled last night's events and the image of him, in a towel, protecting her. She propped her head on her hand and admired the picture he presented.

His blanket rode precariously low on his hips, exposing two delightful dimples at the base of his back while the sun's rays painted him a golden bronze. Sarah's eyes traced the trim, smooth lines of muscles and sinew that formed in his shoulders and across his back.

Anthony cushioned his head on his arms, his thick hair fanning out above him and spilling over the side of the bed. Sarah spotted his pillow on the floor, next to the all-too-familiar towel. Her eyes returned to his naked form and a blanket that kept slipping.

"Damn, he's fine." She touched her hands to her hot cheeks.

Too tempted to resist, Sarah quietly slipped out of bed and knelt beside him. Careful not to wake him, she feathered her fingers across his hair. Its luscious texture slid between her forefinger and thumb. Anthony mumbled in his sleep and turned his face toward her.

Mortified, Sarah jerked her hand away and tumbled onto her backside. She rubbed her offended behind and prayed Anthony didn't wake up.

With her eyes on Anthony, Sarah lifted herself off the floor and perched on the edge of her bed, then breathed a short-lived sigh of relief. In his sleep, Anthony threw the cover off one leg, exposing his hip. If he made any more sudden moves his backside would be exposed. She really should get up and leave.

She knew every inch of his delectable body. It was her reaction to him that had gotten her in trouble in the first place. Those few months of dating had been heaven and hell. Each time they had met, they couldn't keep their hands off each other. And where had that gotten her? Nowhere.

In the end, she'd been the woman on hand to pleasantly fill the time between one deal and the next. She still remembered the deep-seated pain the day she had walked away.

She was torturing herself. Just looking at Anthony set Sarah on fire. She gave him one final look and firmly turned away. Tiptoeing into the washroom, she expelled her breath.

For her peace of mind, Anthony had to leave. Leaving the door slightly ajar, Sarah turned on the shower. Next, she switched on a small radio on the counter and raised the volume loud enough to wake the dead. Stripping off her pajamas, she jumped into the shower and sang at the top of her lungs. She figured if she made enough noise, Anthony would wake up and, being the gentleman he was, leave.

Anthony couldn't figure out where the hell that infernal racket was coming from. It sounded like a boom box was stuck to both ears. He pressed down on his pounding temples. If he found the source, he'd shoot it. Covering his ears, Anthony tried to block out the sound.

"Damn." Sitting up, he rested his elbows on his knees and held his head. The hammers inside pounded in sync with the blasting music. He needed to get a couple aspirins or he wouldn't be in any condition to drive around Rome today.

He flung the sheet off him and walked into the washroom. The music grew louder. Perplexed, Anthony rubbed his face and the room came into focus. Sarah was in his shower?

Then he remembered that it wasn't his room.

Transfixed, Anthony glimpsed her naked silhouette through the translucent glass shower door. The compelling urge to join her and wrap their wet bodies together jerked his body forward. He gripped the doorknob for support, making his knuckles turn white.

What a way to start the morning. He now had two headaches pounding for attention. He shifted his weight and rubbed his temple, the music covering his groan and hiding his presence. He devoured Sarah's lithe movements and soft curves as she soaped herself. His memories didn't do her justice.

Her hands lathered a bar of soap while the hot steam brought a vanilla fragrance to his senses and caressed shivers over his body. Still, he didn't budge. She lathered her arms and ran the soap over her breasts. Anthony swallowed painfully. She raised one leg to soap her ankle, a slender calf and firm thigh before repeating the process on the other leg.

Still humming, Sarah turned her back against the spray of water and arched to rinse her hair. He could distinguish the perfect outline of her breasts as they swayed slightly with her movements. The curve of her pelvic bone and the indentation at her waist enticed Anthony to step into the shower and finish the job for her.

Neither her body nor his reaction to it had changed. He remembered a different place and time when they had stayed so long in the shower the water had run cold. It hadn't mattered—he had carried her to his bed, where they'd warmed up again.

If he even attempted to join her, she'd throw the bar of soap at him and turn on the cold water. He wouldn't blame her if she did. Sarah had been the most stubborn, most exhilarating woman he had ever met.

Now You See It…

Through his own carelessness he had lost someone more precious than all the deals he had closed. The lady had every right not to trust him.

Flushed and uncomfortable, Anthony stepped away from the washroom and closed the door noiselessly, then drew a breath to calm his heightened nerves. He grabbed the towel off the floor and tightened it around his waist to hide his, um…condition. His morning was already topping his sleepless night.

It had been torture sleeping in the same room as Sarah and not being able to touch her. If his door ever locked again, he'd break it down.

Slumping onto the bed, Anthony pressed his palms to his temples. His whole body ached from the inside out. Reaching for the phone, he dialed the front desk for assistance then sat there listening to the shower running. Sarah must enjoy long showers. Walking to the door, Anthony peeked out and spotted a young gentleman in uniform coming at a quick jog.

"You the gentleman that called about a lockout?"

"Yes," Anthony said, stepping into the hallway and closing Sarah's door behind him. "I really appreciate this."

"No problem," he said and opened Anthony's cabin. "Now you're set." He turned and started to leave.

"Wait! Your tip." Anthony grabbed his pants lying on the bed and dug in the pockets for his wallet.

The officer waved it away. "Another time, I'm kinda in a hurry. I've got a seagull boarding and I haven't kissed off the one that boarded yesterday," he said with a grin.

"Excuse me?" Anthony asked. Was "seagull" some nautical term?

"The ladies can't resist a uniform." The officer chuckled. "I've got to see one lady friend off before another boards." With a wink, the officer left.

Shutting his door, Anthony headed straight for the small fridge for a bottle of water before popping two aspirins from his shaving kit.

The ringing of his cell phone jarred him. He grabbed it off the bed and snapped it open. "What?"

His foreman's amused voice came over the line. "You sound worse than when you left to go on that damn cruise of yours. Next time, you stay home and I'll go."

"Dante, when I get back I'll buy you a ticket so I don't have to see that ugly face of yours."

"It's a deal."

Anthony's voice sobered and filled with concern. "Have you heard anything?"

"Things are looking good. We've got them on the run. Unless they've got something else up their sleeves, they aren't touching your baby."

His tension dissolved, taking with it his strength as he dropped onto the edge of his bed. "That's what I needed to hear." For the next few minutes, they went over the details of the jobs in progress and Anthony gave instructions to iron out a few minor things. He rang off, a smile spreading across his face.

Things were running smoothly so he needn't worry. He was glad that his cell phone hadn't rung when he was with Sarah. It would have been another nail hammered into his coffin.

After a shower that didn't ease his headache, Anthony pulled his hair into a ponytail and decided he needed a strong cup of coffee to jumpstart his adrenaline. Throwing on a pair of black slacks and a beige, short-sleeved shirt, Anthony slipped his wallet and his boarding card in his pocket and went to knock on Sarah's door.

Her door opened immediately. "Great, I'm ready," she said, her overbright smile forced. She kept looking over his shoulder instead of meeting his eyes.

Now You See It…

Her defenses were again firmly in place, secure behind a slim wall of determination. How long it took the spell to break through her resistance and help his cause, he couldn't wait to see.

She wore bangles up both her arms with one of his red T-shirts that reached mid-thigh. A scarf held her ponytail in place, and her sunglasses were perched on top of her head. "Why don't you just stick with the clothes I gave you? You know it's a losing battle, decking yourself with everything you can find."

"I still have my shoes and my dignity," Sarah chewed her bottom lip and stole a quick look at him. He wondered what was going on in that lovely head of hers.

Anthony gave her a once-over. "If you put on a belt, people will think it's a dress."

"It's a safety precaution, I have shorts on underneath." She lifted the hem of the T-shirt to prove her point and exposed her lacy black underwear. "Shit, shit, shit." Sarah dropped her hem back down. "It couldn't have taken my bracelets," she complained, waving her arms about, clinking tiny notes. "No, it had to take something I needed."

"I can see that." God, he loved this spell. He chuckled then winced as vibrations echoed in his temples. "It's either the spell or you just flashed me."

Sarah glared at Anthony. "This is not funny."

"Anything's funny after the sleepless night I had."

"Do you realize I'm down to jewelry, underwear and shoes? The rest is yours."

"I don't have a problem with that."

Sarah smiled as a passenger walked by then glared back at Anthony. "Well, I do. I resent that I have to rely on you to keep myself covered."

"You could always return the clothes I lent you," he replied.

"Fat chance."

"Come on." Anthony led Sarah back to his cabin. "You can use a pair of my running shorts. Try on the blue ones, they're a bit tight on me so they should fit you," he said, handing them over.

Without taking off her running shoes, Sarah slipped on his shorts.

"How do they fit?" Anthony asked.

"You be the judge." Lifting her T-shirt, Sarah displayed her shapely behind. "Well?" she asked and peered over her shoulder.

Anthony gave a wolf whistle. "You're lucky I'm tall and thin. Can you imagine if you were falling in love with a short chubby guy? You'd be using a heck of a lot of safety pins right about now."

Sarah's smile disappeared. "Who said anything about falling in love?" She wasn't ready to accept the inevitable. But soon — very soon — she would have no choice.

Anthony's grin slipped. "Have it your way," he said, holding his cabin door open. "Let's go to breakfast."

Stubborn man. Why did he always have to have the last word? If he wanted compliance then he'd have it. Sarah would take Emily's advice and do exactly what the Mancini women did. She'd agree with whatever he said. She'd give him what he wanted.

Sarah didn't want to argue with Anthony. From his pained expression and pallor, she knew he was suffering from a headache. Her hands itched to sooth his brow, but she stopped that impulse.

Instead, she exited the cabin. "Yes, Anthony," she said then walked to the stairs. When she turned around, Anthony hadn't followed.

"Hey Mancini, you coming or not?"

Now You See It...

Emerging from his cabin, Anthony wore a suspicious expression. "What did you just say?" he asked, closing his door.

"I said, 'yes, Anthony'."

He snorted. "That's a first."

She climbed the first step. "Can we please hurry up? We'll be late for breakfast."

"Not so fast." Anthony took hold of Sarah's arm and turned her around. "A minute ago you were ready to argue with me. Did I miss something between my cabin and the stairs?"

Sarah shrugged. "I just changed my mind, that's all."

"Just? All? What are you up to?"

"Why are you so suspicious all of a sudden?"

"Because you've never agreed with me before."

Sarah chewed the inside of her mouth to keep from grinning. Judging from Anthony's glare, it wasn't a good idea. She folded her arms across her chest and glared back. "If I argue with you, you get upset. If I agree with you, you get suspicious. You're just going to have to decide which one feels like the truth." Sarah flung her ponytail over her shoulder and climbed a step. "See you on deck."

Sarah found everyone having breakfast under an umbrella next to the pool. Emily and her aunt were chatting a mile a minute while digging into piles of pancakes smothered in butter and syrup, as Albert quietly enjoyed his eggs Benedict and watched the passengers strolling by.

Sarah pulled up a chair and grinned. "No aftereffects from last night's partying?"

"Couldn't be better," said Aunt Lilly, filling her mouth with another bite of pancake.

"How 'bout you, Albert? I see you survived my aunt and Emily for an entire evening."

"Barely." Alberta winked at them, making them giggle like school girls.

"You'll never believe what happened to *me* last night." Sarah leaned aside so a waiter could pour her a cup of coffee then ordered a basket of croissants.

"Morning." Anthony sat down beside Sarah and ordered coffee and toast. Their orders quickly appeared.

"You were saying dear?" Aunt Lilly took a sip of her coffee then wiped her mouth on her napkin.

Sarah pulled a croissant apart and slathered it with butter. "A drunk banged on my door last night asking for his Dolly," she said, popping a piece of her croissant into her mouth.

Aunt Lilly snorted. "I bet it was one of those inflated life-size models."

Albert covered his cough with his napkin then pretended great interest in his eggs Benedict.

"Aunt Lilly you're terrible." Smiling, Sarah brushed the crumbs off her hands and reached for her cup of coffee. "Dolly was the name of his wife."

Aunt Lilly turned to Anthony. "Where were *you* when all this happened?" she asked.

"I was taking a shower," Anthony said, biting into his toast and swallowing. "But when I heard the commotion I charged out of my cabin—dripping wet and in a towel, I might add—and helped the gentleman realize he was knocking on the wrong door."

Aunt Lilly lifted her knife and fork again, her smile broadening with approval. "Now the story's getting interesting. Let me guess, once Anthony rescued you, you invited him into the cabin to thank him and the rest," Aunt Lilly lifted her hands in a grand gesture, cutlery and all, "is history."

Sarah could feel the uncomfortable heat rising up her neck and scorching her ears. "No, that's not it." She nudged

Anthony under the table with her knee. "We went to bed." Her aunt didn't have to know how close those beds had been.

"What?" Her aunt's mood veered sharply toward anger. "Of all the…"

Aunt Lilly chopped into her pancakes, punctuating her words with her movements.

"…stupid, idiotic…"

She cut more furiously.

"…things I've ever heard in my entire life."

Emily gently touched her arm and shook her head. With a heavy sigh Aunt Lilly put down her cutlery and pinned Sarah with a stare.

"You're telling me you had a naked man at your door and you didn't invite him in?" Aunt Lilly covered her mouth and belched. "I think I just lost my appetite."

"Sarah hasn't finished telling the rest of the story." Anthony ignored the kick she gave him under the table. Instead, he wrapped an arm over her shoulder and played with a strand of her hair. "I ended up locking myself out of my cabin and staying in hers."

Aunt Lilly narrowed her eyes. "You *do* have dark rings under your eyes. Didn't you sleep well?"

"Not a wink."

"Sarah, you had me going there for awhile." Aunt Lilly's eyes lit up, a large grin spreading across her face. "So the whole night you were with Sarah?"

"The whole damn night," Anthony nodded.

Aunt Lilly looked absolutely delighted, whereas Emily seemed confused. "But Antonio, if you were with Sarah and you didn't sleep, why are you in such a bad mood this morning?"

"Good question. Oh my, what a clever girl you are, Em," said Aunt Lilly.

If she could get used to Aunt Lilly and Emily's bluntness, Sarah would find this whole situation funny. Instead, she had two old ladies with sex on their mind and poor Albert who, for the past ten minutes, had people-watched to avoid the conversation. And then there was Anthony, who looked like a bear with a sore head.

"I didn't sleep well because I had a headache." Anthony took his arm away and leaned back in his chair.

Sarah could finally breathe again. Why was the man volunteering more information than was necessary? Hadn't he figured out that her sweet aunt was dangerous when she was blissfully ignorant, but lethal when she knew things?

Emily shrugged nonchalantly. "So romantic. Did she comfort you?"

Anthony just shook his head.

"Oh, for Pete's sake, I fell asleep. Okay?"

Three sets of astonished eyes stared at her.

Sarah blush deepened under Aunt Lilly's knowing smile. "And once Sarah falls asleep only a bomb could wake her up."

Emily patted Anthony's arm. "*Accidente!* You have no luck."

"Can we *please* drop the subject?" Sarah grabbed a croissant and bit into it.

Anthony raised his empty coffee cup to gain the waiter's attention. "Who's picking us up today?"

"Your Uncle Carlo and Zia Roberta will drive us around, while you two will go with your cousin Vincenzo and his wife Ciara," Emily said.

"Last time I saw Ciara she was pregnant," Anthony said.

"She is again," said Emily with a delighted gleam in her eyes. "*La famiglia*, she gets bigger each year. The men in my family are, how you say — very proficient."

Sarah choked on her croissant.

Now You See It...

"Emily, you mean prolific and not proficient," Albert kindly corrected.

Emily frowned at Sarah. "What is the difference?"

Sarah cleared her throat. "Well you see, proficient is when someone is really good at what they do. Prolific is when a person is very productive."

Emily tapped Anthony's cheek. "*Si*, the men in my family are both."

Anthony shook his head at his grandmother's brazenness and stole a warm croissant from Sarah's basket. "Now you'll see firsthand what I meant when I said the men in our family take their women's health personally. Vincenzo is the son of the uncle that I told you about the other day."

Sarah smiled. "This I've got to see."

They were met on the dock by a couple in their late fifties. "So let me get these people straight," Sarah said. "The man hugging the air out of Emily is your uncle Carlo, and the lady impatiently waiting her turn is your aunt Roberta?"

"Correct." Anthony nudged her forward.

"And the guy opening the door to the second car for the very pregnant woman is Vincenzo?"

"Good memory," Anthony said.

Carlo and Roberta embraced Anthony before turning to her. Carlo must have seen the apprehension on her face, for he extended his hand.

"You are Sarah, *si*?" Carlo asked. He didn't wait for her to answer. Instead, he kissed her cheeks then passed her over to his wife.

Sarah extended her hand. "*Signora.*"

"Oh no," Roberta said, brushing her hand away and hugging her. Sarah looked over her head to Anthony. His eyes shone with merriment.

"*Andiamo*, we go." They quickly loaded Aunt Lilly, Emily and Albert while Vincenzo finished helping Ciara out of his car.

"Antonio!" Vincenzo embraced his cousin.

"Look at you." Anthony pulled away from his cousin and patted his stomach. "You're round," he said before turning to Ciara.

"Don't say that." Ciara kissed both of his cheeks. "He's very sensitive about his figure."

"You laugh, but each pregnancy I gain more weight. *Per la misera!* This time I started to grow the first month. Now I can't sleep, my feet hurt and my back is killing me. I tell Ciara that we're going to have the baby this week, but she doesn't believe me."

Sarah looked at Vincenzo's pained face and didn't know if he was serious. He had the same dark eyes as Anthony, only his held a perpetual gleam of mischief. He was also a few inches shorter and much rounder. "He's joking, right?"

"No he's not," said Anthony.

Ciara rubbed her tummy. "The men in this family take their position as papa very seriously." She offered her hand to Sarah. "I'm Ciara, by the way." She was a very beautiful woman, her blunt-cut, chestnut hair exposing a face that glowed. She had light smudges beneath her eyes that told of sleepless nights.

Sarah shook her hand. "I'm Sarah, pleased to meet you." She extended her hand to Vincenzo next, who brushed it away and pulled her into a strong clinch that lifted her off her feet.

He set Sarah back on the ground and kissed her cheeks. "It's about time this good-for-nothing cousin of mine found someone."

"Once our baby is born we come to your wedding," said Ciara.

Sarah blushed. Was the entire Mancini family blind? "You're mistaken," she started as three faces smiled back at her. "We're only on this trip together so Emily and my aunt don't get into trouble." Sarah waved at her aunt as they drove by.

Ciara waved Sarah's explanation away. "If I know our Antonio, he has already told you what he thinks. È furbo, he is sly. But this is normal for the Mancini men. Once they know who they want, there is no stopping them."

With a light touch to Sarah's back, Anthony motioned them toward Vincenzo's car. "We're very persuasive," he agreed.

Ciara threaded her arm through Sarah's and led her to the car. "You mean you tend to bulldoze the other person," she said to Anthony over her shoulder.

Vincenzo laughed. "Bulldozer, this is good. One cousin who acts like a tractor and the other who looks like one." Opening the door to a very small compact car, Vincenzo folded the seat forward. "But now we go. We can continue this discussion in the car as I drive around our beautiful Rome."

Sarah squeezed into the cramped space in the backseat. Anthony bumped her shoulder as he sat next to her. There was absolutely no room to move. Or breathe. Anthony stretched his legs against hers so that his large frame could fit and spread his arm along the backseat. This was terrible.

Every way Sarah shifted she brushed up against Anthony's hard body. She didn't know how to arrange herself so she wouldn't end up lying against him.

"Will you quit fidgeting and relax?" Anthony pulled Sarah against his chest and made the decision for her.

With a sigh, her traitorous body melted against Anthony's to be wrapped in his arms and scent. Sarah relaxed deeper into his embrace and his spell.

"That's more like it."

Vincenzo started the engine. "Where to first?"

"Take us around Rome so Sarah can see some of the sights. Then let's head out to the country to escape the heat," suggested Anthony.

"*Va bene.*" Vincenzo shot into traffic.

As soon as their vehicle surged forward, other small cars and scooters challenged them for space in an already congested street. They zigzagged from lane to lane in a chaotic pattern, grabbing the first available gap. The traffic, the noise and population surged as one.

Competing with the best of them, Vincenzo sounded a long firm blast of his horn then stuck his head out the window. "*Stronzo!*" Vincenzo waved his fist at the offending car to emphasize his point.

Sarah felt Anthony's chest shake with laughter. Sarah tilted her head back and looked into his eyes. "I can't believe he just did that."

"I can," he said and kissed her forehead.

How many times had she yearned for this closeness? To be the center of his attention? She absorbed the moment and blocked her inhibitions, focusing on the passing scenery.

Quick glimpses of narrow streets, all hemmed in with cars and scooters, rushed by. It didn't matter where she looked—everyone blocked each other and no one obeyed the traffic signs.

Sarah opened the small back window and was engulfed by a thick smell of exhaust and a cacophony of sounds. "This is nuts," she exclaimed. And she absolutely loved it.

"I know. Just be thankful we didn't come when it's really crowded," said Anthony.

Sarah's eyes rounded. "It gets worse?"

"In July and August. But most of the tourists have already left."

Sarah returned her attention to the surrounding buildings and statues with their exhaust-darkened faces. In the distance, she could see scaffolding as restorations were being made on a monument.

Over rough roads their car bumped along. Sarah was jostled from side to side. Gripping Anthony's knee, she apprehensively watched cars cut each other off in front of them.

Anthony pulled Sarah's shoulder back against his chest. "Relax. This is normal for Italian driving."

Normal? Sarah thought. Who in their right mind could get used to this? "It looks like everyone is following their own rules. You could have warned me." Her eyes widened when four rows of cars simultaneously made a left turn.

"It wouldn't have done any good. You don't tell people about Rome. You let them experience it."

Sarah couldn't believe how calm Anthony was. "If you can handle this, why were you so nervous when I drove the jeep?"

"Because Vincenzo has years of experience driving in crazy foreign traffic. You don't."

"Holy crap." Sarah applied her imaginary brake when Vincenzo ran a red light and swerved to avoid another car. Sarah leaned forward and tapped his shoulder. "You just ran a red!"

Vincenzo peeked into his rearview mirror and smiled. "No, no, that wasn't for me."

After the initial fright, Sarah began to adjust to Rome's madness. It was contagious. It pulled you in and tempted you to be as spontaneous as the Romans.

Sarah experienced her first look of the magnificence of Rome through this surging chaos. Towering columns and statues of generals on their horses greeted Sarah with an ageless grandeur that reflected the past and the present.

"Look over there." Anthony pointed out villas along the way with their hidden entrances and courtyards.

Along Via S. Gregorio, Sarah got a glimpse of the Arch of Constantine, followed by the inspiring and impressive Colosseum. Driving along Corso Vittorio, they stared at the splendor that was Piazza Navona, with its three monumental fountains. Vincenzo zigzagged along side streets, taking shortcuts as they cut across Rome to reach the Trevi Fountain.

Anthony tapped his cousin on the shoulder. "Vincenzo, dash over to the Spanish steps so Sarah can sample an ice-cream."

"*Va bene.*" Vincenzo changed directions without warning. Anthony tightened his hold around Sarah's shoulders as she grabbed onto the door handle. She held her breath as Vincenzo crossed over the lanes without signaling. Close to the Spanish steps, Vincenzo wedged the car into a tiny space.

Sarah leaned close to Anthony's ear. "He just parked on the sidewalk."

Anthony chuckled. "I know."

Vincenzo hopped out to help Ciara, and Sarah waited for Anthony to unfold himself from the backseat. He tried to exit headfirst, but ended up falling back on his butt. With a grumble, Anthony extended one long leg and pulled himself out, before helping Sarah do the same.

Taking hold of Sarah's hand, Anthony led her down the block to an umbrella-covered table on the sidewalk. "Have a seat, this won't take a moment," he said, before strolling away in deep discussion with his cousin.

"*Uffa!*" Ciara dropped into a chair.

"You all right?" Sarah asked. Ciara was flushed and didn't look too comfortable sitting on the small plastic chair.

Ciara wrinkled her nose. "Not really."

Sarah worried over the way Ciara kept rubbing her back. "Do you want me to call the men back so Vincenzo can take you home?"

Now You See It…

Ciara chuckled. "Now you sound as paranoid as my Vincenzo. I have another three weeks to go. You'd think that after two pregnancies, a mother would know when she was having contract—" Ciara sucked in her breath in surprise as her stomach moved and rolled.

Sarah pointed to her stomach. "Then what was that? Gas?" She started to rise but was firmly pulled back down. "Let me call the men back."

"Nonsense. It's the hot peppers and sardines I ate for breakfast."

That would do it all right, but Sarah still wasn't convinced. "I don't have any children but I think that bun is about ready to pop out of the oven." Sarah scanned the area and hoped the men would hurry up. Ciara was putting on a brave front, holding her hands together to stop them from trembling.

"Not to worry. We have plenty of time." Ciara looked over her shoulder when she heard her husband's and Anthony's laughter.

They each carried spoons and a long oval dish with an assortment of ice cream. "Ladies." With a flourish, Anthony waved Sarah's treat in front of her.

Ciara tried to smile. "I'll move over so Anthony can sit beside you."

Sarah leaned over to stop her when another contraction shook Ciara's body. With a moan, Ciara sank back into her seat and clutched her stomach.

"*Tesoro?*" Vincenzo dropped the dish of ice cream on the table and knelt beside his wife.

Ciara caressed her husband's concerned face. "Maybe I should go home and rest."

Vincenzo threw his hands in the air. "*Accidente!* Now she agrees with me." Placing his hands under her arms, he carefully lifted her out of her seat.

Ciara clutched her husband's arm, her smile strained. "I think my water just broke."

Anthony and Vincenzo both turned green as they said, "Now?!"

Chapter Twelve

෩

Except for the twitch on the side of his eye, Anthony wasn't moving. Totally baffled, Sarah watched him glance at her, then Ciara, then back again. Was this the same man who had a flair for commanding others?

She couldn't get over Anthony and Vincenzo's identical dazed expressions. Horrified, their eyes pleaded with Ciara to tell them she was joking. Like the poor woman had a choice.

"Give me that," Sarah said, jumping up and grabbing the ice cream out of Anthony's hands before he dropped it. "Vincenzo, go get the car while Anthony and I stay with Ciara," she ordered, turning to help Ciara back into her seat.

"Si, si, va bene," Vincenzo agreed, then promptly crumbled into the seat next to his wife.

Sarah grabbed Anthony's arm. "Do something."

He did. He collapsed into the chair next to his cousin.

Sarah gaped at Ciara in disbelief.

Ciara held her stomach and giggled. "It is okay. Vincenzo does this for every baby we have." She opened her purse and pulled out her cell phone. "By the time we reach the clinic, Vincenzo will be fine."

Sarah shook her head, astounded by the men's behavior. "I've never seen Anthony act like this before." He was a little green around the gills.

"This is good. You get to see what happens to the Mancini men when their babies enter the world. It is like a test run for when it is you and Anthony's turn," Ciara said.

"There's nothing serious going on between me and your cousin. You're jumping the gun."

"I'm not going to be jumping anything for a while. Give my sweet cousin a shake."

Sarah waved her hand in front of Anthony's face. "Hello? Anybody home?"

Anthony got unsteadily to his feet. "I need to get the car."

"Good idea, you do that," said Sarah, watching Anthony regain his balance and take off at a run.

Ciara talked to her doctor, informed him they were on the way then shut her cell phone. "*Ecco, tutto fato*, there all done," she said and calmly began to eat her ice cream.

"What are you doing?" Sarah gaped. Were all Italians this crazy? Her father certainly hadn't been.

Ciara pushed Anthony's dish toward her. "Eat. After today, I won't have an excuse to cheat." Ciara spooned a mouthful of ice cream into her husband's mouth.

Sarah shrugged her shoulders and picked up her spoon. Like the saying goes, "When in Rome..." Sarah bit into a roasted almond. "Oh my, this is good." She sampled the flavors Anthony had picked, each one more delicious than the next. She tasted lemon, pistachio and a rich coffee flavor. Sarah moaned. "This is amazing."

"You see? Sweet but firm. Just like our men. They tend to add flavor to our lives." Ciara chuckled, but it turned into a groan when another contraction hit.

Sarah scanned the area. "Come on, Mancini, what's keeping you? Ciara, remember your breathing," she offered, panting in and out quickly like she'd seen a woman do on TV. Ciara copied her until the strain melted from her face, leaving her drained and pale.

"Much better," Ciara said.

Vincenzo slumped further into his seat. "*Dio*, it is time."

"Oh God." *Please don't have the baby here*, Sarah thought. She was a nervous wreck while Ciara continued to enjoy her ice cream. Even with all her bravado, Ciara's hands shook.

Anthony finally sped down the street and brought the car to an abrupt stop in front of them. With sure, steady movement, he rushed toward them, the Anthony that Sarah knew back and in full control, firing commands. "Sarah, get Vincenzo into the backseat while I help Ciara."

Sarah walked Vincenzo to the car and let him stumble into the backseat before stepping in. Anthony closed the door behind Ciara and raced to the driver's seat.

If Vincenzo had driven like a maniac, Anthony drove like a man on a mission. No holds barred. The car shot off on another crazy race.

While Ciara calmly gave directions to the clinic, Sarah braced herself against Vincenzo's shoulder and flattened the other hand against the side of the car. This trick kept both of them balanced.

In record time, Anthony reached the private clinic. Two laughing nurses met them at the main entrance, each pushing a wheelchair. Sarah watched as Ciara and Vincenzo were wheeled away.

Anthony slumped against the hood of the car with a huge sigh of relief. "Now, it's the doctor's worry."

"Were you anxious that we wouldn't make it?"

That green tinge was back again. "That thought never crossed my mind," he deadpanned.

"Liar."

Anthony raised an eyebrow. "You know me that well?"

"Let's just say that when you want something, you don't let anything stand in your way."

"Remember that." Anthony stepped away from the car. "We need to make a couple of phone calls to let everyone know where we are." Anthony guided Sarah through automatic doors and into the clinic's air-conditioned interior.

Within the hour, the waiting room filled with family and friends. Men played cards or snuck peeks through the glass window of the door leading to the delivery room. The women shooed them back to their seats and laughed at their expressions, then resumed gossiping.

Sarah smiled. They were such an adorable bunch. Each time the door swung open, the room held its breath anticipating the announcement. When no news came, they good-naturedly resumed their talking.

She felt the level of energy and anticipation rise. She scanned the room to see how her aunt was doing. Aunt Lilly and Emily were in the thick of a rowdy conversation, with Emily translating for her. Albert was busy learning to play a card game called Scopa.

Sarah looked over the crowded room and said to Anthony, "I think Aunt Lilly, Albert and I should grab a taxi and head back to the ship. That way we're not in the way."

"Nonsense." Anthony's expression darkened. "Besides, this clinic belongs to one of my uncles. He's already used to this."

"Have it your way," Sarah replied.

Anthony sat beside her and adjusted his pant legs. "Don't get too comfortable. Ciara has a habit of delivering quickly. That's one of the reasons I was relieved we made it here in time."

"*Attenzione.*" A short, bald man pushed through the doors and clapped his hands for attention. When all eyes were on him, he stretched out his arms and in a booming theatrical voice announced, "*È una bambina!*"

Instantaneous pandemonium broke out.

"What did he say?" Sarah asked over the commotion.

Anthony leaned over and said in her ear, "It's a girl."

Everyone jumped out of their seats, talking and laughing at once. Sarah was hugged again and again as warm-hearted embraces were exchanged. With each hug, Sarah heard the word *auguri*.

"Hey, Mancini," Sarah called out, "what's that word mean that they keep repeating?" Another member of Anthony's family embraced her.

Anthony tried to explain while a very round aunt grasped his face and pulled it down to her kisses. "It means congratulations," he said before he was set free.

Sarah had never seen Anthony so happy. He patted an old man on the back who tried to inconspicuously wipe his tears away. A cousin stepped up and embraced Anthony before moving on.

People surrounded her on all sides. Feeling vulnerable and confused, Sarah took a step back. This was too much for her. She wasn't used to so many people. Or how touchy-feely they all were. The crush of moving bodies made her heart race with exhilaration and horror all at the same time.

Plastering her back against a cool wall, Sarah took a deep breath to calm herself. She'd had enough. Discreetly edging her way toward the exit, Sarah hoped to leave undetected.

From across the room, Anthony's eyes narrowed. Busted. Her stomach knotted under his stare. He gently moved his relatives aside and advanced on her.

Sarah's eyes widened. "Oh hell." She took a step back and bumped into one of his cousins. "Sorry," she mumbled without taking her eyes off Anthony.

Sarah had nowhere to hide. Trapped. She lifted her hands in defense. Anthony captured them and slid them over his shoulders.

"Anthony, what do you think you're doing?"

"Celebrating," he said, lifting Sarah into the air.

Sarah held onto his shoulders, her cheeks heating up. "Put me down, people are watching."

"Let them." He brought her down, slowly skimming his hands over her body before kissing her. "Coward."

She pushed against Anthony's immovable chest. The kiss left her weak and confused. "I can't believe you did that," she said, tossing her hair over her shoulder. She noticed some of her bracelets were missing. "Now look what you've done."

His smile broadened. "Me? Who were you thinking of?" Anthony slowly released her. "You must be slipping, Santorelli," he said before he was whisked away by another relative.

Sarah looked around at the faces of Anthony's family, each one open and giving as they generously shared the addition to their family with her. She stepped back to the wall as a melancholic craving filled her.

This was what was missing from her life—the chaotic, unconditional love that cocooned this family. Sarah leaned against the wall and unconsciously touched the remaining bracelets for comfort. She wondered if she could share her life like that with Anthony.

She'd convinced herself that her life was full and satisfying. Now, it paled against the brilliance that surrounded her. Could she take what was being freely offered or would her fears of abandonment force her back into hiding?

Sarah covered her face and groaned. Her glimpse of happiness dissolved into uncertainty. All her loneliness and confusion welded together into devouring yearning.

When people started to leave, Sarah made her escape. Following them outside, she waited beside the car for Anthony. She could feel him watching her as he opened her door. Sarah kept her head bent, her hair cloaking the vulnerability she knew was written on her face.

They settled in their seats and drove off. She found his nearness disturbing and at the same time exciting.

Reaching a red light, Anthony leaned over and kissed her.

"What was that for?" Her sarcastic tone concealed the mixed emotions that churned within her.

The car shot forward. "That was to bring you back from wherever you were retreating to. You can't decide if you want to join a very large, very chaotic family or retreat into your safe little world. I'm tipping the scales in my favor."

"Stay out of my head!" Sarah exclaimed, inhaling deep breaths of air to stop the interior of the car from closing in on her.

Anthony accelerated past a couple on a scooter. The woman had her arms wrapped around the driver's waist, her lips pressed against his neck. Sarah didn't know where to look. To her left Anthony tempted her resolve and to her right, the woman continued to caress her companion. She was falling apart.

They left the heat of the city behind and ascended into the cooler mountainous countryside. Off the main road, they climbed a steep winding path that took them deeper into the country.

"I thought we were joining your family at a restaurant?" Sarah lifted her chin and boldly met his penetrating gaze.

Anthony returned his attention back to the road. "That's where we're going. What's the rush?" He maneuvered the car onto another dirt path, this one filled with potholes.

Sarah fidgeted with the strap of her seat belt. "I just thought they would be expecting us."

Anthony steered the car around a sharp curve. "Is that the real reason?" he challenged her.

She stiffened at the provocation. "What else could it be?"

Anthony laughed, the sound cynical and dry. "You tell me."

They were in the midst of an olive grove. Bushes scraped the sides of the car. Sarah could smell the rich, pungent odor of fertile soil. Large branches crisscrossed overhead to shade them as Anthony steered around water-filled ruts, scattering chickens sitting on the side of the road.

A stucco bungalow shimmered in the late afternoon sun. Large doors were flung open, sounds of merriment spilling out to greet them.

Before the car could come to a full stop it was surrounded by family. Anthony jumped out and was immediately encircled. Sarah exited the car at a slower pace and stayed beside it.

She watched the women pass Anthony around as they took turns hugging him. Children clung to his legs, waiting to be thrown in the air.

A woman, bent with age, made her way toward them. The group quickly moved aside to make room for her. With wrinkled hands that shook, she drew Anthony's face to her diminutive height for a peck on her soft, lined cheek.

Laughing, Anthony hugged her and, with a gentle arm, strolled with her to where Sarah waited. "Sarah, I'd like you to meet my great-grandmother, Lucia."

The old woman kindly patted her arm and said something. Sarah shook her head. "I don't understand. *Non capisco.*" The old woman just drew Sarah's arm through hers and clasped her hand.

Each woman kissed Sarah on the cheek, repeating the word *auguri* before departing.

Sarah frowned at their retreating backs. "Anthony, why do they keep congratulating me? I'm not the one who just had a baby."

Anthony awkwardly cleared his throat. "Sarah..."

A warning voice whispered in her head as Lucia escorted Sarah up three flagstone steps to a faded age-old terrace with wicker chairs in secluded corners, and large pots filled with brilliant red snapdragons.

Now You See It…

Everywhere Sarah looked people were eating and laughing. She spotted her aunt, Emily and Albert enjoying themselves at a table covered in a red-and-white checked cloth.

Sarah smiled at Lucia and tried to head to her aunt's table, only to find her arm held firmly by this deceptively fragile old woman.

To her horror, Lucia raised her hand for attention and the room quieted.

Sarah plastered a smile on her face. "Anthony, what is she doing?"

Anthony opened the top button of his shirt and fanned himself. "Sarah, I'd hoped this wouldn't happen." A shadow of regret touched his face.

Judging from the joy on Anthony's great-grandmother's face and the expectant faces of his relatives, Sarah was about to be fed to a roomful of hungry Italians whose main goal in life was to marry off the single members and encourage them to multiply.

"Mancini, I smell a rat." Sarah zeroed in on her aunt's and Emily's ecstatic expressions. She'd bet those two were in on what was about to happen.

Before Sarah could open her mouth and explain, Lucia announced, *"La fidanzata!"* She clasped Sarah's face and kissed both her cheeks.

"Mancini! Tell me she didn't say what I think she said?"

"Oh, you heard right. She just called you my fiancée."

Sarah was passed from one person to another. "Do something!"

Anthony was pulled in the opposite direction. "What do you want me to do?"

"You're the one who usually has all the answers," Sarah yelled over the heads of people as they surged and flowed between her and Anthony.

"For a change, I'm lost for words." Anthony masked his annoyance behind a forced smile as the next relative congratulated him. Sarah felt like a Ping-Pong ball by the time Anthony's relatives returned her to his side.

A gentleman wearing a large white apron placed a glass of wine in Sarah's hand. "Now's not a good time to have nothing to say, Mancini," she said firmly. "Either you set them straight or I will."

"No! Please." Anthony's eyes widened. "It would hurt my great-grandmother's feelings and embarrass my relatives. Let them celebrate and I'll think of something to tell them later," he said, before being dragged away by a group of men to the other side of the room.

She gave in to the tension that had been building all day and collapsed into a chair. Sarah found herself seated beside an uncle who continually filled her plate with food and her glass with wine. Sarah shot daggers across the room, both at Anthony and in the direction of her aunt's table.

She couldn't figure out what she resented more—the fact that her precious control had disappeared, that there was a small chance she wanted it to be true or that Anthony had fared better than she had.

Surrounded by noise and laughter, Sarah surrendered to her sorrow. "Here's to me." She saluted herself with her glass then took a large gulp of wine. She didn't want or need any of this closeness, this bonding. No siree. She drank from her glass again. "This is not for me."

Then why did she hurt so much? Oh God. She drowned her pain with more wine. First the hospital and now this—she was surrounded by a human wall of acceptance and belonging that she didn't feel part of.

Across the room, Anthony winked at her. Anger simmered to a slow boil in the pit of her stomach, churning her insides. She put down her glass, the bitter taste of jealousy filling her mouth as, to his right, a voluptuous brunette leaned forward to spoon food onto his plate.

Bastard. First he convinced her to go along with this charade, now he's sitting next to an octopus. The damn man was supposed to be sitting beside her, pretending to enjoy her company.

Sarah fisted her hands on top of the table. "Men."

If this was the way Anthony treated his fiancées, then she was lucky it was a farce.

Picking up her glass, Sarah saluted Anthony. Taking another huge slug of wine, she resumed her nodding to the uncle beside her. She hadn't a clue what he saying, but whatever she agreed with was making him happy.

"Do you know what you just agreed to?" Anthony's amused voice asked.

Sarah stood up and squinted at Anthony's wavering figure. "Well, if it isn't my fidizooo." Her tongue refused to cooperate.

Anthony chuckled. "You're drunk," he said, steadying her.

"I beg to differ." Sarah swayed gently on her feet. "Mancini, will you quit moving so I can talk to you?"

Anthony wrapped his arm around Sarah's waist. "I think we've had enough for one night. Let's go. Everyone's waiting in my uncle's van."

The day had been an unmitigated disaster for Anthony. Getting stuck next to one of his uncle's "friends" at dinner hadn't helped the situation either. Based on the scowls Sarah had sent across the room and her dark disposition, Anthony had burned his bridges.

He hadn't wanted the situation to progress this far, but to protect his great-grandmother from embarrassment, he had landed Sarah in quite a predicament.

Sarah pulled out of his arms and stumbled. "You could always stay behind you know. From what I noticed, that woman was serving you more than food." Sarah carefully navigated the first step that descended from the terrazzo.

Anthony clasped Sarah's arm so she wouldn't fall. "She was only being hospitable."

"Very accommodating." Sarah weakly shoved against Anthony's chest. "What was her name? Madame Holiday Inn or McDrive-thru?"

Anthony pulled Sarah's body against his. "She was my uncle's guest."

"That's just as well, Mancini." Sarah let Anthony help her into the backseat of the van next to her aunt, who was snoring. "I can't take much more of this." She grabbed the seat belt and saw that her arms were bare. "Look." She raised her arms under Anthony's nose. "I'm losing everything to you."

Anthony leaned over to fasten her seat belt as her eyes drifted shut. Leaning over her in the open doorway, Anthony tucked Sarah's hair behind her ear. His sadness was a huge knot inside of him. "What about your heart?" he whispered.

Her soft breathing answered him. Sarah had fallen asleep. He shook his head and sighed. Emptiness shrouded his body, leaving him disappointed.

At the docks, Anthony found himself in a predicament. All of his fellow passengers were sound asleep. Including Albert, who was quietly snoring beside Emily.

Anthony smiled at his uncle. "I'll wake them up one at a time." He roused Aunt Lilly, then his grandmother and Albert. He helped Lilly to her cabin while Albert and Emily held each other up.

Going back for Sarah, Anthony leaned over her and unsnapped the seat belt before gently shaking her. "Come on Sarah, time to wake up."

Now You See It...

Nothing. She moaned, but refused to wake up. With no other choice, Anthony hugged his uncle goodbye and lifted Sarah out of the car.

"Jeez." Anthony shifted Sarah in his arms. She was heavier than she looked. He took a deep breath and adjusted her body as he walked.

With all of his jiggling, Sarah slowly came to her senses. "What are you doing?" she groggily peered up at him.

His forehead was covered with sweat. "I'm trying to carry you to your cabin." He adjusted his grip again and shifted her weight.

Her eyes cleared of some of her sleep. "You can put me down you know."

He gladly placed her on her feet but wrapped his arm around her waist. "Come on, it's bed for you." Anthony led her along the deck to her cabin. They passed a group of partiers with Yarmilla in their midst.

Sarah waved. "Oh look, there's Cruella De Vil."

Anthony hurried her along. Just a few more steps and he'd have her inside her room. Anthony propped her up against the wall and slowly released her. When Sarah remained standing, he unzipped her purse to retrieve her key.

Sarah started slipping sideways and giggled. "Oops."

Anthony quickly righted her, opened the door then slammed it shut with his foot once they'd entered. "What a disaster this cruise is turning out to be."

From the foot of the bed, Sarah grumbled, "You know Mancini, you talk too much. I liked you better when you were asleep."

Deflated, Anthony leaned against the door and ran his fingers through his hair.

Sarah dropped onto her back and blindly searched for a pillow. Once she found it, she tucked it under her head.

"You want to know a secret?" she asked, her eyes drifting shut. "You have a great body. I should have joined you this morning when I had the chance." She sighed into her pillow.

Anthony shut his eyes, leaned his head back against the door and moaned. "Just shoot me." He dragged his feet over to the bed and stood over Sarah's sleeping body.

It was going to be another long night. He thought about changing her clothes, but decided against it. Instead, he threw a cover over her.

Anthony took off his clothes and threw them onto a nearby chair. As he crawled into Sarah's spare bed, the phone rang.

Anthony gripped the telephone and barked, "Hello!"

"Anthony? Is that you?" Amanda's astonished voice came over the wire. "Did I catch you at a bad time?"

He rubbed his tired eyes. "No, couldn't be better." He looked over to where Sarah slept peacefully.

After a telling silence, Anthony heard Amanda chuckle. "Maybe I should call back later."

"Amanda, don't hang up. It's not what you think."

Amanda cleared her throat. "Where's Sarah?"

Anthony lay back and closed his eyes, then replied in mock resignation, "In the next bed, drunk and sound asleep."

Amanda laughed. "Oh dear, now I understand. Between the alcohol and my sister's tendency to sleep like a brick, you're not doing so well."

"I don't think it's that funny."

"I'm sorry." Amanda sobered but Anthony could still hear the smile in her voice. "I'm sure you don't. The reason we were calling Sarah's room was to try to find you anyway. Hang on, Mark wants to talk to you."

"Anthony?" asked Mark.

"Who else?" he replied.

Now You See It…

"Okay, I get the picture. I'll make this short and sweet. You know that monster of a house next door to Aunt Lilly's?"

"What about it?"

"It went on the market this morning."

Maybe the day wasn't a total write-off after all. He remembered Sarah once saying that if she ever had the chance, she'd buy the big Victorian house next to her aunt's.

"Buy it." He named his top amount.

Mark gave a long whistle. "You got it. And Anthony?"

"What?"

"Good luck, buddy."

Anthony glanced at Sarah who was snoring quietly into her pillow. "Thanks, I'll need it."

Chapter Thirteen

Sarah woke with nausea rising from the pit of her stomach. "Oh God." She covered her mouth and stumbled to the bathroom. Leaning over the toilet, she paid retribution for the drinking she had done.

Breaking out in a cold sweat, Sarah waited for her stomach to settle. "I'll never drink wine again." Her head pounded. Her eyes burned. Closing the lid of the toilet, she rested her forehead against the cool porcelain.

Groaning, Sarah pulled herself up and in the darkness, felt her way to the cold-water tap. She washed her face, then blindly located the mouthwash bottle and rinsed her mouth.

Through the dimness, Sarah peered at her pale reflection and groaned at her appearance. She still wore yesterday's clothes.

After stripping them off, she pulled on the T-shirt that was hooked on the back of the door. "This is all Anthony's fault." She lifted her hair away from her face.

"Who are you talking to?"

Sarah screamed, the sound vibrating against her temple.

"You scared the hell out of me!"

"Sorry," Anthony replied groggily, turning on the bathroom light.

She covered her eyes. "Turn it off." She waited for the click of the light switch.

When no sound came, Sarah slowly peeked through her fingers. Anthony stood in the doorway, bare-chested, hair disheveled and wearing a pair of black boxer shorts, totally unaware of his appeal. His body was flushed from sleep, its hard lines relaxed and smooth.

He disappeared briefly and returned. "Here." He handed her two tablets and a bottle of water.

Sarah popped them into her mouth and drank from the bottle.

"How does your stomach feel?" Anthony took the bottle and left it on the counter.

"Better." Sarah rubbed the goose bumps on her arms. Maybe the air-conditioning was too high.

"Okay then, let's hit the sack. We still have a few hours before we have to get up." Anthony led Sarah back to her bed, covered her then turned off the lights.

Sarah huddled underneath her cover. She couldn't stop shivering. "What are you doing here anyway?"

"I figured you'd need my help."

"Thanks." Another shudder racked her body. She clutched the extra pillow to her chest and huddled deeper under the covers. Her teeth chattered like castanets.

"Are you all right?"

"I can't seem to get warm."

The mattress dipped. "What are you doing?" Sarah peered over her shoulder, instantly aware of Anthony's warm body as he crawled under her blankets and stretched out behind her.

"I'm warming you up." Anthony drew her close and gave a tired sigh. "Just close your eyes and sleep."

"In that case…" Sarah pressed her frozen feet against his warm shins.

"Jeez!" He jerked his legs away. "Your feet are like icicles."

Sarah's body liquefied as Anthony's heat seeped into her. Gradually, her shivers subsided. She relaxed into Anthony's chest and sighed. His hot, moist breath fanned the back of her neck.

His warmth surrounded her. She melted further into his delicious heat. It was as though her body recognized his and slipped back into acceptance.

Sarah also remembered how a look would ignite a spark that would smolder the whole evening and flare the minute they were alone. And each morning, she'd wake up alone. How she'd hated those moments.

Just because he had taken this trip didn't mean Anthony had changed. To open herself to uncertainty when she had reclaimed control of her life was ludicrous. Destructive. She couldn't go through it again. And yet, when they had dated, she had almost convinced herself that she could have it all.

"Anthony?"

"Mmm?"

"Can I ask you something?"

Anthony sighed. "Shoot."

Rolling over, Sarah looked into a pair of eyes whose lids were closing. "Did you say anything to your grandmother to make her think we were engaged?"

Anthony stilled. His eyes opened, sleep slowly clearing from them to be replaced with a guarded expression. Sarah had his full attention now.

He bent his elbow and rested his head on his hand. "No, I didn't."

Sarah didn't dare move as she tried to decipher the tone of his voice. The shadows of the room hid the depths of his eyes but she nevertheless became increasingly uneasy under his stare.

"Then someone has some explaining to do." Sarah decided she would have a talk with those two troublemakers tomorrow morning.

Anthony touched her arm. "Would it be so bad?"

Now You See It…

Would it? Her fears rose to the surface, gripping her insides. A warning at the back of her mind refused to be stilled. Desperate to keep in control, Sarah turned her face away, suddenly unsure.

Anthony felt like someone had kicked him in the stomach. Furious over her continuous rejections, he clasped her chin and turned her face back to him. "Why can't you give me a straight answer?"

Her body stiffened against his. She refused to meet his eyes. Damn, what was a guy supposed to do? It didn't matter what he did, he couldn't push past that last barrier of hers. Maybe he was doing it all wrong, or maybe she just didn't want him.

"You haven't got a clue what you want. It bothers you to see other women show their appreciation, yet you don't want me for yourself."

Sarah hugged the blanket to her chest. "That's not true."

"Either you're interested or you're not." He leaned away and switched on the bedside lamp so he could see the truth. "If you're not, just say the word and I'll shove off. I'll make room for the next poor sucker. Maybe I should warn the unfortunate bastard about your arm's-length rule. That way he'd fare better than I have."

Sarah's face flushed with anger. She stared at him as though he were something that had gotten stuck on the bottom of her shoe.

Tough. This meant too much to him.

She pushed against his chest and plastered her back against the wall. "Who the hell do you think you are? Setting time limits for when I have to make up my mind? Quit trying to set ground rules. They don't work."

Anthony threw the covers off, marched to his pants and grabbed them. "Nothing works, does it princess? You've locked yourself in a little tower so you can watch the world pass you by."

Sarah clasped the blanket to her chest. "You have no idea what you're talking about."

"Sure I do, princess." He angrily thrust his legs into his pants and pulled them on. "If you want to experience life, then I suggest you climb out of your tower," he yanked at an uncooperative zipper, "and get your hands and feet dirty just like the rest of us."

Sarah gasped.

Bingo. He'd finally hit a raw nerve.

Sarah straightened farther. "I've got news for you Mancini, I've lived most of my life in the middle of that so-called dirt. And you know what? It stinks! You're no different, hiding behind your authority, moving people around like chess pieces. Who are you to judge me?"

Her chest rose and fell with each rapid breath she took. Her hands clenched at her sides as her eyes darkened with pain. Wounded. If she was feeling as desolate as he was, she was breaking inside.

Anthony felt himself weaken. Damn. He ground his teeth and stiffened his resolve. He wasn't giving in. Thrusting his bare feet into his shoes, he grabbed his shirt and stormed toward the door.

He gripped the handle, his knuckles turning white. He heard Sarah's hiccup as she controlled her battered emotions.

He'd done this to her. Anthony felt low, disgusted with himself. He should have listened to Sarah's wishes, accepted them and left her alone.

Fury almost choked him. Opening the door he glowered at her. "I wasn't judging you. I thought I was strong enough to breach that wall of yours. Obviously I was wrong." With a flourish he bowed. "You win, princess." He didn't care whether he hurt her or not. "Hope you enjoy your own company."

Now You See It...

With a final contemptuous look, he slammed out of the cabin.

"Damn you, Anthony!" Sarah threw her alarm clock at the closing door.

Pulling her other pillow under herself, Sarah tightly hugged it as silent tears of betrayal fell. She felt split in two. When push had come to shove, Anthony hadn't wanted to understand how she felt.

In the end, he had left. Just like she knew he would. She had tested him, pushed him to his limit. She didn't know what frightened her more, the urge to run after him or the panic that held her back.

Sarah watched the endless night gray into dawn as the sun slowly chased the cabin's shadows away. There was movement outside her door as the crew quietly prepared for the day and passengers headed for early-morning walks.

Frustrated, she threw her covers off and dragged herself into the shower. Emerging, Sarah changed into one of Anthony's clean T-shirts and shivered. Tentatively lifting the fabric, she smelled the clean scent that reminded her of him.

She had no choice but to wear the same shorts she had worn yesterday and slipped her feet into a pair of low open sandals. What was the use? If she wore her own shorts and thought about him, she'd find herself enjoying some unexpected breezes.

Her short moment of humor was dashed when she closed her eyes and relived the pain of their last scene. It didn't matter how many bracelets, rings or layers she put on—he had broken through her control.

With half a heart, Sarah tied her hair back and added the useless bangles, five on each arm. She'd keep putting them on and she knew that they'd keep coming off. She kicked her alarm clock out of her way and closed the door behind her.

On deck, a clean fresh gust of wind welcomed her into another exhilarating, cloudless day. All around her, the early morning bustled with activity. The crew set up for the day's events while passengers jogged by. Music from an on-deck aerobics class reached her.

Strolling to the breakfast buffet, Sarah poured herself a coffee and headed for the railing. Resting her foot on the lower rung, she sipped from her cup. The beauty of Livorno, Italy, lay before her.

A ghostly mist clung to the chiseled mountain peaks as the early-morning sun melted its weak resistance. Sarah's eyes traveled down the mountain, where flowers flourished and terra-cotta roofs huddled together. Somewhere in the city, church bells chimed out to one another.

A thousand questions crowded her mind. How should she act? Would it be better not to say anything? Would he even want to listen? Each doubt hammered at her emotions as they competed to gain her attention.

Taking another sip, Sarah mulled over the previous evening's events. She couldn't continue on this destructive path. It was tearing her apart. Staring unseeingly over the water, lost in confusion, Sarah was startled when a comforting hand touched her arm.

"You didn't hear me calling," Lilly said. "Emily spotted you over here and thought you'd like to join us for breakfast."

Sarah rubbed her gritty eyes. "Sure."

"Are you all right?"

"I'm a little tired," she said as they walked to their table.

Emily smiled at her. *"Buon giorno."*

"Morning. Where's Albert?" asked Sarah.

Aunt Lilly pulled out a chair and sat down. "He's staying on board today to recuperate from yesterday."

Sarah took a seat. "I don't blame the guy." Trying not to grimace, she slipped her sunglasses over her burning eyes.

Now You See It…

"Where's Anthony?" Aunt Lilly unfolded her napkin on her lap. "I thought he'd be with you."

"Don't know." Sarah ordered pancakes and fruit.

Aunt Lilly shrugged her shoulders and cast a worried frown toward Emily.

About to reach for her coffee, Sarah heard her aunt gasp. It was Lilly's dramatic expression and the hairs that stood up on her own arm that gave Sarah an initial warning. The sound of Anthony's laugh, followed by a woman's chuckle, gave her only seconds to prepare herself.

"Good morning everyone. I'd like you to meet Rachael." Anthony leaned over and kissed his grandmother's cheek. "I met her the first day of our cruise while I admired the Palma de Mallorca scenery. I've invited her to spend the day with us."

A beautiful brunette with laughing blue eyes extended her hand. "I've heard so much about everyone. From Anthony's description, you must be Emily," she shook hands with the right person, "and you two are Aunt Lilly and Sarah."

"The one and only," Sarah replied. It just about killed her to smile politely.

"I have to thank you," Rachael said before smiling at Anthony.

"Why is that?"

"If it weren't for you, Anthony said he wouldn't be on this cruise."

Anthony acknowledged Sarah with a curt nod.

Sarah kept her smile in place. "I finally did something right." Behind her glasses, her eyes stung with unshed tears. Had she been that easy to replace? She clutched her napkin on her lap to stop her hands from shaking.

Anthony touched Rachael's waist and gestured as they moved away. "If you need us, we'll be at the next table."

"Sarah?" Her aunt's look of confused hurt said it all.

Sarah raised her hand to halt her aunt's questions. "Not a word." Sarah glanced at Anthony as he helped Rachael into her chair. With her yellow halter-top and white shorts and her hair in a pigtail, she looked very young. And pretty.

Sarah pretended to enjoy her breakfast. They could have been the fluffiest pancakes she had ever eaten, but they tasted like sawdust. She should be happy that Anthony had moved on. Wasn't that what she'd pushed him to do?

Then why did their laughter grate on her nerves? Their heads were bent close together as they read a magazine. Each time he turned a page, Sarah was aware of his hand movement. The same hands that had warmed her body last night.

Ping! Sarah looked at her bracelets. One chimed softly as it bounced against another before disappearing.

The soft sound traveled up her arm, sending shivers down her spine.

The flutter of the magazine quivered against her nerves. When Anthony picked up his cup and clinked it back down on the saucer, it felt like a pebble hitting her broken heart.

Ping.

She didn't have to look this time.

On the ship's railing, a seagull squawked while it danced from one spindly leg to the other. Was fate teasing her?

Rachael looked over and smiled at her, a friendly, open smile, welcoming her to join in. Oh hell, not only was she pretty, she was also nice. She'd lost Anthony and this was what freedom tasted like. Bitter.

The scrape of a chair drew Sarah's attention as Rachael rose to go the juice bar.

She caught her aunt's and Emily's perplexed expressions.

Turning the page, Anthony caught her staring and raised an insolent eyebrow. His slight gesture reminded her that this was what she had wanted. Cold blankness painted his features, his jaw inflexible and his eyes frigid points of blackness. She'd never seen Anthony like this before. Distant. Unapproachable. Cold silence thundered between them.

Breaking the hold he had on her body, she took a deep breath and looked away to find herself under the shrewd scrutiny of her aunt. She fidgeted with the napkin on her lap.

From the determined tilt of her chin, Aunt Lilly was about to butt in where she wasn't wanted.

"What's put the two of you in such a pickle?" she asked loudly. "It would have been better if you hadn't joined us on this cruise."

Anthony's head snapped up.

Aunt Lilly waved a fork loaded with eggs about. "At least we wouldn't have to look at such long faces first thing in the morning," she said and stuffed her mouth.

Now that Aunt Lilly had their attention, she wrapped her arm around Sarah's shoulder and glared at Anthony. "What have you gone and done this time?"

Anthony snapped his magazine shut. "Wait a minute—"

Emily jumped in like a mother bear defending her cub. "Maybe Antonio hasn't done anything wrong. Maybe it is Sarah who needs her head examined. And maybe my Antonio is too good for her."

Aunt Lilly confronted Emily over the breakfast table. "I'll have you know that Sarah has lines of men coming to call on her."

"Maybe that is why Antonio doesn't want her. How do you say…she is *consumata*, used goods," Emily smiled at Aunt Lilly's furiously red face.

"Enough!" Anthony's eyes widened at their spiteful jabs.

Sarah noticed that Rachael had returned. From her embarrassed flush, she must have thought she had gotten herself mixed up with a bunch of nuts.

Anthony took one of the juice glasses from her hands and pulled out her chair for her. "What's gotten into you two? You're on holiday, so act the tourist."

Aunt Lilly flashed Emily a guilty look.

Anthony cleared his throat. "I suggest that we concentrate on where we're going today."

"How about a tour of Florence?" Rachael suggested. "It's really quite lovely."

"We"? When had it become "we"? And what a lovely "we" they made, Sarah thought resentfully.

"Sounds fine by me," said Aunt Lilly.

Anthony pushed his chair back. "So it's settled. Let's get going or the bus will leave without us."

Sarah gulped the last of her coffee. She didn't want to go on a tour of Florence and endure Anthony's cold shoulder for the rest of the day.

But she also didn't want to ruin Aunt Lilly's vacation. She sighed and stood up. Nothing else would have gotten her off this ship.

She warily kept her distance so she wouldn't have to contribute to the conversation. Sarah watched Rachael use natural charm to draw her aunt and Emily out. She had them talking like old friends in no time.

Why couldn't Anthony have picked someone I can find fault with, Sarah thought miserably? He was absolutely relaxed walking beside Rachael as he paid close attention to what she was saying. He had that about him. He made you feel special just by listening.

Ping.

Sarah could feel a tension headache growing at the back of her eyes. As she waited to board the bus, pinpricks of strain traveled down her neck. She was conscious of Anthony's words, of his gestures as he spoke to Rachael and his grandmother.

Now You See It…

During the hour-long ride to Florence, Sarah stared unseeing out her window, aware of the low, intimate whispers that were coming from Anthony and Rachael in front of her. To her right, Aunt Lilly and Emily had their heads bent together as they chatted away furiously, not paying attention to the guide's narrative of the beauty of Italy and its ruins.

At Piazzale Michelangelo, Sarah leaned against the railing and tried to lose herself in the perfect panorama of the surrounding countryside of Florence, the Arno River flowing silently by.

"Beautiful, isn't it?" Rachael leaned on the railing close to Sarah.

"Yes, it is." Sarah watched a group of tourists click away with their cameras before they moved on.

Rachael nudged her with her elbow. "And Italian men aren't so shabby, either."

God, she had a sense of humor. Could this day get any worse?

"Anthony tells me you do bookkeeping work from home."

"Yes. What do you do?" asked Sarah.

"I'm a teacher at a school for special-needs children. I've been doing it for the last five years."

"That's great." So she looked younger than she was and loved children. She was perfect for Anthony. Her heart squeezed in anguish with the thought of them together.

Ping.

Everyone quickly boarded the bus once again and they moved on to the Duomo. Its entire exterior was made of hand-carved marble that glistened in the sun, while its immense interior dwarfed the many visitors inside. Each footstep, each cough, each whisper echoed and magnified within its cavernous dome.

Sarah craned her neck to admire the stained glass windows and frescoes in the main dome. "It's amazing."

"I know," said Anthony, admiring the sun shining through the stained glass.

Startled, Sarah glanced over at him and quickly looked away. She hadn't expected him to answer.

"You see how creative Italian men can be with their hands," said Emily.

Aunt Lilly chuckled. "Now that's a loaded sentence if I've ever heard one."

Anthony drew closer to them. "You're going to embarrass Rachael."

"You are a prune. You don't think I married your grandfather for his cooking skills, do you?" asked Emily.

"That's a 'prude', *nonna*, which I'm not. And the only time grandpa ever cooked an egg, he forgot to turn on the stove. I do remember how happy you were together. But I also remember the way you loved to argue."

"And your grandfather enjoyed those arguments just as much as I did. That way we had an excuse to make up," said Emily.

"Smart man," said Rachael, joining the group.

Sarah watched Rachael's smile slip into one of sad regret. She held a painful breath as Anthony took Rachael's hand and squeezed it.

Ping.

Leaning over, he whispered something into Rachael's ear that encouraged the smile to return to its original brightness.

Ping.

Too distraught to watch, Sarah looked away as they continued to talk.

Emily gave Anthony a gentle push. "Who do you think you took after?"

Now You See It…

Anthony kept his arm around his grandmother's shoulder and strolled from the cool, dark marble interior back into the bright sun. "Now I understand why I act the way I do. It's a defective gene I've inherited."

A clock in the piazza chimed twice. "Anyone for lunch?" Sarah asked.

Maybe she could drown her sorrows with food.

They were able to get a small table in a crowded open café under a white-and-blue canvas cover, where they ordered a pizza. A small breeze teased Sarah, but had little effect on the moisture that trickled between her breasts. Aunt Lilly and Emily fanned themselves with napkins, while Sarah used a paper plate.

A tall, thin waiter delivered their pizza and cold lemonades before dashing off again. With the weight of the heat and Anthony's body so close, Sarah couldn't eat.

Each time she moved, her knees bumped into his, jarring her frazzled nerves. It wasn't that she was doing it on purpose. She felt hemmed in.

Ping.

Shifting away, Sarah only made it worse by bumping into the table leg, nearly toppling their lemonades.

Anthony stopped a glass from falling. "Damn it, Sarah, would you relax?"

A hysterical laugh slipped from Sarah's lips. "Of course I'm relaxed." Sarah's voice edged higher. So did Anthony's eyebrow and the posture of the other three at the table.

Oh hell, Sarah felt utterly wretched and disgusted with herself. Rachael looked cool in the middle of all the heat, while Sarah felt irritated and tired. Dressed in Anthony's baggy T-shirt and shorts, she looked a mess.

"The heat getting to you Santorelli?" asked Anthony.

"Not at all." Sarah knew they weren't talking about the weather. "I'm used to worse."

Anthony stood up and threw some notes on the table. "It's time we left."

At the Palazzo Vecchio, Sarah looked around a small square surrounded on all four sides by time-faded buildings and a towering clock with taupe-colored stone walls.

She purchased birdseed from a woman dressed in black and meandered through the square feeding pigeons. Statues stood like sentinels throughout, a fountain sang in an isolated corner, while a horse-drawn carriage carrying Anthony, Emily and Rachael lethargically clattered over cobblestones.

Sarah headed toward a fountain where her aunt sat in a corner of shade. "How are we doing?"

Aunt Lilly pointedly glanced at the passing carriage. "I could ask you the same thing."

"I don't know what you're talking about."

"I'll have none of that, missy." Aunt Lilly wiggled on the marble edge of the fountain. "Last night you were almost an engaged woman and this morning you don't even have a date. Give your aunt some credit here. What are you waiting for?"

"I have some thinking to do."

"What were you thinking about, letting a specimen like that slip through your fingers?" Aunt Lilly slapped her forehead. "What am I saying? Of course you weren't thinking. We only have a few days left before opportunity boards a plane."

Sarah frowned at her aunt. "What do you want me to do? Jump his bones?"

"Now there's a thought. It's a shame you and your sweet sister didn't take after me more."

Sarah squirmed under her piercing attention.

"Where's the little girl I once knew who could take on the world?"

Now You See It…

Sarah's lips quivered. "Stuck in her tower without a key, trying to chip at the walls from the inside."

Aunt Lilly's scowl melted into a tender, sad smile. "Oh, now I see," she said in a soft whisper and shook her head. "You're going to have to let go of the past. You can't go around trying to control everything. We all end up leaving, be it by choice or fighting and kicking on the way out."

A tear fell down Sarah's cheek. "Oh God! That's what I do, isn't it?"

Aunt Lilly passed her a tissue. "Since you were a little girl. I'd watch you try to make your sister's world perfect after your parents passed away." Aunt Lilly squeezed Sarah's hand in hers. "It's a losing battle."

Sarah blew into her nose. "I can't simply stop being who I am. I thought I had more time."

Aunt Lilly grunted. "Oh Lord, help me. That's what I've been trying to tell you. You've almost run out of chances." She wiggled her behind off the rim of the fountain.

Sarah pointed to where Anthony was gently handing his grandmother from the carriage before helping Rachael out. From their delighted grins, Sarah knew they were enjoying themselves. Even Emily liked her. "If you haven't noticed, I already have."

Each time Sarah thought of letting go of her protective mantle, that same suffocating fear overwhelmed her. What if Anthony turned away?

"Rachael's just a minor obstacle."

"If that's what you call minor, what would you consider a major difficulty?"

"A man's stuck zipper."

"Oh Aunt Lilly." Sarah embraced her aunt and hugged her tightly. "I do so love you."

"It's about time you moved your caboose," Aunt Lilly said, straightening her dress. "I thought by now you'd be sharing a cabin. I even brought a whole damn bag of condoms for this trip and I have no intention of taking them back home."

Sarah's hand froze in midair as she threw the last of her birdseed. "You did what?"

Aunt Lilly turned red. "Not for me, you idiot. For you."

Sarah looked toward Anthony and opened the floodgates of her mind.

Ping.

Ping.

Ping.

Chapter Fourteen

☙

Defeated.

The alien emotion left a bitter taste in Anthony's mouth. When he returned home, he'd bury himself in the mindless solitude he found in his work.

With half an ear he listened to his grandmother and Rachael chat as their carriage slowed down. His sunglasses and the smile he cemented on his face were the only things that hid his vulnerability and cultivated the image of a happy tourist.

"You can keep your damn tower," he mumbled beneath his breath. "See if the princess likes it this way." Fury tightened his gut as her rejection came flooding back.

He'd had enough. He was shoving off and God help the next sucker that came along. Sucker? Unfortunate bastard? They both added up to the same thing—defeat.

He fidgeted in his seat as nervous energy surged through him like an army of ants trying to find a tunnel of escape. Before the carriage came to a halt, he jumped down.

"Hold tight." He held onto his grandmother's hand and let her down gently. "We have one more stop before returning to the ship." Rachael accepted his outstretched hand and jumped down.

"That was lovely," Rachael said.

"My pleasure." He continued to smile as terrible regret assailed him. He'd served himself up like a charbroiled fish, crisp on the outside and tender on the inside.

From across the square, Sarah and Aunt Lilly drew near. Anthony nodded in their direction. "Why don't you join them while I pay the driver?" he asked his grandmother and Rachael, needing a few minutes to close the pain behind an iron resolve.

A few yards away the women chatted, their faces alive with excitement as giggles and snippets of their conversation reached his ears. He could hear Sarah and Rachael planning the evening's activities once they returned to the ship.

That was another miscalculation. He'd brought Rachael as a safety net so he could stay away from Sarah. Instead, they got along like a house on fire.

What a fool he'd been. To think he could convince Sarah of his love in the short span of a week had been ridiculous. Anthony pinched the tense muscles on his shoulder and sighed. The weariness of his body could not compare to the disillusionment in his soul.

"*Quanto?* How much?" Anthony asked the old man who held his hat in his hands. Anthony handed over the sum with a generous tip added.

"*Grazie! Grazie!*" The driver flipped his hat back onto his head and assisted another waiting couple into the carriage.

Anthony clenched his teeth and slipped his wallet back into his pocket. Enough stalling. His resignation veered sharply to anger. If Sarah had been a business, he'd have cut his losses and moved on to the next venture.

He'd give her what she wanted by staying out of her way. He just hoped the remainder of this damn cruise would move quickly. He'd be relieved to get off that floating circus of a ship and the merry-go-round Sarah had put him on and get back to his life again, his feet back on solid ground. It was time to move on.

With determined strides he ate the distance to where they stood. "If you've seen enough, we can start back to the bus." Anthony placed one hand on his grandmother's back and the other on Rachael's. "Some of the other passengers have already boarded."

"Anthony," Sarah said, tentatively touching his arm and offering a smile. "Could I have a word with you?"

Her carefree attitude triggered an earthquake of fury he barely contained. "Not now," he snapped. At the look of shock on his grandmother's face, he quickly reverted to the happy tourist and lowered his voice. "The buses are about to leave."

A knot formed in Sarah's throat. His curt reply lashed at her, leaving bleeding, open wounds. She swallowed and stared at where Anthony rested his hand at the base of Rachael's spine. Always the gentleman. Sarah had lost something precious in order to gain her solitary, controlled existence.

She grasped what little courage remained and tried again. "This will only take a moment."

"Then it can wait."

She felt her throat closing up as she stared at their retreating backs. Could she blame him? A suffocating fear of loneliness tightened its grip.

She tried to remember how many days were left to plead her case. Two? Three? The pounding of her heart made it difficult to think.

When she'd first boarded this cruise, she'd wished the days would go quickly. Now she would like nothing better than to turn back time and start this trip with a clean slate.

On legs that shook, Sarah followed Aunt Lilly and Emily as they chatted away. This was not going to work. Anthony's snubs cut too deep. With her hands clasped behind her back, Sarah followed her aunt at a slower pace.

Emily's hands were waving about as she spoke. When Lilly pulled Emily to a stop, Sarah halted and waited for them.

Lilly waved Sarah away. "We'll meet you back at the bus."

With a shrug, Sarah turned to the bus, her lead feet crossing what seemed an overwhelming distance of sun-drenched cobblestones, their penetrating heat unable to reach her numb heart.

"Nuts." Lilly watched Sarah drag her feet like she was going to her own execution before turning to Emily. "Things are not working out."

"Yes, they are," contradicted Emily.

"Are you blind? Sarah is miserable and Anthony is with another woman."

"I know," Emily replied, her knowing smile grating on Lilly's nerves. "Sarah has realized how much Anthony means to her. And my Antonio has another woman as a cover. They both peek at each other when the other isn't looking."

Lilly grunted. "If we leave it to those two, I'll be buried before the first of my grandnieces comes along." Aunt Lilly slipped her arm through Emily's. "Drastic times call for drastic measures."

Emily pulled her arm away and frowned. "Oh, *mama mia*, not again. We pestered them enough to come on this trip. Let fate run its course."

Lilly squared her shoulders. "I am. I'm just giving it a healthy shove in the right direction."

"*Sei na pazza*—you're crazy." Emily pinched Lilly's arm for good measure, her eyes filling with disapproval. "No."

"Ouch." Lilly rubbed her arm. "Will you keep your voice down?" Lilly peered at Anthony and Rachael as they boarded the bus, while Sarah kept her distance. They were acting like complete strangers. "Would you just look at those two? How's our plan supposed to work if they're not even talking?"

Emily gave a disappointed sigh. "Maybe it's not meant to be."

"Not meant to be? Nonsense." Lilly took hold of Emily's hand and dragged her toward the bus. "I lit all the candles I had in the house, pulled half the flowers in my garden and cast a magic spell and things *still* aren't turning out like I expected."

"*Cosa?*" Emily pulled her hand away and looked at her suspiciously. "Did you put something in my Antonio's coffee, too?"

"Don't be ridiculous." Lilly nudged her forward. "I did magic on Sarah, but I failed."

"You're going to send me to an early grave," Emily complained, wiping her neck and pocketing the handkerchief. "I'll find Antonio's grandfather at heaven's gates asking me what the hell I'm doing there."

"No you won't." Lilly pushed Emily up the bus steps. "Think of our future grandkids." Lilly waved at her niece at the back of the bus as she moved down the aisle. "How we doing, dear?" she asked across a sea of heads.

Sarah watched Lilly and Emily leisurely stroll to their seats. They took the one across from her, Aunt Lilly giving Emily the window seat before settling beside her.

"All set." Aunt Lilly winked at Sarah, then immediately turned her back to her.

Their heads glued together, Aunt Lilly and Emily frantically whispered. Sarah could tell that Emily was agitated from her rapid hand movement, while Lilly kept shaking her head.

Sarah leaned forward. "Is something the matter?"

Her aunt gave a guilty start. "What could possibly be wrong? We've spent a wonderful day together. We have one more stop before we head back to the ship and a night of food and entertainment."

"A glass of wine and some cheese and crackers would hit the spot right about now," Rachael said, looking back at Sarah while Anthony, who sat beside her, didn't bother to turn around. "Besides, I don't know about you but my feet are killing me. What if Emily and I stayed on the bus while you enjoy our last stop?"

Aunt Lilly jumped in her seat. "That's out of the question."

"Excuse me?" Sarah eyes widened at her aunt's rudeness. She wore an innocent smile that would alert anyone to trouble.

"I'm sorry, dear. It's just that I've enjoyed myself so much that I want to share as much as possible with the people I've come to care about." Lilly gave them a puppy dog stare. "I'm sure a ten-minute walk won't hurt us. Once we get back to the ship, we can put up our feet and enjoy the evening breeze."

"Count me in," said Anthony, oblivious to the undercurrents.

When they reached Ponte Vecchio, a bridge that crossed the Arno River, everyone went in different directions. Sun-kissed, earth-colored stucco buildings lined the bridge's sides, creating a narrow alleyway where people browsed. The afternoon sun shone down on stamp-sized wrought iron balconies filled with rows of potted plants. White paint-chipped shutters remained closed to the heat and prying eyes.

Spotting a bench, Sarah crumbled onto it and wrapped herself in a cocoon of anguish. Everywhere she looked, couples young and old strolled hand in hand. Right now, Anthony would be sharing this with Rachael. His smile would widen and his eyes would mischievously light up as he teased her.

All her well-thought-out plans and precious control had flown out the window the day Aunt Lilly had cast her spell, allowing her past to walk through their kitchen door. Sarah took several deep breaths and finally stood up.

Now You See It...

She should never have come on this cruise. Her life would have remained the same boring routine of work, dating and home without having to consciously submit to the whirlwind of emotions that Anthony had awakened. The bliss of ignorance was no longer an option.

She remembered all too well that his take-charge attitude hid a marshmallow interior that he generously shared. Top it off with one heck of a sweet body and hands that created delicious, mouthwatering magic and you had yourself one hell of a package.

A package she had stupidly returned to sender.

A tingle started at the top of her head and ran to the tips of her toes. She looked down and, in a blink of an eye, her sandals vanished.

She bounced from one foot to the other. "Oh shit. Oh hot." The heat of the cobblestones was uncomfortable, but bearable.

Hysterical laughter bubbled from her mouth, startling a Chinese couple who scurried away and looked at her suspiciously. God, how she resented the spell and what it had done to her life.

She clasped and unclasped her hands as fear and anger knotted inside her. Now what should she do? Think! She was a logical, well-ordered person. Panic would get her nowhere.

How long she walked staring at nothing, immersed in her own thoughts, Sarah didn't know. A tourist bumped her, jolting her back to reality and the realization that she had only moved two stores down from her original spot.

Sarah scanned the vicinity looking for her aunt. "Where did that old busybody get to?" She was certain they hadn't gone far.

Close by, she spotted Anthony coming toward her with a troubled expression. It was an effort not to look away and pretend she hadn't seen him. Each step he took brought a cold front that froze her.

"I can't find Aunt Lilly and my grandmother," Anthony said.

"I'm sure they're around here somewhere." Sarah couldn't see them. "They must have stepped into one of the shops."

"I thought the reason you came was to look after them?" His cold, abrupt words were abrasive. "If I can't find them, I'll come back this way." With a curt nod, he walked away.

Dark eyes had looked right through her, as if she was a stranger to be dismissed and forgotten as soon as his back was turned.

She rushed in the opposite direction from Anthony. Overwhelmed, she rubbed her burning eyes as she checked each store. Nothing. She couldn't spot the top of her aunt's curly white head anywhere. Heart pounding, Sarah scanned a nearby restaurant in the hope that her aunt had stopped to eat again. No such luck.

"Where the hell are you?" Sarah gripped the hair at the top of her head and tried to squeeze the tension that was building.

Her body broke out in a cold sweat as she frantically searched the area. She needed to find her aunt and Emily fast. Sarah prayed her aunt had slowly made her way back to the bus and this topsy-turvy search was all for naught. Turning back in the direction she had come from, she found Anthony zooming in on her.

"I think we should go back to the bus and check if they're—" Sarah stepped on a stone and yelped.

"Where are your sandals?"

"More than likely back on the ship."

His frown cleared into a bittersweet smile. He knew she had been thinking about him.

Now You See It…

Anthony pulled his fingers through his hair, leaving it disheveled. "This is just great. We don't have time to shop for sandals."

"I never asked you to. Besides, dirty feet never killed anyone." Sarah sidestepped a sticky ice cream wrapper.

Anthony looked at his watch and swore. "Come on." He touched her arm and immediately dropped his hand as though he had been burned. "They're more than likely already sitting on the bus waiting for us."

When they reached the bus, Anthony leaped aboard and she was right behind him. He swiftly scanned the passengers, who inquisitively stared back. Out of breath, Sarah moved Anthony aside and hoped to see her aunt.

Nothing.

Rachael looked up and smiled.

"Have you seen Lilly and Emily?" Anthony asked.

Rachael frowned. "They told me to wait on the bus while they went to the powder room. When they didn't return, I thought they would be with you."

"Damn!" Anthony threaded his fingers through his hair. "We'll never find them at this rate."

"Wait here." Sarah jumped off the bus, her feet slapping the hot pavement as she ran to the public washrooms. "Aunt Lilly? Hello? Are you here?"

When no one answered, she made sure to watch where she stepped and checked the stalls. When she came to a stall that was locked she knocked on it.

"*Occupato,*" said a woman's voice.

"Sorry."

Out of time and out of breath, Sarah dashed back to the bus. "They weren't there."

"What should we do?" Rachael looked to Anthony.

Again with the "we", thought Sarah. Too bad Sarah liked her so much.

"Rachael, you stay here in case they show up." Anthony and Sarah moved back to the head of the bus. "Sarah and I will make one last dash along the bridge."

They blocked the other passengers trying to get to their seats. "Please take your seats," the tour guide said. "We'll be leaving in ten minutes."

Sarah's apprehension built. "But we're still missing two people!"

"I'm sorry, but we're on a tight schedule to get back to the ship." The guide directed the last of the passengers into their seats.

"I don't want to take the chance of leaving them behind." Sarah descended the bus steps onto hot asphalt and cringed. "Think how scared they'll be if that happened."

"How much time do we have left before the ship leaves?" Anthony looked up at the guide standing on the bus' step.

The tour guide looked at her watch. "You have two more hours. The ship sails at six. But remember, it takes an hour to get back to the dock, so don't cut it too close."

"Then we'll catch a taxi back. It will give us time for a quick search." Anthony stepped off the bus.

A cold numbness settled around Sarah as she watched the bus close its doors and pull away. Just thinking of what might happen to her sweet aunt caused the blood to drain from her face, leaving her pale and swaying on her feet.

"None of that." Anthony took hold of Sarah's hand and steered her back to the shops. "If we're going to find them we need to put our differences aside and work as a team or we'll never make it."

Tears of frustration and sadness fell from her eyes. "You were right. You said that something could go wrong and it did. It's all my fault for insisting we come on this cruise. The

Now You See It...

more you pushed not to come, the more pigheaded I became." Sarah wiped her tears with the back of her hand.

"Watch your step." Anthony abruptly pulled her away from a discarded pop can. "I knew what you were doing. My trouble is that I enjoy watching your temperature rise so much that I cornered myself into this trip."

"You too?" Sarah sighed. "If anything happens, I'll never forgive myself."

Anthony clasped her hand and gave it a gentle squeeze. It should have given comfort—instead, Sarah felt more depressed.

"We can't think that way. They may have gone back to the ship. You take one side of the bridge while I take the other. It's more than likely they're holed up chatting and have lost track of time."

By this point, she really didn't care what she stepped on. Her main priority was the safety of two sweet, innocent, simple-hearted old ladies.

Sarah quickly inspected the shops on her side. By the time she reached the end of the bridge, she was flushed with heat and breathing heavily. Her sense of dread increased.

Hearing her name, Sarah looked up and saw Anthony jogging over, carrying two water bottles. He was just as flushed as she was. "They're not here," he said, passing her a bottle.

"I know." Sarah took a large gulp from hers. "We would have been able to see them now that the tourists have thinned out and some of the shops have closed. Let's head back to the ship."

Anthony drained his bottle and threw it into a trash can. "Let's go," he said and flagged down a battered old taxi. Climbing into the cramped and heated backseat, Anthony talked to the driver before settling back. The old taxi driver rapidly nodded and shot into traffic.

Surprised, Sarah grabbed hold of the door handle. "What did you say?"

"That if we made it back to the ship in time I'd give him a large tip, so hang onto your seat," Anthony said, grabbing the rim of the open sunroof.

Sarah thought she knew what to expect after her ride through Rome, but this didn't even come close. Anthony agreed, if Sarah correctly deciphered his incredulous expression. Sarah braced her hands against the ceiling and her feet applied pressure to a set of imaginary brakes and some candy wrappers.

She switched her grip to the edge of the sunroof, and her knuckles turned white. Up ahead, she watched as the taxi squeezed through a tiny space in the road, connecting their door handle with the side of a parked car. A grating sound filled the interior of the taxi. "Oh hell."

The taxi driver chuckled at Sarah astonishment. "*Non ti preoccupare.* Don't worry," he said with a very heavy Italian accent. "I drive for forty years." He honked at a motorist before cutting him off.

Closing her eyes only made it worse—Sarah's oversensitive ears tuned into the constant flow of Italian that was being directed through the driver's window as he hurled insults at the other drivers.

Sarah gasped as the car swerved to the right. "Are we almost there yet?" She could feel drops of water trailing down her back as she stuck to the dirty old leather upholstery.

Anthony placed his hand over hers, squeezing it reassuringly. Opening her eyes, Sarah noticed that Anthony's shirt stuck to his body and that he was flushed with heat. "We're in the home stretch."

No sooner had he spoken than Sarah was thrown forward, hitting her forehead on the backrest of the front seat. She screamed as stars burst behind her eyelids.

Now You See It...

The jarring sound of steel connecting with steel rang in the taxi as it chewed away at the oncoming cars, locking them in an unrecognizable mass of tangled metal and chrome.

Sarah held her head and watched in horror as the sides of the taxi seemed to move in on her in slow motion. She felt her blood drain as the already small space continued to shrink.

In the blink of an eye, Anthony pulled her away from the crumpling walls to protectively wrap her body on his lap and shield her bent head from shattering pieces of glass with his arms.

"We're going to die!" she screamed, holding her breath until the car came to a thunderous stop.

Where before the loudness of the crash vibrated through Sarah's bones, now a breathless silence settled around her. She remained unfocused as the world stopped in shock, then picked up speed.

"Sarah? Sarah, can you hear me?"

Anthony's concerned voice seemed to come from a muddled distance. "Sarah, look at me. Sweetheart, are you all right?"

Her hair was gently brushed from her eyes as Anthony tilted her head up to him and talked her back to the present.

Disoriented, Sarah looked around her. They were sandwiched between a parked car and another that stuck into the side Sarah had been sitting on.

The taxi driver had climbed through the sunroof of the car and jumped to the ground. Like a conductor, he rapidly waved his hands around as he yelled at the other drivers, who yelled right back.

Horns blared. Tempers flared. Pedestrians walked by without the slightest flicker of curiosity, as though this was a normal occurrence.

A loud sigh of relief escaped Anthony. "How do you feel?"

"Like the crash occurred inside my skull." She tentatively rubbed the bump she felt forming on the side of her forehead.

"We'll get that looked at. If I give you a hand, can you climb out through the roof?" Anthony cleared the pebbles of glass on the seat and wrapped his hands around her waist to get ready.

"Piece of cake." Sarah tried to stand, only to fall back onto Anthony's lap.

"Take your time."

Time. That one word caught Sarah's attention. With shaking hands, she pushed herself off Anthony's shoulders and grabbed his arm to look at his watch. "Did you say time?"

Anthony frowned. "Calm down. You must have suffered a concussion."

"Calm down?" She thrust his wrist under his nose. "How the hell can I be calm when we're going to miss our ship?"

"Damn! Come on." Anthony stood up on their seat and climbed out of the sunroof. "Maybe the ship is running late and we'll still make it."

Anthony gently helped her through the roof. "I doubt it." To her dismay, her voice broke slightly.

Before she could find a place to put her feet down on, Anthony swung her into his arms. She instinctively wrapped her arms around his neck.

As though she was light as a feather, Anthony jumped off the hood without letting her go. He scouted the area then issued a piercing whistle. Before another taxi could come to a complete stop, Sarah opened the door and Anthony handed her in.

"What time does your watch say now?" Sarah asked.

"Ten to six."

She agitatedly dragged her hands through her hair and winced. Her whole body shook on an adrenaline high. She was angry with herself for having lost control of the situation.

Now You See It...

Feeling totally helpless, Sarah continued to blame herself. "I should have paid more attention to my aunt and your grandmother's whereabouts."

Anthony took one of Sarah's hands and clasped it in his. "I could say the same thing about myself. My mind was elsewhere."

Sarah slipped her hand out of Anthony's and looked out the window to hide her hurt. She bet his thoughts had been on Rachael and moving on with his life.

Her mind was in turmoil as she went over all the problems they'd faced. And now they didn't know where their relatives were. Sarah prayed they could still make it to the ship.

And if the ship had left? How would she know if her aunt was on board? Once they found Lilly and Emily, she would still have to figure out how the hell they were going to get to their next stop. This trip was a disaster.

When the taxi stopped next to the docks, Sarah jumped out and froze. The blood drained from her face as her heart gave a terrified jump. She looked to Anthony for reassurance but found only disappointment written on his face—only one of many emotions that churned and bubbled inside of her.

Only the clear blue ocean sparkled under the late afternoon sun where the gleaming white hull of the ship had been. Out on the horizon, Sarah saw its glistening silhouette.

"Now what?"

Chapter Fifteen

ঞ

Anthony banged on top of the taxi. "*Aspetti, un momento.* Wait here," he told the taxi driver and ran into a nearby office, determined to straighten out this havoc.

He remembered reading in the daily schedule that each port had an agent who took care of any ship's passengers that were left behind. Any stragglers would have to pay to get to their next port of call.

Bursting into the tiny air-conditioned office, Anthony spotted a pretty brunette in her late forties in a navy blue uniform. Before he could speak, she was out of her seat.

"You are Anthony Mancini?" The agent rushed around her cluttered desk.

"Yes." Finally, someone who knew what to do.

"Come, we don't have much time." She handed him his passport. "Is Miss Sarah Santorelli with you?"

"Yes, she is."

"Good." She passed over a second passport. "Let's go." Anthony followed her out the door.

In typical Italian style, the agent smiled down at the taxi driver and rapidly fired instructions. She opened the taxi door so Sarah could step back in. "You must return to Pisa and go to the train station for the connecting train to Nice." She slammed the taxi door and stepped away. "You must hurry."

"Wait." Sarah leaned out her window. "What about my aunt and Anthony's grandmother? We can't leave without knowing what happened to them."

Now You See It...

"I had only two passports placed in my safekeeping. That means the other passengers made it back to the ship," reassured the agent. "I was here 'til the ship set sail. Describe your aunt to me, maybe I'll remember."

"She's a short, stout woman with white curly hair, wearing a flowered dress."

Regrettably, the agent shook her head. "No, I'm sorry."

Apprehension radiated off Sarah's body like heat waves off a desert. Anthony leaned toward the open car window and tried again. "She was with my grandmother, who wore this really large straw hat with yellow roses on it."

A grin of recognition lit the agent's face. "Oh *si, si,* now I remember. Your *nonna,* she kept telling the woman with white hair to prepare her *cassa di morte,* her funeral casket. Her name was Emily, *si?*"

Oh Lord, what had her aunt done now?

"That would be my grandmother all right."

"Now you must hurry up," the agent banged on top of the taxi to signal the driver to get a move on. "Good luck," she yelled at their departing taxi as they waved their thanks through the back window.

Sarah sagged into her seat with a sigh of relief. "That's one less thing to worry about," she said, rubbing her tired eyes.

"Santo cielo!"

Anthony's sudden bark of harsh laughter startled her. Uncovering her eyes, Sarah frowned at him, his eyes conveying his fury within. "I don't think I want to know what you just said."

Anthony swatted the hair that the wind kept flopping in front of his eyes. "For the major part of this week we've baby-sat two seniors who never sit still. I don't know from one minute to the next if I'm coming or going."

He waved his hands around as he expressed his emotions. From the determined look in his eyes, Sarah figured he was just warming up.

"*Porcha misera!*" Stains of scarlet appeared on his cheeks. "How could two women just vanish from under our very noses?"

Sarah let him vent his anger and frustration. She knew it overflowed more from embarrassment than anger. From his self-mocking chuckle she knew he was mortified that two seniors could slip through his surveillance, and angry with himself for letting it happen.

"Those sly dears are smarter than we thought."

"You can't actually prove that," she replied. Yeah, and pigs could fly. Sarah watched the scenery zoom by and waited for Anthony to start back in. She didn't have to wait long.

"You want evidence? Let's put the past couple of days into perspective, shall we?"

Sarah shrugged. She already knew what was coming. "Be my guest."

"This is supposed to be a relaxing week. *Si?*"

He didn't wait for her answer but ploughed on. "Instead, we're dodging traffic to catch a train that might have already left because they purposely went back to the ship without us." With each point Anthony made his voice grow louder.

Sarah fidgeted in her seat as his frown darkened. So what if they'd had some minor incidents? Things always turned out fine.

"To top things off, your aunt and my grandmother booked us on some sort of Love Boat where women keep hitting on me." Anthony deflated against the seat. "Have I missed anything?"

Sarah ticked off her fingers. "You forgot the mugger you chased, the nudist beach our respective relatives found quite entertaining, the irate husband looking for his Dolly, being locked out of your cabin and having to sleep with a drunk female."

Anthony grunted his agreement.

"And last but not least, don't forget the spell. I wouldn't have to borrow your small supply of clothes if mine wouldn't keep disappearing." Sarah dropped her hands on her lap and clasped them together to stop them from shaking.

"I should have stayed at work."

As soon as they came to a stop at the train station, she jumped out while Anthony threw a large roll of euros at the driver before grabbing her hand. "Let's go."

Sarah tried to keep up but stumbled on some rocks. "Ouch. Can you cut me some slack?"

"No time," he replied, swinging her into his arms, making the air whoosh through her lips. He pushed open a door with his back and dropped her on top of the ticketing agent's counter. "*Due biglietti*, two tickets for Nice."

The smiling ticket agent gave Sarah a conspirator's wink and handed over their tickets. Again, Anthony scooped her into his arms, the pounding of his heart beating against her own frantic rhythm as they went back outside. He didn't put her down until they made the train.

Sarah dropped into her first-class seat as the departing whistle sounded. "Just in the nick of time." Her body shook with waves of relief as they pulled out of the station.

He collapsed into his chair and pushed against the back so his footrest would pop up. Sarah did the same as the last of her energy deserted her. They had five hours to travel before they could connect with their next train, which would take another hour to reach Nice in the early morning hours.

She tried to admire the ragged mountain slopes of Tuscany as they flew past her window. It was impossible. Her body solidified into a block of pain as the heat from her scorched and battered soles pulsed with each mile that passed. The grime that clung to her body made her even more uncomfortable, spoiling her enjoyment of the extremely old villages that embraced the bell towers and castles in their midst, and olive groves that colored the mountains with a rich green tapestry.

She'd run barefoot with the sun beating down on her. The interior of that first taxi hadn't helped either. Sarah shifted in her seat and grimaced when her dirty T-shirt stuck to her damp skin.

She couldn't figure out why her aunt had left without letting them know. But her sixth sense warned her that something wasn't adding up. Once she got back to the ship, she would get to the bottom of things. This type of behavior had to stop.

Taking a peek at Anthony, Sarah found him smiling and wondered if he had come to the same conclusion she had.

"Do you think they did it on purpose?" Sarah asked as a waiter approached, carrying two glasses of sparkling white wine.

Anthony removed the drinks from the waiter's tray and handed her a glass. "First drink, then talk."

She took a couple fortifying sips and looked apprehensively at Anthony. To her amazement, he chuckled.

"It took you this long to figure it out?"

Her mouth dropped open. "You knew?" She took a large gulp of wine.

"I wasn't sure, but the more I thought about it the more it made sense. My grandmother would never leave Florence without me." Anthony calmly sipped his wine. "Then there's the small matter that she kept telling your aunt she'd better order her funeral casket."

Sarah melted back into her seat with a resigned sigh. "That about covers everything."

"Those two meddling matchmakers outthought, outmaneuvered and succeeded in a hostile takeover without us even realizing what they were up to." Anthony shook his head. "I should appoint them to my board of directors."

Sarah put down her empty glass. "What I'd like to know is what we can do to stop them from meddling again?"

"The way I see it, we have two options." Anthony shifted in his seat and faced her. His eyes didn't mirror his smile. "If we confront them, it'll only upset and embarrass them. Then the dears will logically reason away their guilty consciences and start meddling again."

"That sounds about right."

"On the other hand, if we pretend that their scheme worked, the meddling will stop and we can enjoy the remainder of the cruise."

Sarah heard a heavy dose of sarcasm in her voice. "Hey, don't knock yourself out on my account." Fact was she liked his suggestion too much. "Look, they're grown adults. We just tell them enough is enough." She nervously twirled the stem of her empty glass and prayed that Anthony's stubbornness would kick in.

"And you honestly think that will stop your aunt?"

"No, but it's better than having to watch you grimace like you've got a pickle stuck up your butt for the rest of the cruise." She motioned to the steward for more wine.

Anthony folded his arms over his wide chest. "What is it about even pretending to be in love with me that scares you?"

"There's nothing about you that frightens me," Sarah said with false bravado. "But what about Rachael?"

He shrugged. "She was at a loose end and I helped her out. I enjoy her company but we're just friends. Now that that's settled we can stick together for the remainder of this cruise." He offered his hand for a handshake. "Deal?"

Sarah looked at Anthony's offered hand then up to his closed expression. "This would just be acting, right?"

"Sweetheart—you made that absolutely clear."

Never one to back down, Sarah firmly grasped his hand. "It's a deal."

Wrapping her hand in both of his, a satisfied smile spread across Anthony's face. Sarah instinctively tightened her grasp and held his stare.

"You've just placed yourself in a pair of very capable hands," he said and released her.

One second her hand had been surrounded by a boiling heat, and the next the air was teasing the cold sweat off Sarah's palm.

Glancing out at the darkening sky, Sarah concentrated on a distant clusters of lights gathered along the water's edge. Other scattered, isolated dots shimmered on the mountainside.

In his capable hands? she thought. *Tell me about it.*

After changing trains in Ventimeglia, they arrived in Nice just after midnight. Descending from the train, they stepped into a balmy darkness filled with the smells and sounds of France.

Newly washed roads shone like oil under welcoming streetlights that greeted them outside the station. Anthony grabbed a waiting taxi, opened the door and helped Sarah in so she wouldn't have to limp on her sore feet.

"Come on," he said, climbing in beside her.

"Now what?"

"We're going to the Carlton and in the morning we'll put on the best act those dears have ever seen," he said as the taxi drove into the heart of Cannes.

Now You See It...

Anthony watched the breeze ruffle Sarah's hair and blow loose strands against her face. She valiantly tried to stay awake, but every so often, her head would lull back as sleep tightened its grip on her tired body. Their ordeal wrung her final ounce of energy as Sarah dropped into the slumber her body craved.

He had to hand it to her. From the moment Lilly and Emily had gone missing, she had been magnificent. She hadn't complained once. Not from discomfort, being filthy or hungry. With no makeup on, her hair frazzled, her clothes rumpled — she was still the most beautiful woman he'd ever seen.

The taxi drew up to the Carlton's steps. Later in the day Sarah could admire the carved white sun-washed walls and turrets, but right now he leaned her against his body as they entered an opulent lobby. Crystal chandeliers lit the high elaborate gold ceilings, held by red and gold marble pillars.

A party of guests, women in designer gowns and expensive jewelry and men in their tuxedoes, exchanged grimaces as they judged Anthony and Sarah's appearance before moving on. He was happy that Sarah was oblivious to their surroundings.

"Ah, this feels good on my feet." Her sigh echoed in the cavernous room as she walked over gleaming, cool, diamond-patterned marble floors.

He gestured to an ornate gold-gilded chair near the check-in counter. "Have a seat."

Sarah dissolved into it, supporting her head on her hand as it rested on an armrest.

His platinum card and a generous tip quickly obtained them a room. Anthony lifted her to her feet. "Come on."

He wrapped her against his body and led her onto the elevator. "Don't fall asleep on me, we're almost there," he said, watching the floor numbers climb. He supported her to their room and straight to the washroom. "Will you be able to look after yourself?"

Sarah leaned forward and turned on the shower. "Of course I can, I've been doing it all my life." She waved him to the door. "Ring me from your room in the morning and we'll meet," she said and closed the door.

For a long moment, Anthony listened to Sarah moving around in the bathroom. He wanted to make sure she was okay. When he heard her step into the shower, he turned away and walked out onto the balcony overlooking the sea.

A full moon gifted the ocean with diamonds of lights as private yachts and sailboats rocked on a gentle lullaby of waves. A soft breeze massaged his tired muscles.

Hearing a noise behind him, Anthony turned from the balcony and stepped through the doorway to correct Sarah's misconception about their accommodations. The moon's rays penetrated the room from the open balcony door, casting Sarah in shadow and light, hinting at her beauty. Before he could open his mouth, Sarah stripped out of her robe and crawled into bed without noticing him.

A low growl rumbled from his chest and erupted into the silent room. Rubbing his face, Anthony allowed the day's events to finally rob his body of the remainder of his energy. Sitting down on the bed, he gently brushed her damp hair away from her angelic face. He knew that under that adorable, peaceful look lay a holy terror of volcanic proportions. Her Irish temper matched his Italian temperament any day.

He just couldn't figure out why he kept coming back for more. Since the day she'd crashed back into his life, his sanity had flown out the window and total chaos had reigned.

There was never a dull moment, but God, how much could one man take?

Sarah slowly awoke to high, cream-colored ceilings and remembered where she was. Bright sun streamed through open balcony doors as the ocean breeze played with the billowing sheers. The soft roar of waves crashing against the shore reached Sarah's ears.

Grasping an extra pillow against her nakedness, she rolled over and bumped into Anthony's shoulder as he slept. One of his hands lay above his head while the other rested on his stomach.

Like a Roman statue, Anthony was pure symmetry. From his wide forehead, down the cords of his neck to the large tanned hands, he was absolutely sinful.

This was her chance to take him off guard and sneak her way back into his heart. She'd use one of his strategies and storm his defenses. This was her point of no return.

Sarah traced her finger along his shadowed cheek, making his nose twitch. Gently holding a strand of his long hair, she feathered it along his sculpted cheeks and around the cleft in his chin.

An irritated expression flitted across his face as he absently swatted his hair away and settled deeper into his pillow. Sarah waited to see if he would awake. No sign of life yet.

Anthony's muscular upper body was bare for her enjoyment. With the tips of her fingers, she traced his ear and teased his earlobe where his diamond stud blinked at her. She lightly skimmed his collarbone, across his soft chest hair, gathered her courage and feathered her way down to his flat stomach.

Anthony's hand firmly grasped her wrist and stilled her flat palm against his stomach. Startled, Sarah's head jerked up in surprise and met Anthony's penetrating eyes.

"Good morning," he said.

Anthony's quiet stillness vibrated against Sarah's tightly held sense of anticipation and dread.

"Good morning." She swallowed her rising anxiety and cemented her courage and determination within her.

Slumberous, dark eyes focused behind long lashes, capturing her in their direct stare. Without breaking eye contact, Anthony raised her palm to his lips, kissing the fluttering heartbeat at her wrist.

It was the only spot he touched, but the excitement radiated from that point and filled her body, making her crave more. Her sensitive breasts brushed against the pillow, raising the urge to touch skin to skin.

Tugging her wrist free, she watched wariness enter Anthony's eyes as he narrowed his focus and waited to see if she had changed her mind.

With the smile of a temptress, Sarah traced her tongue along the soft fullness of his lips. "I wanted to see if you were still a morning person."

"And your conclusion?"

Sarah lifted her pillow away from her body, revealing her hardened nipples and exposing her state of arousal to Anthony's hungry eyes.

Sliding over, she brought her body flush against his. "Definitely a morning person." She enjoyed the pure male grin that replaced the lingering darkness in his eyes.

She buried her face against the corded muscles of his chest and whispered the rusty words that had been locked away in her heart for so long.

"I love you."

Anthony pulled her roughly, almost violently into his arms. A dam of passion broke as he grasped Sarah's hips and ground his arousal against her. Rolling her onto her back, he threaded his fingers through her sleep-rumpled hair and captured her lips, firm and hard. Anthony devoured her as Sarah matched his hunger with her own.

She wrapped her arms around his back and arched off the bed. He needed her with a desperation that frightened him. He could smell her arousal, could feel her fast shallow breaths as his chest rubbed against her swollen breasts. Her soft curves melted into the lean contours of his body as she softened further with desire.

Her heated reaction excited and fueled him. Sarah wrapped her legs around his waist and rocked back and forth, cradling his hips, letting the friction in their lower bodies build. His hands cupped her breasts and his lips and tongue laved her nipples as they swelled within his gentle grasp.

His hand seared a path over her quivering stomach, through her curls and gently separated her folds to find her swollen. Slipping a finger into her wetness, Anthony found her more than ready for him as her walls convulsed around his finger.

Softly moaning, Sarah lifted her head, joining their open mouths. With her tongue she showed Anthony exactly what she wanted. "More," she panted into his mouth.

Anthony pulled a condom from his wallet that sat on the nightstand and put it on. Supporting his weight on his elbows, he thrust forward into her tight welcoming center. Sarah's nails raked over his shoulders as her inner walls flexed around him, sending them spiraling higher.

Arching his back, he groaned in pleasure. He captured a nipple in his mouth and sucked hard as he continued to move in and out of her warmth. Increasing his pace, her impatient whimpers grew. Moisture gathered on Sarah's body as he gently wiped her hair from her face. She was absolutely beautiful lying there below him, trusting him.

When they had dated they had taken their pleasure in hurried snatches. This time was for Sarah's enjoyment. Clenching his jaw, Anthony slowed their tempo and brought his hand in between their bodies and pressed on her clitoris.

She screamed her release. Only then did he shatter in her arms, soaring higher and higher as his delight peaked.

Spent, Anthony dropped onto his side, rolling Sarah with him. He gathered her close to him and kissed the top of her head where it rested on his chest, certain she listened to the thunder of his heart quieting down as the storm of his reactions subsided. "You know, we'll never hear the end of it from Lilly and my grandmother."

"Speaking of the busybodies..." Sarah slid up Anthony's chest and smiled down at him. "The ship should have docked by now. Shouldn't we hurry back so that Aunt Lilly and Emily don't worry?" She played with Anthony's cleft.

"There's no need to rush over. Last night I sent a message to the ship. They're to meet us here for brunch at eleven o'clock." He looked at his watch. "It's ten-thirty, so we have plenty of time," he said and relaxed back onto his pillow, enjoying Sarah's caresses.

"No, we don't." Sarah rolled off Anthony and jumped off the bed, wrapping herself in the robe she had used the night before.

Anthony made a lunge across the bed. "Get back here," he said, but wound up empty-handed as she waltzed toward the balcony.

Moving the sheer curtains aside, she stepped out onto the balcony. "God, you should come and see how beautiful it is." He could hear the awe in her voice.

Anthony put his hands behind his head and sank back into his pillow. "I saw it last night—or early this morning. It's your turn to enjoy."

Wrapping her arms about herself, Sarah's joy bubbled into laughter. Today, the world was beautiful to her. Angel Bay sparkled a bright blue, a thousand twinkling lights played on the water as the morning breeze caressed the waves. Blue and white umbrellas flapped happily as guests set up their towels and beach paraphernalia before setting off to have breakfast.

Now You See It...

The thought of food reminded Sarah that she hadn't eaten since yesterday morning. Returning to the room, Sarah found Anthony sprawled on the bed, unconcerned with his nakedness.

"I'm hungry." Sarah eyes traveled down Anthony's aroused body back to his lecherous grin and chuckled. "For food."

"Who said that we couldn't satisfy two appetites?" He slowly unfolded his body from the bed.

Sarah scurried half-heartedly around the room's sofa.

"Anthony, be reasonable. We don't want to be late."

"After what they put us through, they can wait," Anthony said, circling the sofa. "In fact, a little waiting would be excellent penance."

Snatching one of the decorative gold pillows off the cream sofa, Sarah flung it in his direction. Miscalculating his position, she hit Anthony lower than she expected.

"Hey!" His fast reflexes saved him.

Sarah covered her giggles. "I'm so sorry." She stumbled as she tried to anticipate Anthony's next move. The playful smile he had worn a moment ago had been replaced with a lion's snarl.

Sarah raised her hands. "Now Anthony, don't go doing anything crazy," she said as she looked for an escape.

With lightning speed, Anthony captured her arms and within the blink of an eye, Sarah found herself flung over his shoulder. He bit her hip through the robe and purposely walked toward the washroom door.

"Cut that out." She held onto his sides as she bounced on his shoulder. From this angle, she had a great view of Anthony's backside. Each step he took flexed muscles she didn't know he had.

"I owe you one for that pillow incident."

Breathing heavily, Sarah made one last-ditch effort to reason with Anthony. "What about our clothes? We still have to buy a set for this morning." Her playful tension was replaced with sexually charged electricity that sparked excitement.

Anthony grunted. "It's been taken care of. There should be a bag already attached to our door filled with two sets of shorts and T-shirts, sandals and other miscellaneous items from one of the shops downstairs. Anything else, Santorelli?" Anthony slipped his hand under her robe and ran his fingers up her inner thigh, not missing a step.

Sarah squeaked as she tightened her muscles around Anthony's roving hand. "What if we compromise?"

"I'm listening." Anthony brushed his finger along her curls as he entered the bathroom. "I'm willing to negotiate," he said in his best boardroom voice.

Sarah lifted her head and turned to smile at Anthony's reflection. "You put me down and I promise to kiss it better."

Anthony's eyebrows disappeared under his hair.

Sarah found herself standing in front of Anthony with lightning speed. Lightheaded, she grasped his arms and held on as she adjusted to the topsy-turvy trip she'd just experienced. Once her head stopped spinning, Sarah caught her breath as she stared into a pair of still, deep eyes.

"I love the way you compromise."

Chapter Sixteen

"Ten bucks says my plan worked." Lilly eyes scanned over the tables located at the front of the hotel, overlooking the magnificent view of the bay. Still no sign of Anthony and Sarah.

Instead, she eyed the two women in tennis whites with artificially enhanced breasts and lips at the next table. She compared her dish—piled high with pastries, sausages, ham and eggs—to the fruit and cottage cheese they were eating, and snorted. If you asked her, keeping a size two was too much work.

Albert pulled out a chair for Emily then sat next to Lilly under a large white square umbrella. "Here." He slapped his money down on the table and Emily did the same. "If you're so sure your plan worked, then why are we sitting the farthest from the entrance, away from the line of fire?"

Lilly leaned to the side as a waiter poured her coffee. With each suspended minute that passed, she became more uncomfortable. "That way we can spot them first. If they're upset, I'll think of an alibi." Lilly took a large bite of her omelet. "It's either that or fake a heart attack."

"No heart attack and no more lying." Emily handed her cup to the waiter to top it off again. "If my Antonio is upset, we confess. *Capisci?*"

Lilly moved the food around on her plate. "We can't just give up so late in the game."

"Enough is enough." Emily bit into a croissant covered in chocolate.

"Ah, ladies," Albert pointed with his fork, "here they come."

"Here goes nothing." Lilly crossed her fingers.

Sarah stepped out of the hotel and came face-to-face with the brilliant blue sea. A row of umbrella tables followed the front of the hotel so that guests could enjoy the ocean's breezes.

"They're down near the end," Anthony said.

Looking down the length of tables she spotted three pairs of eyes, like deer caught in a car's headlights, staring back. None of the occupants at the table moved.

"How do you want to play this?" he asked. "I can wrap my arm around you and kiss you or not."

What Sarah wanted was to drag him back to the hotel room. Blissfully happy, she felt a warm glow flow through her. Her body had been shaken and was, for the first time in a long time, awake.

Sarah caressed a potted palm as she walked by tables filled with guests eating their breakfasts. "I'm looking forward to evening the score with my aunt."

Conspiring *with* Anthony, instead of against him, was refreshing. Goose bumps formed on her arms just thinking of joining forces with this beautiful man. And connecting in more ways than one.

Finally feeling secure in their relationship, her tower's walls had begun crashing down, liberating her locked soul to spiral upward with confidence.

Her aunt looked ready to bolt by the time they reached the table. "Good morning," Sarah said, her tone cold and devoid of her usual friendliness. "Did you sleep well?" she asked as Anthony pulled out her chair.

Her aunt played with the food on her plate and tried to change the subject. "My, don't we look special. With your matching white shirts, blue shorts and men's sandals," she frowned at Sarah's feet, "you look like two happy tourists."

"We're far from happy," Sarah said.

"Sarah?" Lilly's cheeks flamed red. "We can explain."

Sarah placed her elbows on the table and balanced her chin in her hands. "Please do. I'd like to hear what you have to say."

"Me, too." Anthony pinned his grandmother with his stare. "Were you sick?"

Two curly white heads shook. "No."

"Did you have an argument and didn't want to ruin the day for the rest of us?" Sarah asked.

"Neither." Aunt Lilly's answer came grudgingly.

"Were you tired?" Anthony asked.

Lilly's eyes latched onto that excuse, only to have Emily's dark scowl dash her hopes.

"None of the above," his grandmother stated.

Sarah was finding it difficult not to cave under their pathetic expressions. Anthony's leg nudging hers under the table wasn't helping any. "You do realize that if we hadn't been able to catch the train to Nice, you would be completing this cruise on your own?"

Emily folded and unfolded her napkin. "I need to explain—"

"No, I do, since it was my stupid idea," Aunt Lilly interrupted.

"Go on," Sarah said. Their guilty faces showed remorse. She'd let up on them soon.

"It was my idea to leave the two of you in Florence," Aunt Lilly said.

"We figured as much." Anthony's foot traveled up her calf and back down again.

She shot him a "stop that" look and turned her attention back to her aunt.

"We had hoped if you spent some time together by yourselves, without us in the way, you'd start talking," Emily said.

Aunt Lilly snorted. "Try more than talking."

"What these lovely ladies are trying to say is that they're sorry for sticking their noses where they didn't belong," Albert said and resumed his eating.

Lilly glared at his bent head. "Something like that." She stabbed a piece of grapefruit, dropped it into her mouth and grimaced. "I've learned my lesson. I'm minding my own business because all my plans are a dismal failure."

"Not all of them," Sarah said, nudging a basket of steaming hot rolls toward her aunt.

Aunt Lilly continued as if she hadn't heard. "I'm not as good at matchmaking as I am at casting spells."

"All in all, I think you did pretty good." Sarah smiled and waited for her words to sink in.

"I—" Aunt Lilly gasped. "What was that last thing you said?"

Sarah finally put her out of her misery. "Your plan worked."

"Oh my." Aunt Lilly deflated into her seat. "Oh my." She looked at Emily who was grinning and at Albert who continued to enjoy his breakfast. It took but a moment for the storm clouds to gather in her eyes.

"Of all the low-down, good-for-nothing—" Her mouth opened and closed. "Do you know what you just put me through?"

"Do you know what you put *us* through?" Anthony asked, standing and pulling Sarah out of her seat. "Let's get our own plates."

Now You See It...

Aunt Lilly bit into a roll. "Touché. How come you made such a hullabaloo about us taking this cruise anyway?"

Anthony patted Sarah on her behind. "I had to make a stink, otherwise she wouldn't have come."

Sarah rubbed her offended part and enjoyed the admiration that gleamed in her aunt's eyes.

Aunt Lilly swiped the money off the table, waved it under Emily and Albert's noses and stuffed it down her top. "I like this guy's style. For a moment there, I thought you were up to no good trying to stop us from coming."

"My type of trouble is the good kind." Grasping Sarah's hand, Anthony led her to the covered, hot chafing dishes. Waiters stood behind the table, ready to serve.

"That worked out quite well," Sarah said, handing him a plate.

"Yes it did." He accepted it and placed eggs Benedict on one side. "Now for today's plans." He dipped his finger in the hollandaise sauce and licked it. "If we take them to the village of Eze, they'll be able to see Villefranche and Beaulieu from there. We can browse through the flower market and tire them out quickly."

"Let's drive by Nice first to get a glimpse of the big homes and their gardens," Sarah suggested. "It's going to be a very full day."

There was a glint of humor in his eyes that promised devilment tonight.

"Here." Sarah piled a half-dozen slices of bacon onto his plate. "You're going to need all the energy you can get."

Anthony rented an air-conditioned minivan and everyone piled in, Sarah in front and the others in back, and they headed along the coast. They traversed over time-darkened bridges crossing gentle, tumbling streams that kissed steep lush banks, and entered another age.

Sarah sighed in contentment. This is what she'd always wanted with Anthony. Time together, to do everything or nothing. Just time spent together.

No cell phones, no cancelled dates and no interruptions while they made love. He was enjoying their time together just as much as she was.

"Why don't we head toward the mountains then turn back along the ocean?" Sarah suggested, looking out her window at the castles with turret towers and steep-pitched roofs crowning hilltops, their many sparkling windows blinking in the afternoon sun.

Anthony reached for her hand and peered into the rearview mirror. "Okay?"

"You're the driver." Aunt Lilly settled her ample body deeper in her seat. "So long as we don't have to walk a lot, don't get lost and can eat, you can take us wherever you want."

By late afternoon, Anthony pulled into a charming village so they could meander through an open marketplace. A cacophony of sounds and smells drew Sarah out of the van and onto the cobblestone streets.

"I'm starving," Aunt Lilly said.

"We'll buy some food and eat as we walk," Sarah said, hooking her arm through Anthony's and admiring the stands.

"Stick close by," Anthony said as he purchased fresh baguettes.

"There's no worry these ladies will get lost this time," Albert replied, buying a basket of dried fruits, nuts and cheeses.

A Frenchman with a white bushy moustache tipped his red beret at Emily as he rode by on his bike. *"Enchanté,"* he said as he rode on, his wicker basket brimming with cheese wrapped in green leaves and crusty loaves of bread ready to topple out at any moment.

Now You See It…

"Oh mamma mia." Emily followed the gentleman's progress 'til he disappeared through the stands.

"It's the Mancini blood," Anthony explained, tearing the end off the bread and popping it in his mouth. "It has a magnetic effect on the opposite sex."

Sarah contributed farm-churned butter and a bottle of rich red wine grown locally to complete a wonderful cornucopia to tantalize their taste buds. "Let's keep walking."

They strolled through artistically arranged fresh produce displayed next to the fresh catch of the day, and Anthony fed her bread covered with butter and shared his cup of wine. The day was perfect, not a cloud in the sky or shadow in her heart.

Sarah let her heart and mind run wild. Since she wore the extra set of clothes Anthony had bought for himself, she didn't have to worry that she'd end up naked in the middle of the street. She could give her full attention to Anthony.

With each caress and each morsel he fed her, Anthony stoked the fire that lay waiting for the briefest huff of air to bring it to life. The air crackled with anticipation each time they exchanged knowing smiles. Basking under his attention, Sarah felt cherished, special.

What a fool she'd been to waste so much time. From here on in, it was full steam ahead. She could really enjoy the day knowing that her clothes wouldn't disappear on her. She flexed her toes in the men's sandals she wore, very roomy and quite comfortable.

Sarah inhaled the heated aroma of the sweet bougainvillea flowers that draped the balconies, their trellised doors open.

Near the lapping water of this quasi-French cove, painters and artisans worked and displayed their wares.

Sarah admired a quaint streetscape in oils depicting a long sloping set of stone stairs ascending to an open doorway covered in brilliant bougainvilleas. Ivy-covered sun-kissed walls reached a terra-cotta roof. The fading sunrays lit on a dormant cat as it lazily passed the waning hours of the afternoon away.

She felt just like that cat. Warm. Content.

Anthony draped his arm around her shoulders. "Thinking of buying it?"

"Yup." She opened her purse.

Anthony stopped her hand from reaching into her bag. "Let me buy it for you," he said and handed the smiling old man the euros in exchange for the wrapped painting.

He tucked it under his arm and smiled. "This is where you're supposed to kiss me for my generosity. Besides, we should show your aunt how well her plan worked."

Sarah wrapped her arms around his neck, stood on tiptoe and kissed him. Under the hot sun, their bodies melted together. Out of breath, Sarah finally leaned back. "Do you think that convinced her?"

Anthony glanced sideways and shook his head. "Not quite." He tipped her chin with his finger. "Let's give it another go."

Sarah closed her eyes, letting her body radiate toward Anthony's, magnifying the feeling of belonging. Anthony slanted his lips across hers as her world shrank until only the two of them existed. Somewhere between arguing over the sensibility of this cruise and waking up together in Nice, she had fallen in love again.

She knew he cared deeply for her, but even after making love a second time in the shower, he hadn't said the words she wanted to hear. Tightening her shaking fingers around Anthony's neck, Sarah slowly pulled away and stared with rounded eyes at his endearing face.

"Are you all right?" he asked.

Sarah nodded. She wouldn't let her dwindling insecurities ruin a perfect day. She cleared her throat only to have a soft squeak emerge. "Sure, couldn't be better."

"I don't know. You've gone pale and I can feel your body shake."

Sarah wet her suddenly dry lips. "It must be all the sun. Let's sit in the shade with my aunt." She dropped into a rattan chair and ordered ice water.

The aroma of strong fresh coffee filled the air as waiters bustled around taking orders and refilling baskets with croissants. Breathing in a fortifying gasp of air, Sarah plastered a smile on her face and looked up. Four pairs of eyes smiled back at her. Her aunt's old eyes crinkled with a wise smile.

"Sorry, what was that you said?" Sarah gulped her water and felt it cool her parched throat and mouth. "Too much sun."

Aunt Lilly chuckled. "It's not the sun that's making you lightheaded."

When it was time to climb back into the van, Aunt Lilly casually maneuvered everyone. "Emily dear, why don't you sit in front this time next to Anthony and enjoy the view? If no one minds, I think I'll sit quietly in the back next to Sarah, while Albert catches a snooze in the middle seat."

No sooner had they left than soft music and Albert's gentle snores filled the van. Her aunt's gentle touch drew her attention. As they drove toward the docks, her aunt's patient eyes waited. Sarah lowered her voice. "How'd you figure it out?"

"That you're in love?"

Sarah nodded.

"You have that same look that your dear mother had when she first met your father." Aunt Lilly shook her head and chuckled. "It was like she was standing on tracks as she stared at the train coming toward her. She wasn't sure if she should jump out of the way or wait for it to hit her."

"What did she do?" Sarah loved hearing about her parents.

"She went into hiding. But your father, being the smart cookie that he was, pretended that he didn't notice her."

"That's really stupid Italian thinking." That earned her a slap on her knee. "How could it work if they were both avoiding each other?"

"You have to understand that your mother was like your sister Amanda. Reserved and timid. She'd settled into her job at the library and never ventured out much. She lived her fantasies through the books she read. Then one day, in walked your dad." A soft sigh escape as a far-off look entered her aunt's eyes. "Tall, dark and one-hundred percent Italian with his accent and old-fashioned manners. He was a true gentleman."

"So what did he do?"

"He pretended that he didn't speak English that well and was looking for books to read so that he could improve. He showed up week after week after week. Eventually, he started waiting for your mother at the end of her day. He told her that it wasn't wise for good girls to walk alone at night."

Sarah smiled. "What a smooth operator."

Aunt Lilly's eyebrows rose. "Sound familiar? Anyway, each night that he dropped your mother off at the house, he'd take a step or two closer. At first, he would stop at the end of the walk and watch your mother wave as she entered the house. Then the bottom of the porch steps. Until finally he was invited through the front door. And like they say, the rest is history."

Sarah grinned. "He played the waiting game and made my mother come to him."

"So now that you know you get your reluctant streak from your mother and your tenacity from your dad, what do you intend to do?" she asked as their ship came into view.

Now You See It...

"I'm going to let Anthony walk through my cabin door tonight. And speaking of tonight, can I have that famous bag of condoms you have stashed away?" In her mind, she was already planning Anthony's evening and early morning hours.

Aunt Lilly hooted, startling Albert from his nap while Anthony peered through the rearview mirror and Emily looked over her shoulder. Aunt Lilly gave Emily a thumbs-up. "I thought you'd never ask."

Sarah wrapped her arm around her aunt's padded shoulders and gave her a big hug. "You're too much."

"So where do you want me to deliver the goods?"

"To my cabin," Sarah said as Anthony parked the van at the rental dealer close to the ship.

"Consider it done."

Anthony swiped his boarding pass. "Anyone up for a drink on deck before we head to our cabins?" He adjusted Sarah's painting under his arm.

"Count us out." Aunt Lilly threaded her arms through Emily's and Albert's. "Emily and I have things to do and Albert is going to his cabin to recharge his batteries for the evening ahead."

Albert scratched his head. "I am?" He dropped his hand and shrugged. "Sounds like a plan to me." Arm in arm, they left for their cabins.

Anthony offered his other arm to Sarah. "Let's go."

Passing the front desk, one of the stewards recognized Anthony. "Mr. Mancini? There's a message waiting for you."

"This shouldn't take long." He drummed his fingers on the check-in counter, his eyes clouding with uneasiness.

"Do you want me to stay?"

Anthony handed her the painting. "Why don't you go to your cabin and freshen up and I'll catch up with you."

With winged feet, Sarah floated to her cabin. From the chuckles of the passengers she passed, she knew she wore a stupid grin. She shrugged. What the heck, she was finally happy. And tonight there would be no shadows across her heart. It would be just her, Anthony and the brilliance of all her tomorrows.

In her cabin, she leaned the painting against the wall and pulled from her closet a gold organza evening skirt that fell in folds around her ankles. From another hanger, she took a sheer camisole and from the bottom of her closet she grabbed evening sandals.

This was one time she would finally get to use the spell to her advantage. She could really strip in style. She wouldn't have to lift a finger and her clothes would return to their original spots. No hanging, no folding, no cleaning.

From a chest of drawers she selected a skin-colored lace bra and panty set. "This is going to be great." She'd pin up her hair so the spell could do the honors of unclipping it. It would set the mood for the evening to come.

Sarah turned on her shower and was kicking off her sandals when she heard a knock on the door. If it was Anthony, she'd send him to his cabin so she could get ready, she decided as she opened the door.

"Here you go." Aunt Lilly passed her the bag. "Have fun," she said, hurrying away.

"Thanks," Sarah called out to her aunt's retreating back.

She gave a backward wave, acknowledging that she had heard and kept on walking.

Sarah quickly showered and patted herself dry, sprayed her body with the perfume Amanda had given her then dressed with the clothes she had laid out. She blow-dried her hair and pinned it up.

She could hear Anthony moving about in his cabin and that's where she wanted to be. Goose bumps of eagerness rose on her arms as impatient shivers of delight shook her spine.

She wiped her damp palms on her skirt. This was it. Grabbing the bag of condoms from her night table, Sarah left her cabin in high spirits. Once in the hall, she found Anthony's door slightly open. Smart man.

Her body vibrated with new life as she stepped over the threshold. Just as she expected, her clip disappeared, making her hair cascade in front of her face. "Oops." She threw her hair away from her eyes so she could see and laughed.

He managed a small, tentative smile. "I'm glad you're here. I have a Lear jet waiting and I don't have much time."

She found a shirtless Anthony throwing clothes into the luggage that sat on his bed.

"What are you doing?" she asked, following his agitated movements from one side of the cabin to the other. *What are you doing?* Stupid question. She could see he was packing. She closed the door and leaned against it as her heart sank into the ground. This couldn't be happening.

"Sweetheart, I'm about to lose my company." Anthony ran into the washroom, grabbed his shaving kit and threw it into his luggage. "I'm so glad you're here so I don't have to worry about anyone while I straighten out what's going on back home."

Fear and anger knotted inside her, turning her body into a block of ice. She pushed off the door and on legs that shook, followed him around the room as he opened drawers.

When she touched his arm to gain his attention her sandals disappeared. *Damn spell*, she thought. "Not now." She ground her teeth.

"I *have* to leave now. Carmichael's finally made their move to become a major shareholder in my company." Anthony threw on a clean white shirt and buttoned it up. "They're house builders and my carpentry company would go hand in hand with their operation."

"Oh God, I'm so sorry." She opened her arms to hug him when her camisole vanished. "I said not now," Sarah yelled at the ceiling.

"Oh God," Anthony groaned. "Sarah you're so damn beautiful and I hate that I have no choice." He clasped her face in his hands and kissed her. He nodded to a pile of clean T-shirts, silk shirts and shorts on his bed. "Those are for you," he said and tucked his shirt into his pants. "I knew I shouldn't have come on this cruise."

Stunned and sickened, she repeated his words. "You shouldn't have come on this cruise?" Hadn't the time they shared meant anything to him?

Sarah pulled on a T-shirt that reached mid thigh and flipped her hair out. With both hands on her hips, she confronted him. "Since I've known you, you've worried that someone would take your company away. Well, it's finally happening." She took a step toward him. "Let it go, can't you see how much it's destroying your life?"

His features hardened. "You don't get it. You've never understood. This company *is* me." He jabbed his finger at his chest. "My blood, my sweat, my life."

She grabbed his arm when he tried to pass. Sheer anger swept through her. "You don't have a life."

He threw her hand off his arm. "I'm not going to lose my business." With a swift jerk, he zipped up his suitcase. "If I hadn't put off my phone calls for days this takeover wouldn't have happened."

"But you're willing to throw our relationship away—again!" Sarah fisted her hands at her sides, engulfed in anger and sadness. "I'm always going to come in a distant second, aren't I?"

He tried to pull her into his arms but she blocked him. "Don't do this to us," he pleaded, putting his hands on her shoulders and holding her still. "You've got to trust me. Please."

He hadn't changed. "I promised myself that I wouldn't go through this hell again." Tears fell down her face. Her dreams had burned to ashes.

She tried to pull out of his hands. "I hate you."

His complexion paled as she continued, "But I hate myself more for being so gullible a second time."

"Once you get back from the cruise, things will be different." He looked at his watch and swore. "I have to go. The plane is on standby."

The last drops of hope drained from her body, leaving her hollow.

"Anthony, this is goodbye." She wiped at her tears as raw grief overwhelmed her.

His pained gasp sounded like someone had stabbed him. He pulled her to him and kissed her. "I'm sorry."

With a final kiss, he ran out the door.

Damn him. Damn his stupid, thick Italian hide. He'd made his choice. Again, she'd come in a poor second.

Moments later, the blast of the horn signaled that the ship was setting sail. Sarah lifted her skirt and raced onto the deck to get a final glimpse of him. Heart pounding, her body wrenched into a million pieces, she raced along the railing but he was nowhere in sight.

The wind pushed small dark puffy clouds swiftly across the sky, forming them into a storm. Below, the sea looked shadowy as waves slapped the sides of the ship. Sarah tucked her wind-whipped hair behind her ear, oblivious to the cold.

A single tear trickled down Sarah's cheek to be promptly dried by the wind. The sky was now a blanket of gray. The sea looked menacing as the ship slowly left its docks. Deeper and more turbulent, the waves rushed the sides of the ship then retreated.

What a fool she was.

He was sorry? What had he meant by that? Sorry that he'd had to leave? Sorry that he hadn't changed? Sorry that he didn't return her emotions? She was sure by the time Anthony reached home he would consider this cruise a write-off. He wasn't coming back.

Gripping the railing, she realized she still held the package her aunt had given her. "This is what is called being left holding the bag." Sarah threw it overboard into the churning waves below, along with her dreams.

Chapter Seventeen

One moment Sarah was leaving her suitcase outside her cabin for early morning pickup, and the next she was anxiously searching around the milling people pulling their bags off the moving carousel in Toronto.

Since Anthony's departure, time had flown in a misty haze for the remainder of the cruise. She'd felt detached, watching everything go by as though she were an outsider. Time's steady passage had moved her closer to home. Tomorrow had come too soon.

Heart pounding, Sarah pulled her bag away from the waiting crowd. *Keep smiling, keep smiling.* All she had to do was hand Emily over to Anthony and then she would never have to see him again. Each time she thought of him, a nervous flutter took hold of her heart. She was of two minds. One half wanted to see him and the other half wanted to run as fast and as far as she could.

"You see anyone yet?" she asked.

"You're a foot taller than we are." Aunt Lilly stuck close to Emily. "Keep looking."

Sarah looked at their sad faces. They had said their goodbyes to Albert in Spain with the promise of reuniting.

Sarah wiped her moist palms on her shorts and, with her suitcase, ploughed forward. A piercing whistle caught her attention, making her stomach end up in her mouth. She took a fortifying breath and straightened her back. "Here goes nothing."

A second later, Sarah was looking into the grinning faces of Mark and Amanda. She gritted her teeth. *What a stupid fool I am.*

Her strength melted into the floor, leaving her numb and tired. She'd been on pins and needles for nothing. Hurt and relief confused her already muddled mind, while self-loathing grew for putting so much importance on this moment. She'd psyched herself up for nothing.

Sarah held back while Aunt Lilly and Emily exchanged jubilant hugs with Mark and her sister and excitedly recounted their adventures. When it was her turn, Sarah hid her disappointment behind a smile and joined the fold. But it didn't wash with her sister.

"Welcome back." Amanda gave her an understanding look.

Sarah bravely returned her hug. "Thanks."

"Sorry, I know we're second-best, but Anthony couldn't make it," Mark said as he tightly embraced her.

She stepped back and shrugged. "It's no big deal."

"So who will take me home?" Emily asked.

Amanda smiled. "No one."

"*Cosa?*"

"Anthony's in New York so you're staying with Aunt Lilly and Sarah and me, until he can pick you up."

A wave of apprehension coursed through Sarah. Now the suspense of their next meeting would start all over again. This was torture on her nerves.

As one day led into another, Sarah's moods swung between anger and agitated worry. She was so upset that she couldn't concentrate on her work. "Shit." She pushed her chair away from her computer and pulled her fingers through her hair.

Now You See It...

The ruckus outside her window wasn't helping either. Someone had bought *her* house. That's what she'd called the large Victorian inside her head. Another lost dream. An odd twinge of disappointment filled her heart.

Hammering and sawing started first thing in the morning and lasted into the evening. Today was no exception. She just hoped that tomorrow, being Saturday, they wouldn't work.

Sarah covered her ears in frustration. She could still hear the insistent pounding. "I give up," she said and went to the kitchen.

There, she found Aunt Lilly and Emily happily chatting as they ate omelets and salads for lunch.

"Hungry?" Aunt Lilly stood up.

Sarah waved her away and stuck her head in the fridge. "Keep eating, I'll fix myself something," she said and pretended to search for ingredients for a salad. "Has Anthony called?"

"No, dear. Why don't you call him?" Aunt Lilly asked.

Sarah shut the fridge door with a snap. Forget about it. She might as well go upstairs and practice wearing her own clothes. Her longest record before they disappeared was three hours.

"What about lunch?" Aunt Lilly asked.

Sarah waved her question away. "I'm not hungry anymore," she said and walked out of the kitchen.

"Stubborn puss," Aunt Lilly griped, watching Sarah walk out of the kitchen. Something had to be done.

"Hmm." Emily crossed her arms over her chest.

Lilly met her accusing stare. "What?" She took a bite of her omelet.

"Why did you lie? We talk to Antonio every day while he works next door."

"I know. And each time we go over to bring drinks and cookies what does Anthony ask?"

Emily sighed. "If Sarah is home."

Those two were pathetic. "And each time we tell him to go check for himself, what does he say?" Lilly drummed her fingers against the table.

Emily deflated in her seat. "'Maybe later', but later never comes."

Lilly rubbed her hands together. "I have an idea."

Bright and early Saturday morning, Sarah awoke to the sound of sawing and hammering. "Damn it." She buried her head under her pillow. "Can't a person get any sleep around here?"

She threw the pillow across the room. "I should walk over there and give them a piece of my mind."

Instead, she grabbed a cup of coffee and escaped to a day of serious clothes shopping. Maybe by the time she got back, the workers next door would have left.

She felt much calmer and in control by the time she got back home. Her bedroom was littered with shopping bags sporting designer labels, and shoe boxes.

She smiled at her reflection. "This is it." She twisted her hair into a French bun and added a touch of makeup.

She straightened her new red pantsuit. "I can do this." Sarah ignored the shadows of doubt that lingered in her eyes.

Come hell or high water she was going out with a group of friends for dinner. In her own clothes. And she wasn't bringing any spares along. She'd impose an iron will on her mind and not one thought of you-know-who would slip through.

Practicing the breathing exercise she'd learned for her fear of flying had worked better on her nerves than she'd thought possible. "Keep focused. Think of work. Of dinner. Of anything."

Anything but him.

She could do this. Folding her jacket over her arm, she walked into the kitchen. "I'm off—" she started, her grin, along with her jacket, vanishing when she spotted Anthony seated between her aunt and his grandmother, eating sunflower seeds.

Shock ran through her. "Son of a bitch."

"It's nice to see you too."

"Like hell it is." This is where he'd come into her life the last time. In her kitchen, right after Aunt Lilly had cast her spell. And he could just walk back out again.

"Did you see that?" Aunt Lilly sat up in her seat. "Where'd your jacket go?"

Sarah looked up at the ceiling. "In my room."

Anthony patted Aunt Lilly's hand. "It's okay," he said and continued to eat sunflower seeds. "You just saw the result of your spell."

"My spell makes your clothes disappear?" Her aunt's face lit with excitement.

"Unfortunately." Sarah took a step toward the kitchen door.

"Yup." Anthony balanced his chair on its back legs and grinned at her. Didn't the man have any meetings to go to?

"And no one thought to mention this to me?" Aunt Lilly waved her hands about, scattered sunflower seeds on the floor.

Sarah fisted her hands on her hips. "There was no way in hell I was going to hand over such incriminating information."

"Why not?"

"Because I know you. You did enough conniving on the cruise without me adding fuel to the fire. It would have only made you more unpredictable than you already are."

Aunt Lilly sank back in her seat and grinned. "Your clothes are disappearing. How lovely."

Sarah snorted.

"And I bet that's why Anthony gave you his clothes on the cruise," Aunt Lilly said.

"You catch on quick," he said.

Aunt Lilly pinched him. "*You* don't."

"Ouch." Anthony dropped the chair forward. "What was that for?"

"He was a gentleman and you pinch him?" Emily asked.

"Think." Lilly tapped the side of her head. "One small cabin and a convenient spell that makes clothes disappear." She threw her hands up in the air. "I don't believe this. They could have been naked for a week and we wouldn't have had to lift a finger."

Emily hit Anthony on the side of his head. "*Stronzo!*"

"Hello? People?" Sarah tapped her foot. "I'm still here you know. And nothing more has vanished."

Anthony stood up. That was one problem he would soon fix. It was time to put the spell to good use. "The two of you stay put," he said to Lilly and Emily as he walked around the table. "I've got some groveling to do." He advanced as Sarah back-pedaled out of the kitchen.

"Enjoy your visit." A shadow of alarm touched her face. "I have to go," Sarah said, aiming for the front door.

"Not so fast." He clasped her wrist and the clip vanished from her hair, toppling her hair in front of her face. Good, the spell was working.

Sarah threw her hair over her shoulder and glared at her aunt, who had followed them into the hallway. "Do something."

Aunt Lilly chuckled. "Oh, you're doing just fine."

Anthony backed her up the stairs. "You," he said, looking down at Lilly and his grandmother at the bottom of the stairs, "not a step more." He turned his attention back to Sarah.

"That's it, Mancini, I've had enough." She pushed against his chest and her shoes disappeared.

"With you it's never enough." He wouldn't let her freeze him out. "We need to talk."

She climbed the final step. "I don't want to talk to you."

He joined her on the landing. "Things have changed."

"What kind of fool do you think I am?" She took a step backward. "You've said that before."

"I know you're mad and you have every right to be." He edged her toward her bedroom. "If you want to punch me, go ahead." He tightened his abdomen. "Take a swing, you've earned it."

"You idiot!" She pulled her arm back and socked him in the stomach, making the air whoosh out of his lungs. She cradled her hand against her chest and marched toward her room.

"Damn, that hurts," he exclaimed, rubbing his stomach. He opened his mouth to say more but her pants disappeared, leaving him speechless. He closed his eyes and swallowed a groan. "Nice bottom, Santorelli."

Sarah screeched and pulled at her short shirt to cover her. "Go to hell." She ran down the hall, dodged into her bedroom and tried to close the door in his face.

Anthony stopped it with his hand, stepped into her room and slammed the door behind him. How was a guy supposed to apologize when she kept running away from him? Turning the key, he pulled it out of the lock and slid it under the door. "Just hear me out."

"Get out." She pointed to the door with a finger that shook.

"Can't." He took a step toward her and she put the bed between them. He raised his hands in surrender. "Listen to me."

"No," she said, covering her ears.

He stormed up to her and pulled her hands down. "I sold my company."

She yanked her hands out of his, her shock passing quickly. "Good for you."

"Don't you get it? I'm finally free to do what I want, when I want."

Sarah narrowed her eyes. "What's to stop you from turning around and building another company 'til it consumes you again?"

He rubbed his face and sighed. "Because I won't. All I'm asking is that you give me another chance. You've never let me down and—"

"I wish I could say the same of you." Sarah hugged her arms around herself. "I'm not ever coming in second again." Tears shimmered in her eyes. "You broke my heart."

Her jacket reappeared on the bed. Oh, hell. Anthony pulled his fingers through his hair. Her clothes were supposed to disappear as her feelings grew for him, not come back. Icy fear twisted him in knots. He was losing her.

"I'm going to invest in our relationship. Have you forgotten what we shared on the ship?" he asked.

Sarah laughed sarcastically. "That was sex."

Sarah's anger transformed her, made her vulnerable as layers of her disguise melted away. It made her all the more beautiful and reinforced what Anthony knew. Buried inside was a woman of deep emotions. He knew that her fury hid her fear of abandonment, her vulnerability. Just the thought of how she was suffering tore at his insides.

He read her stubbornness in the tilt of her chin, the glower of her eyes. He had to demolish her walls, once and for all. Not reaching her wasn't an option. She left him no choice.

"Liar." He dragged her into his arms. "You feel the same things I do." Anthony focused his dark penetrating stare on Sarah.

Sarah blushed. "I have no idea what you're talking about." She wouldn't look at him, but from the flush of her skin he knew she felt his length press against her stomach.

Anthony gently shook her and watched those damn shutters close over her emotions. "The only difference between the two of us is that I can't hide what you do to me."

"It's only a physical attraction that will soon go away," Sarah refuted. "What you're feeling is lust. It's common when people are on holiday. You'll soon hop to the next lady you fancy."

"Don't insult me." Anthony's body heated with anger. "Would a man in lust buy the house next door?"

She gasped with surprise.

"Would he sell his company so it doesn't come between the women he loves and his dreams with her?" He brushed her hair away from her face while lowering his own. "It's one-hundred percent, all-consuming love."

Her eyes filled with hope. "You solemnly swear no more deals?"

"Only if we've talked them out and we're both on board."

The jacket vanished again. The tight knot in the pit of his stomach unraveled.

"God, even to contemplate this is crazy. This will be your third strike. If you fail you're out."

"I have no intention of failing." He unbuttoned his shirt and threw it across the room. "Now that I've worn your stubbornness down, I intend to lick this spell. So where were we?"

"Not so fast." Her infectious grin challenged him. "You can work for it, buster."

Sarah took a step back and began reciting accounting principles. "When reconciling your bank statement, tick off your debits and credits and input all remaining items." She looked anywhere but at him.

Trying to distract herself only made him want to up the ante. He wasn't going to cave from such a small hurtle. "You're going to run your hair all over my body after I've done the same to you."

Her eyes drew wide and her skin flushed. "Stop that." Sarah stuck her fingers in her ears and sang.

He pulled off his boots, socks and pants. His arousal filled the front of his boxers. "You're going to wrap those lovely legs around my waist."

Her top disappeared. "Quit putting thoughts into my head," she exclaimed, gripping the sides of her bra and holding on for dear life.

"They've always been there." He rested his hands on his hips. "I'm waiting."

Sarah looked up to the ceiling. "If a difference is divisible by nine you have transposed two numbers." She peeked down to her chest. Her hands were her only cover.

Anthony chuckled. "I knew you wouldn't let me down."

He pulled her against his chest and plundered her lips. Shock waves traveled through her as she absorbed Anthony's heat.

Their lips meshed, sweeping Sarah deeper into the celebration. Emotions flared as Anthony's kisses forced her emotions higher.

Secure in the warmth of Anthony's arms, Sarah was overwhelmed as a feeling of being cherished washed over her.

Anthony threaded his fingers through her hair and, tilting her head, thoroughly tasted her lips. He was taking control of her body. Her mind.

A crack formed around her heart, letting feelings of belonging seep in. The remaining doubts soon took flight, leaving an inner peace that left her weightless.

Sarah wet her lips and took a step back so he could see what was going to come next.

"Now you see it…"

With a blink of an eye the black thong underwear she had been wearing disappeared.

"…and now you don't."

Anthony's eyes widened. There was no escaping the message she was sending him. She believed in him completely. Their timing was finally perfect.

"Lady, it's about time," Anthony discarded his boxers and swung Sarah onto the bed.

Her body greedily took what it craved. Sarah moaned and lost control. Threading her fingers through his hair, Sarah held him tightly. "God, I love you." Her shivers transmitted themselves from her body to his.

Anthony rolled her over, captured her hands above her head and slid his leg between her thighs. He trailed quick hot kisses over her cheeks, down her neck and past her collarbone until he reached her breast.

He licked a turgid nipple, laving it at his leisure before gently blowing it dry as his fingers found more pleasure points. Tremors of need shook her body as currents of pleasure coursed from her breast down to her hot, wet center, liquefying her body.

Her nails bit into Anthony's skin. Her head moved from side to side. She made tiny frantic sounds of surrender as she drew closer to her climax.

In the throes of passion, Sarah looked into Anthony's earnest eyes and greedily grasped what they offered, rediscovering small parts of herself that she'd locked away. He'd freed her heart and healed her soul.

With shaking hands, Sarah reached up and pulled his beautiful face down for a kiss filled with hope and promise. He moved his mouth over hers, devouring what she freely gave.

Her gentle kiss quickly filled with longing then escalated to one of urgency. Sarah channeled all her old feelings of abandonment to ones of fulfillment. Flames engulfed her body to cauterize old wounds.

The fire inside her burned out of control as his skilled hand pressed on her lower abdomen, causing quivers beneath his palm. Sarah sucked in her breath. "Anthony!"

She peered into warm, trusting eyes. "I'm here. I'll always be here for you."

Together, they shattered in each other's arms.

Moist warmth cocooned her body as he gathered her in his arms and held her snugly. Her heart pounded against his as their breathing returned to normal. He brushed the hair away from her face, his gaze a loving caress.

She traced his lips with her finger. "You think we licked the spell?"

Anthony buried his face in her neck and shrugged. "It doesn't matter."

"It does to me." Sarah pulled out of Anthony's arm and got out of bed.

"Where are you going?"

"I want to see something." She picked the jacket up off the floor and slipped it on. "Or more precisely, *not* see something."

Anthony sat up in bed. "You want me to do anything?"

She nodded as she buttoned up the jacket. The silk fabric barely covered her thighs. "Talk dirty to me."

Anthony threw his head back and laughed. "With pleasure."

He slipped out of bed, his intention all too obvious. "I'm taking you for a long, wet ride." He pointed to the bathroom behind them. "Only after you've begged me and can't stand up any more, I'm going to bend you over in the shower and enter you from behind."

"Oh my." Sarah's cheeks heated, but the jacket remained. "It's still here. The spell is broken!" she laughed. "That's a big relief." She looked up and came nose to nose with Anthony. The gleam in his eyes promised a wicked future. "The disappearing act is officially over."

"That's easily remedied." With torturous slowness he unbuttoned his way down the jacket.

"Now you see it…"

He brushed the jacket off her shoulders and let it fall to the ground.

"…and now you don't." He kissed his way up her shoulder to her neck and gave her a love bite.

She sucked in her breath. "You're not disappointed?"

"No." He led her into the bathroom and turned on the shower. "I like stripping you myself." He pulled her with him under the warm spray of water. His hands grasped her bottom as he rubbed against her.

She brought her hand between their bodies and cupped him. "So long as I can do some divesting of my own." She ran her hand up and down his shaft. "Deal?"

His Adam's apple moved up and down. "Deal."

"Now we're in business."

Downstairs, Lilly sent dark looks at the ceiling. "I can't stand the suspense any more. If they don't come down soon

I'm liable to go up there." She touched her hot cheeks with her cool hands. No she wouldn't.

"*Pazienza,*" Emily said, rearranging her cards.

"You're cheating," Lilly said.

"Just like you taught me." Emily moved two more cards about.

"After everything those two have put us through you'd think the least they could do is let us know what's going on." Lilly opened a box of chocolates and started eating.

Emily chuckled. "We know what they're doing."

"That's not what I meant. They've been an hour in the shower."

"We wanted them together and now they are. For once just sit and be quiet."

"I can't." Aunt Lilly stood up. "Come on."

"Where you go?" Emily followed.

"This is making me nervous."

"*You're* making me nervous," Emily retorted, following Lilly to the washroom door.

"Watch and learn." Lilly flushed the toilet and they heard banging on the walls.

Emily grinned. "Oh *capito*, may I?"

Aunt Lilly waved Emily toward the toilet. "Be my guest."

With relish, Emily flushed the toilet again. This time a loud shriek was heard. "They'll come down soon."

Laughing, the two old women toddled back into the kitchen.

"My plans always work," Lilly bragged, preparing a pot of coffee. "So, how many grandchildren do we want?"

Why an electronic book?

We live in the Information Age—an exciting time in the history of human civilization, in which technology rules supreme and continues to progress in leaps and bounds every minute of every day. For a multitude of reasons, more and more avid literary fans are opting to purchase e-books instead of paper books. The question from those not yet initiated into the world of electronic reading is simply: *Why?*

1. *Price.* An electronic title at Ellora's Cave Publishing and Cerridwen Press runs anywhere from 40% to 75% less than the cover price of the exact same title in paperback format. Why? Basic mathematics and cost. It is less expensive to publish an e-book (no paper and printing, no warehousing and shipping) than it is to publish a paperback, so the savings are passed along to the consumer.
2. *Space.* Running out of room in your house for your books? That is one worry you will never have with electronic books. For a low one-time cost, you can purchase a handheld device specifically designed for e-reading. Many e-readers have large, convenient screens for viewing. Better yet, hundreds of titles can be stored within your new library—on a single microchip. There are a variety of e-readers from different manufacturers. You can also read e-books on your PC or laptop computer. (Please note that Ellora's Cave does not endorse any specific brands. You can check our websites at www.ellorascave.com

or www.cerridwenpress.com for information we make available to new consumers.)
3. ***Mobility.*** Because your new e-library consists of only a microchip within a small, easily transportable e-reader, your entire cache of books can be taken with you wherever you go.
4. ***Personal Viewing Preferences.*** Are the words you are currently reading too small? Too large? Too… ANNOYING? Paperback books cannot be modified according to personal preferences, but e-books can.
5. ***Instant Gratification.*** Is it the middle of the night and all the bookstores near you are closed? Are you tired of waiting days, sometimes weeks, for bookstores to ship the novels you bought? Ellora's Cave Publishing sells instantaneous downloads twenty-four hours a day, seven days a week, every day of the year. Our webstore is never closed. Our e-book delivery system is 100% automated, meaning your order is filled as soon as you pay for it.

Those are a few of the top reasons why electronic books are replacing paperbacks for many avid readers.

As always, Ellora's Cave and Cerridwen Press welcome your questions and comments. We invite you to email us at Comments@ellorascave.com or write to us directly at Ellora's Cave Publishing Inc., 1056 Home Avenue, Akron, OH 44310-3502.

Cerridwen Press
Monthly Newsletter

News
Author Appearances
Book Signings
New Releases
Contests
Author Profiles
Feature Articles

Available online at
www.CerridwenPress.com

Cerridwen Press

Cerridwen, the Celtic goddess of wisdom, was the muse who brought inspiration to storytellers and those in the creative arts.

Cerridwen Press encompasses the best and most innovative stories in all genres of today's fiction.

Visit our website and discover the newest titles by talented authors who still get inspired—much like the ancient storytellers did...

once upon a time.

www.cerridwenpress.com